SPACE BAT and the FUGITIVES

TACOS @ THE END OF THE WORLD

D1441687

BY CHRIS SHERIDAN

**For Kirsten,
a beautiful, patient, and peaceful
partner that makes the world more fun!**

Spacebat and the Fugitivies: Tacos @ The End of the World © & ™ 2017 Chris Sheridan.

Editor-in-Chief: Chris Staros.

Edited by Chris Ross and Zac Boone.

Published by Top Shelf Productions, PO Box 1282, Marietta, GA
30061-1282, USA. Top Shelf Productions is an imprint of IDW
Publishing, a division of Idea and Design Works, LLC. Offices:
2765 Truxtun Road, San Diego, CA 92106. Top Shelf Productions®,
the TopShelf logo, Idea and Design Works®, and the IDW logo are registered
trademarks of Idea and Design Works, LLC. All Rights Reserved.
With the exception of small excerpts of artwork used for review purposes,
none of the contents of this publication may be reprinted without the
permission of IDW Publishing. IDW Publishing does not read or accept
unsolicited submissions of ideas, stories, or artwork.

Visit our online catalog at www.topshelfcomix.com.

ISBN 978-1-60309-414-6

Printed in Korea.

17 18 19 20 21   5   4   3   2   1

ISSUE ONE:
BAD OPENING

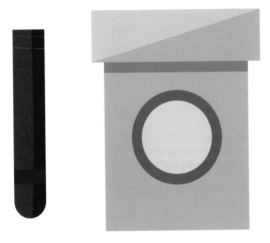

CACAO:
The cacao is a thing of utter perfection, crafted by man and, while perhaps not in God's image, made into a thing of beauty all the same.

-SAMUEL CLEMENS

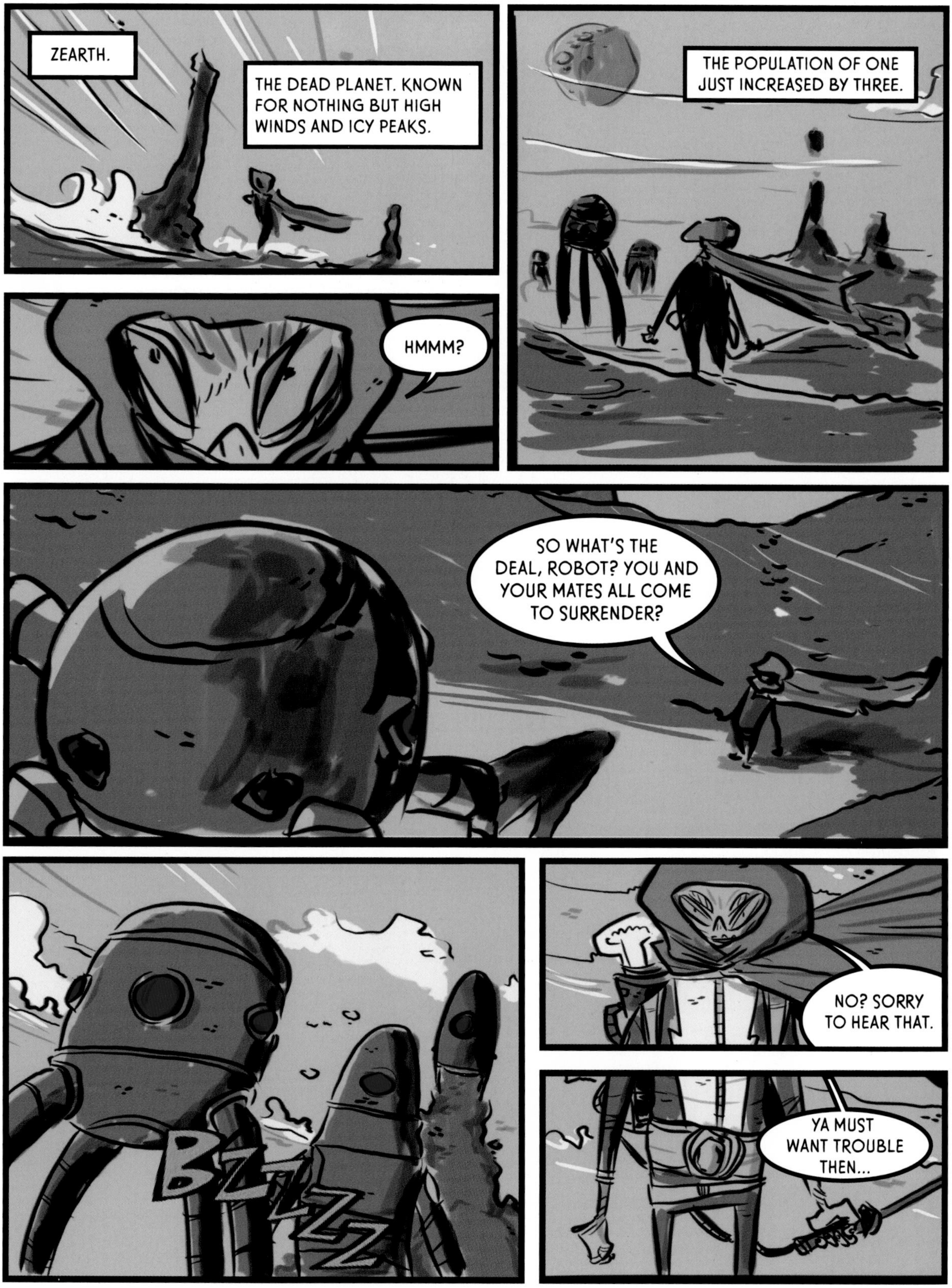
ZEARTH.
THE DEAD PLANET. KNOWN FOR NOTHING BUT HIGH WINDS AND ICY PEAKS.
THE POPULATION OF ONE JUST INCREASED BY THREE.
HMMM?
SO WHAT'S THE DEAL, ROBOT? YOU AND YOUR MATES ALL COME TO SURRENDER?
BZZZZ
NO? SORRY TO HEAR THAT.
YA MUST WANT TROUBLE THEN...

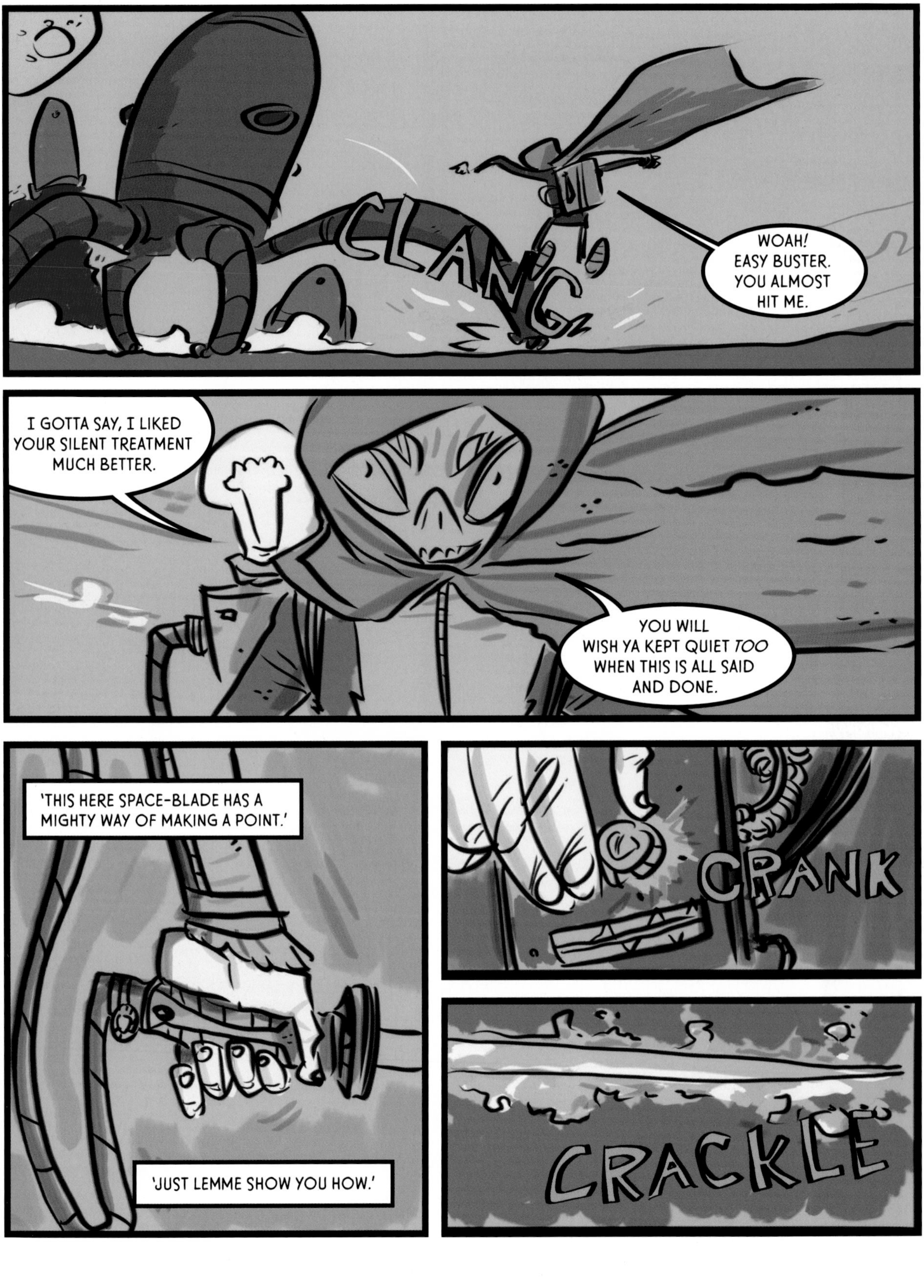
CLANG
WOAH! EASY BUSTER. YOU ALMOST HIT ME.
I GOTTA SAY, I LIKED YOUR SILENT TREATMENT MUCH BETTER.
YOU WILL WISH YA KEPT QUIET *TOO* WHEN THIS IS ALL SAID AND DONE.
'THIS HERE SPACE-BLADE HAS A MIGHTY WAY OF MAKING A POINT.'
'JUST LEMME SHOW YOU HOW.'
CRANK
CRACKLE

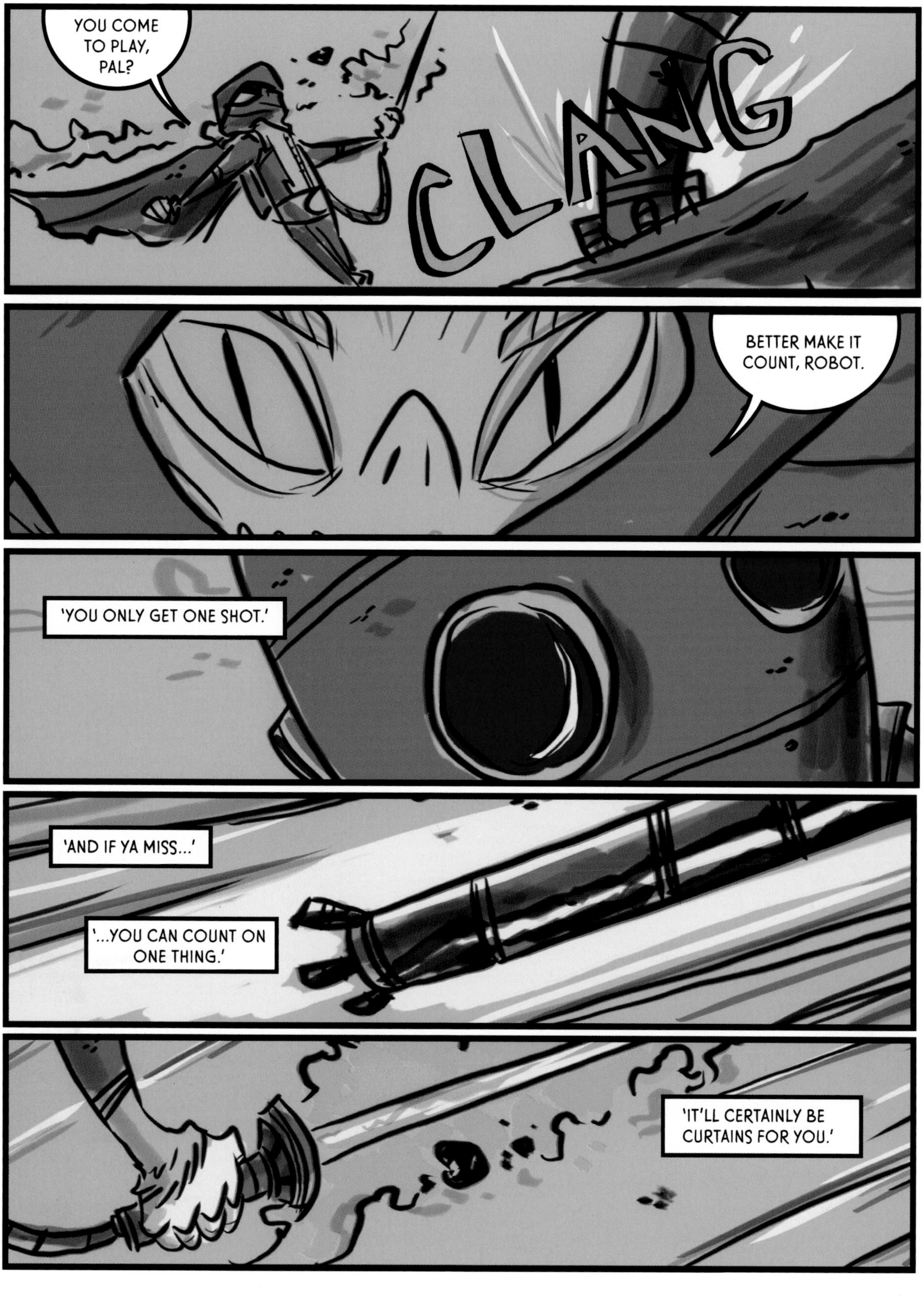
YOU COME TO PLAY, PAL?
CLANG
BETTER MAKE IT COUNT, ROBOT.
'YOU ONLY GET ONE SHOT.'
'AND IF YA MISS...'
'...YOU CAN COUNT ON ONE THING.'
'IT'LL CERTAINLY BE CURTAINS FOR YOU.'

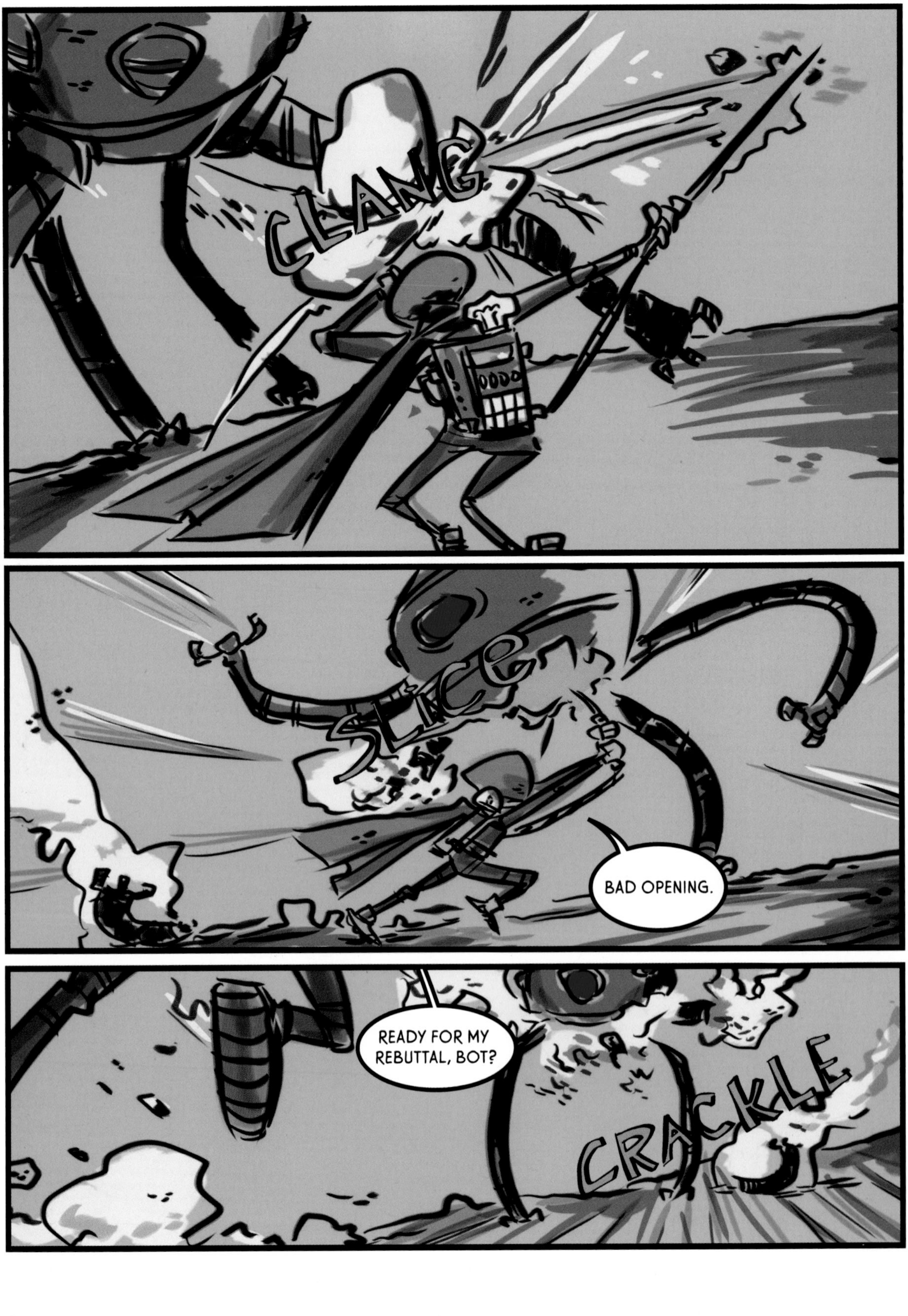
CLANG
SLICE
BAD OPENING.
READY FOR MY REBUTTAL, BOT?
CRACKLE

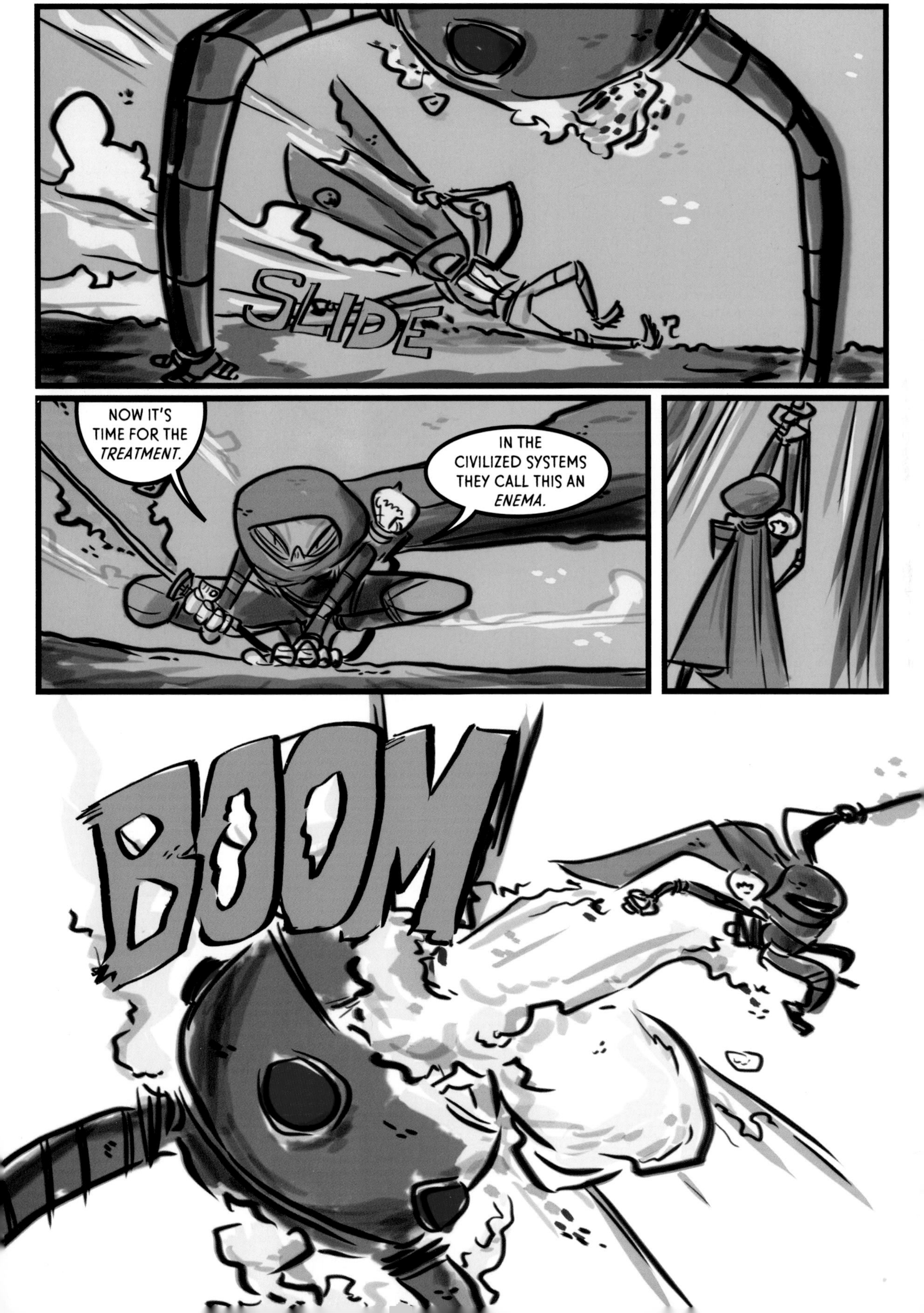
SLIDE
NOW IT'S TIME FOR THE *TREATMENT.*
IN THE CIVILIZED SYSTEMS THEY CALL THIS AN *ENEMA.*
BOOM

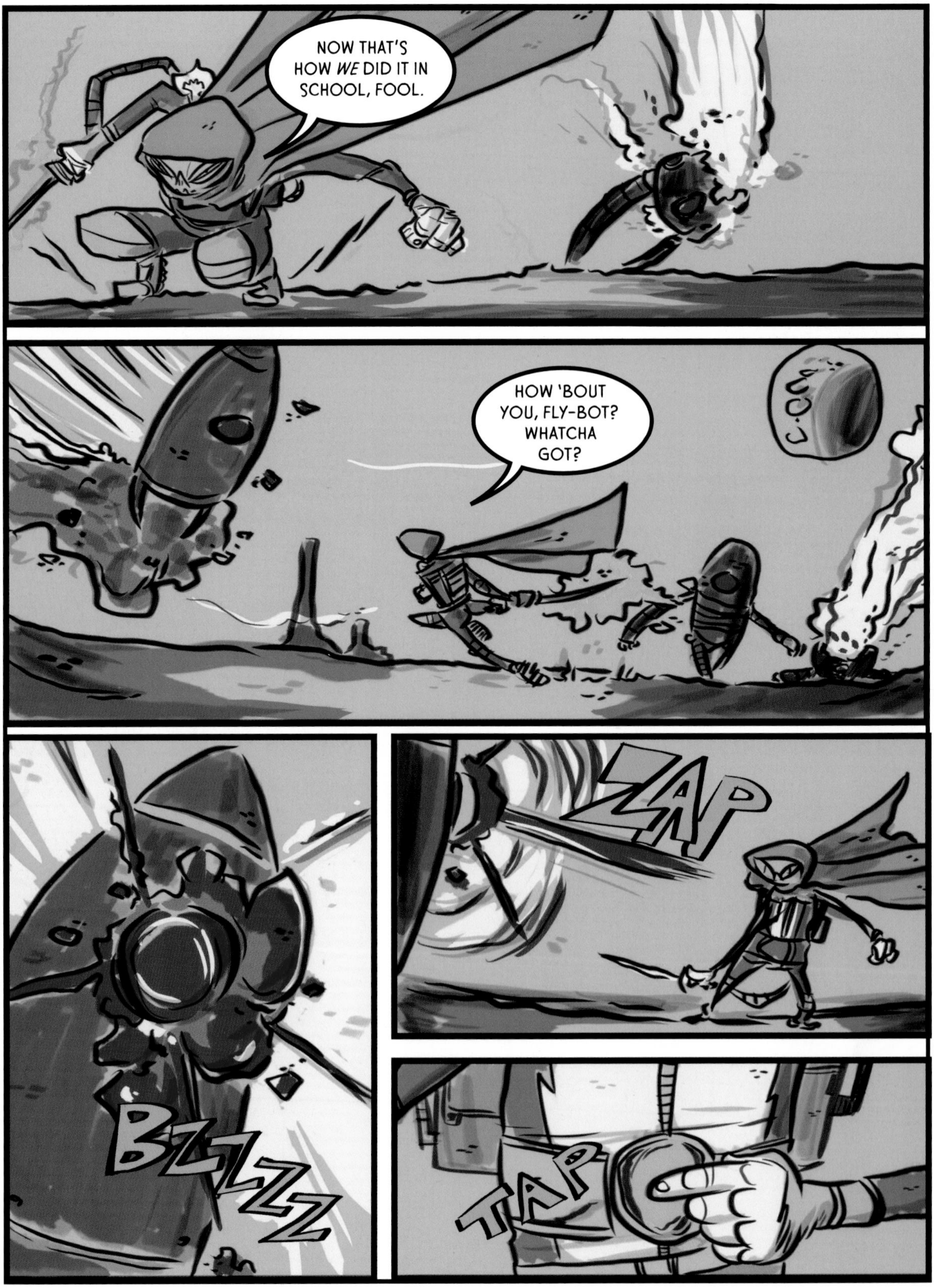
NOW THAT'S HOW *WE* DID IT IN SCHOOL, FOOL.
HOW 'BOUT YOU, FLY-BOT? WHATCHA GOT?
BZZZZZ
ZAP
TAP

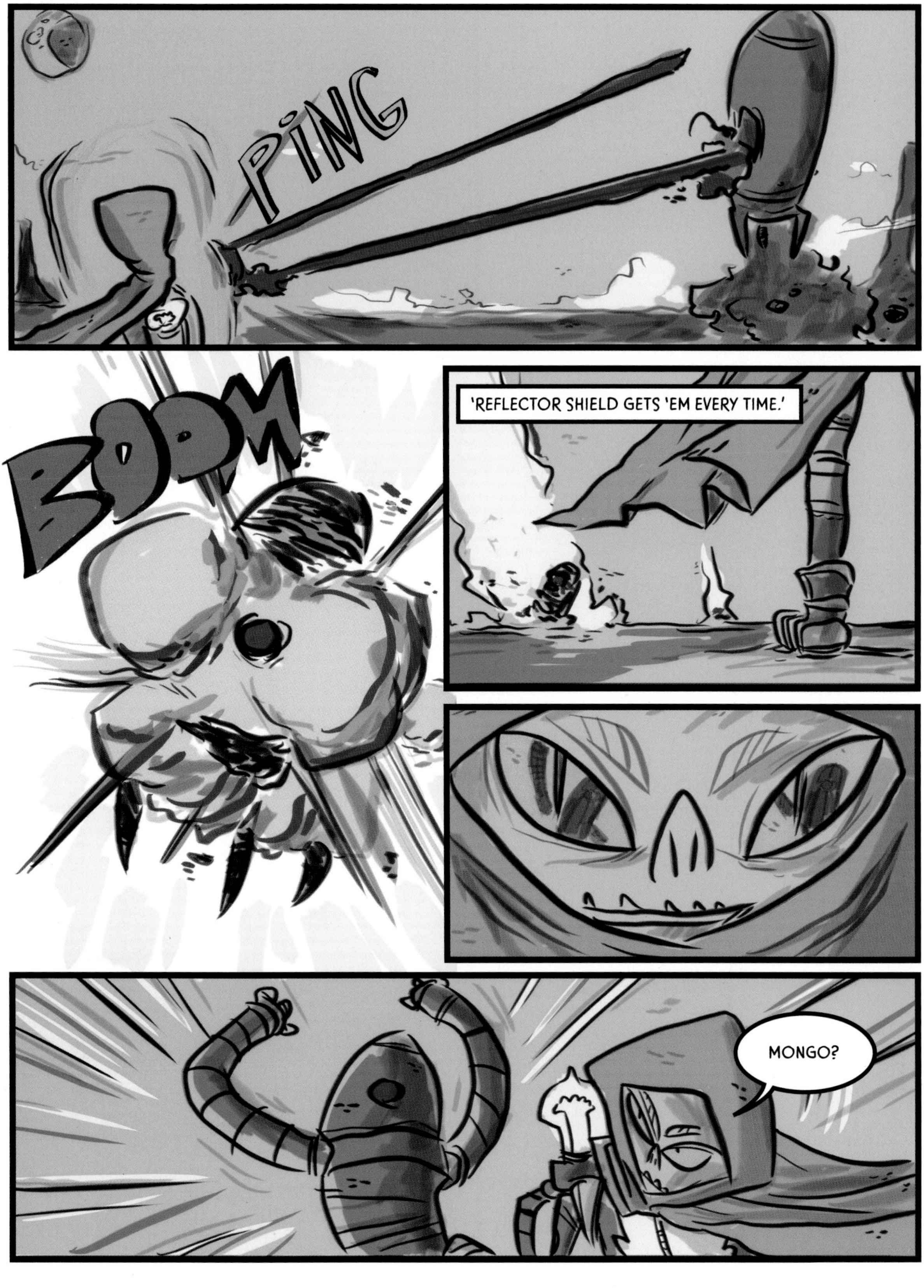
PING
BOOM
'REFLECTOR SHIELD GETS 'EM EVERY TIME.'
MONGO?

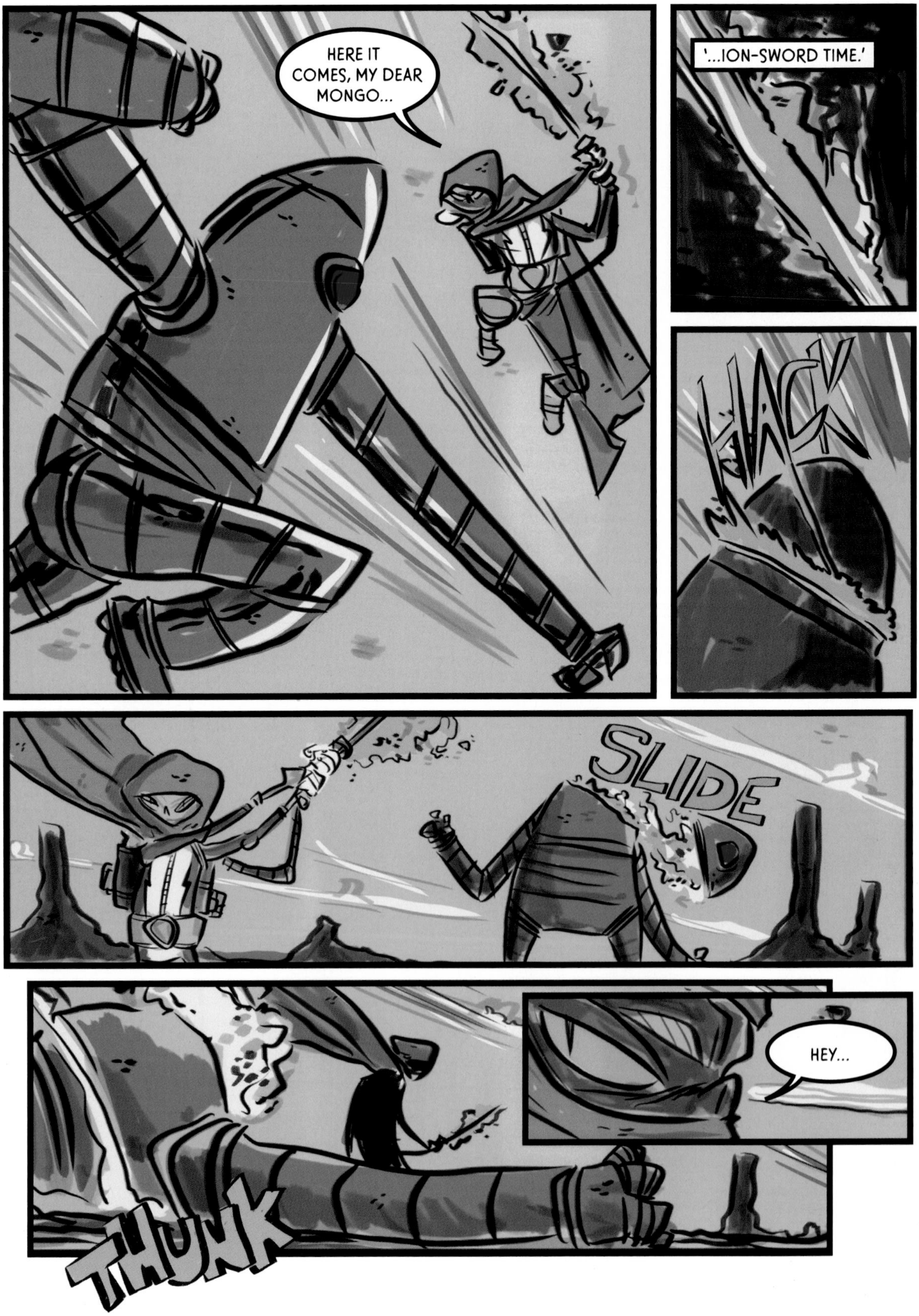
HERE IT COMES, MY DEAR MONGO...
'...ION-SWORD TIME.'
HACK
SLIDE
HEY...
THUNK

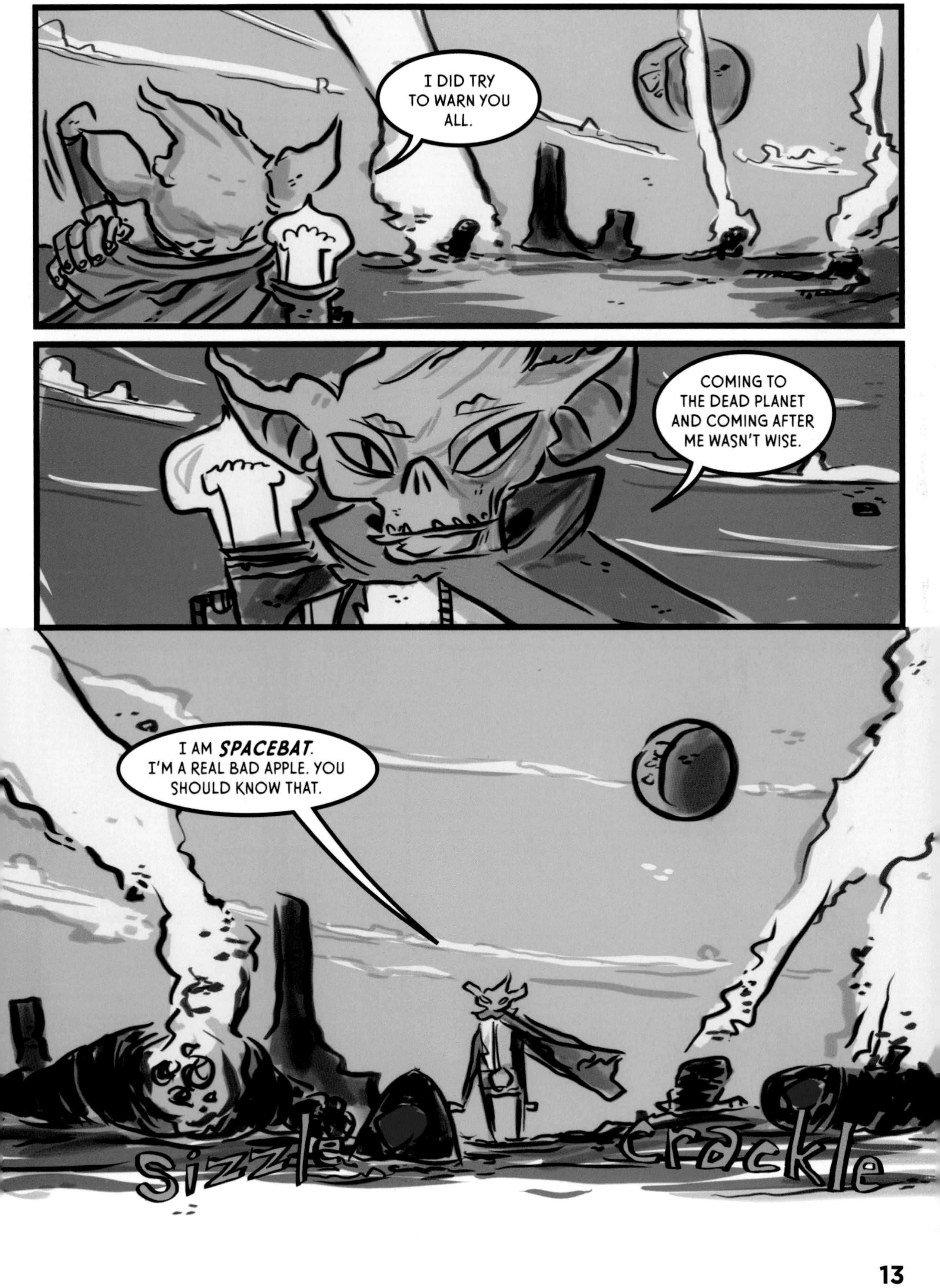
I DID TRY TO WARN YOU ALL.
COMING TO THE DEAD PLANET AND COMING AFTER ME WASN'T WISE.
I AM ***SPACEBAT***. I'M A REAL BAD APPLE. YOU SHOULD KNOW THAT.
sizzle
crackle

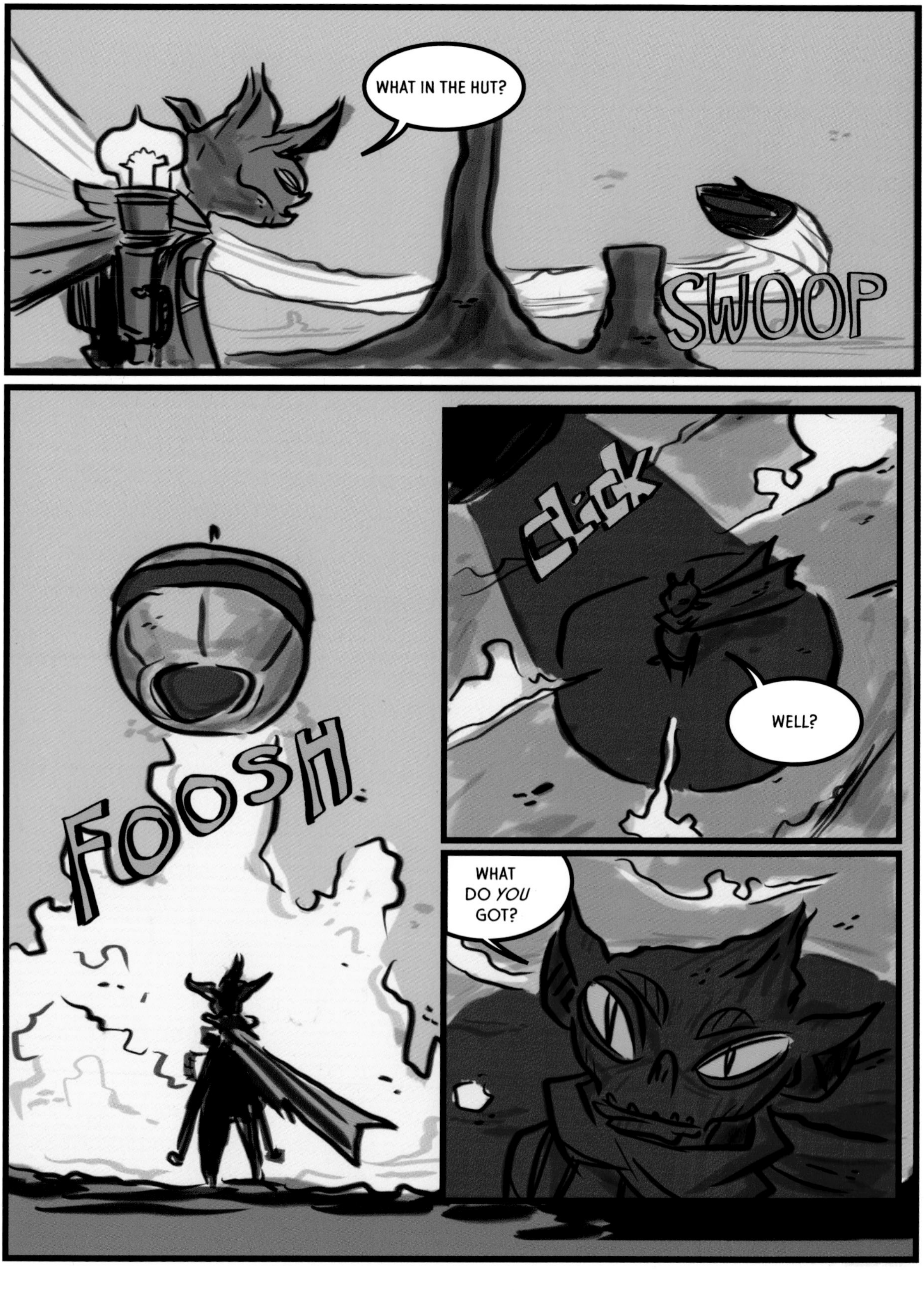
WHAT IN THE HUT?
SWOOP
FOOSH
click
WELL?
WHAT DO *YOU* GOT?

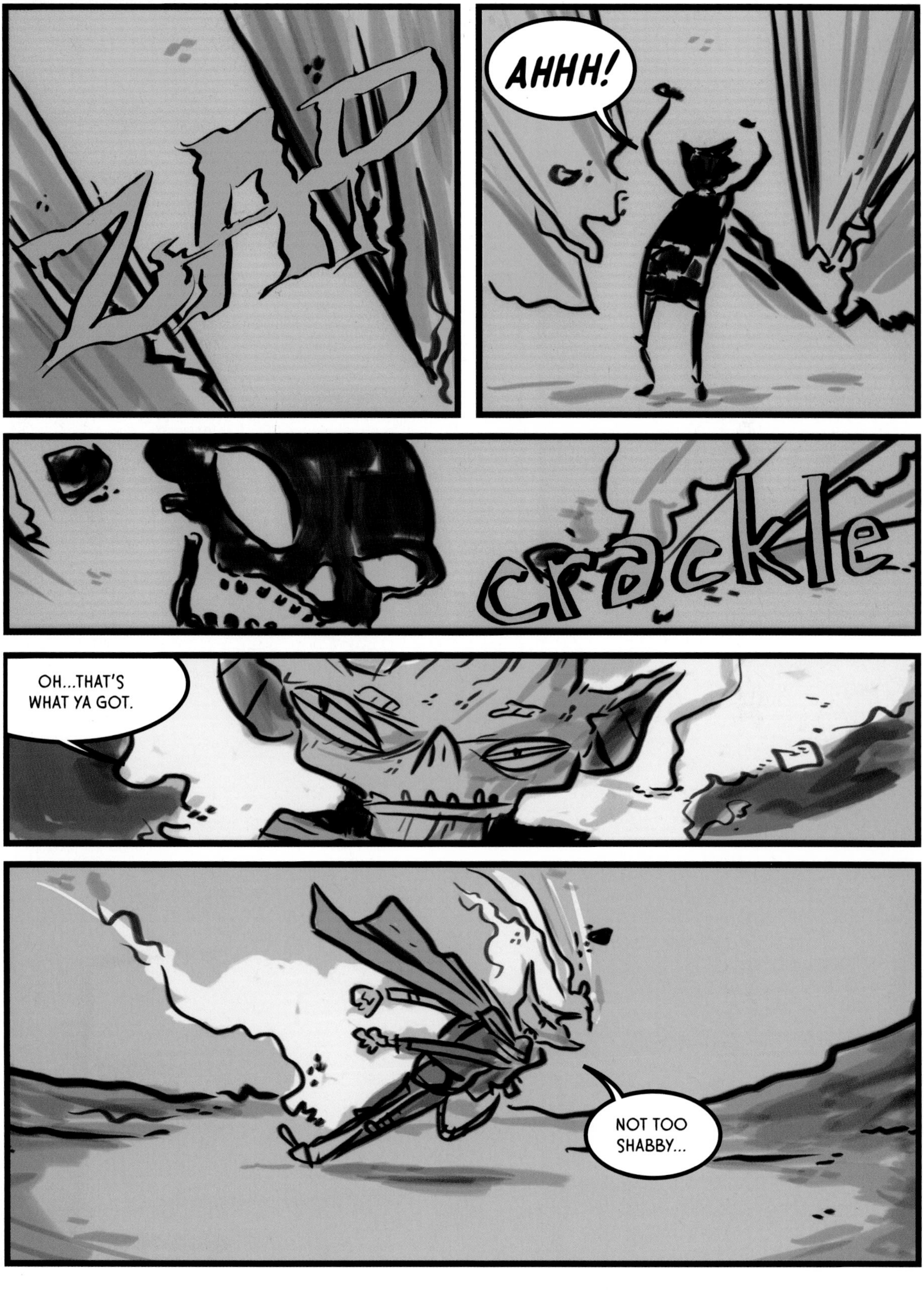
ZAP
AHHH!
crackle
OH...THAT'S WHAT YA GOT.
NOT TOO SHABBY...

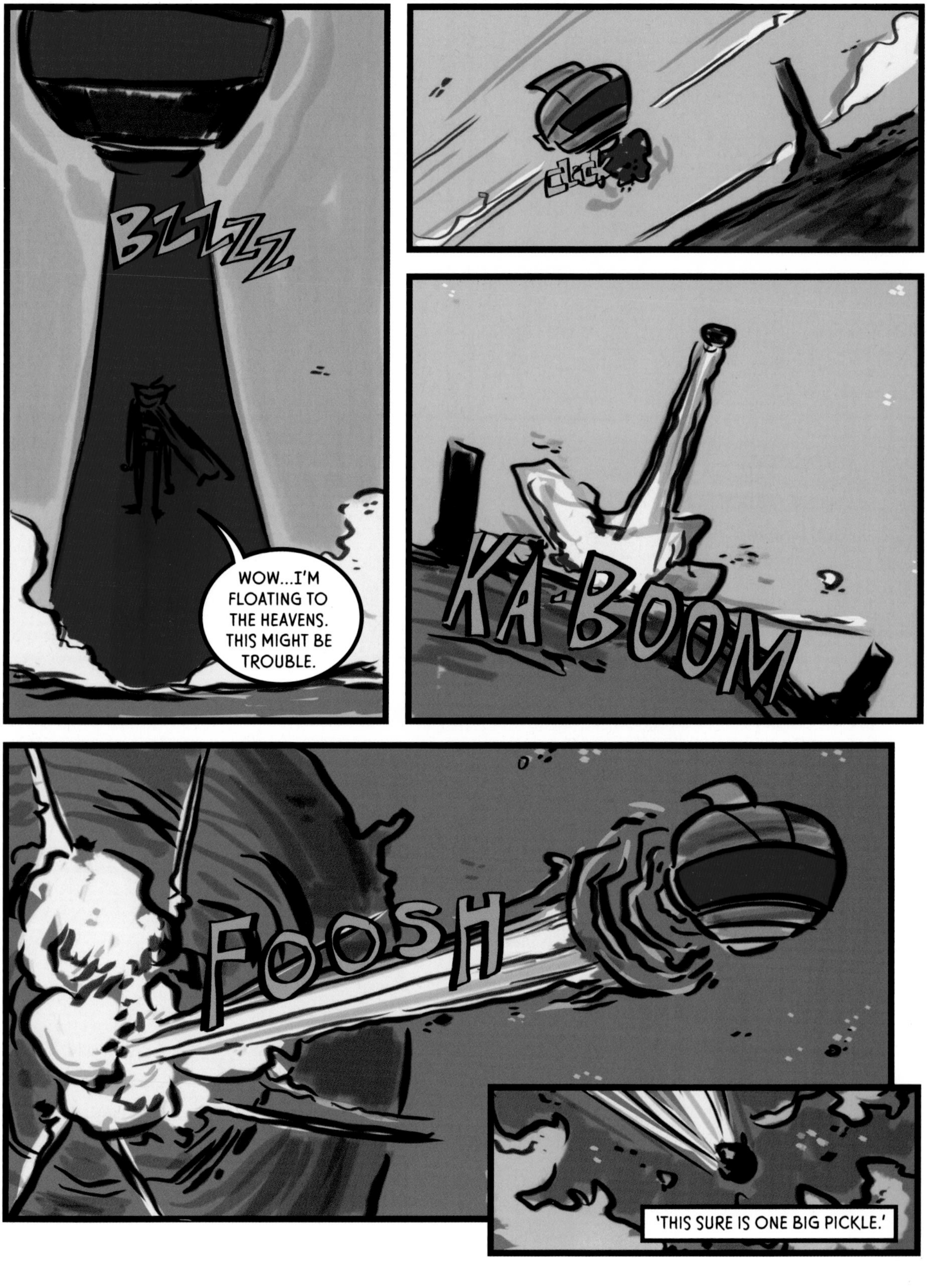
BZZZZZ
WOW...I'M FLOATING TO THE HEAVENS. THIS MIGHT BE TROUBLE.
click
KA-BOOM
FOOSH
'THIS SURE IS ONE BIG PICKLE.'

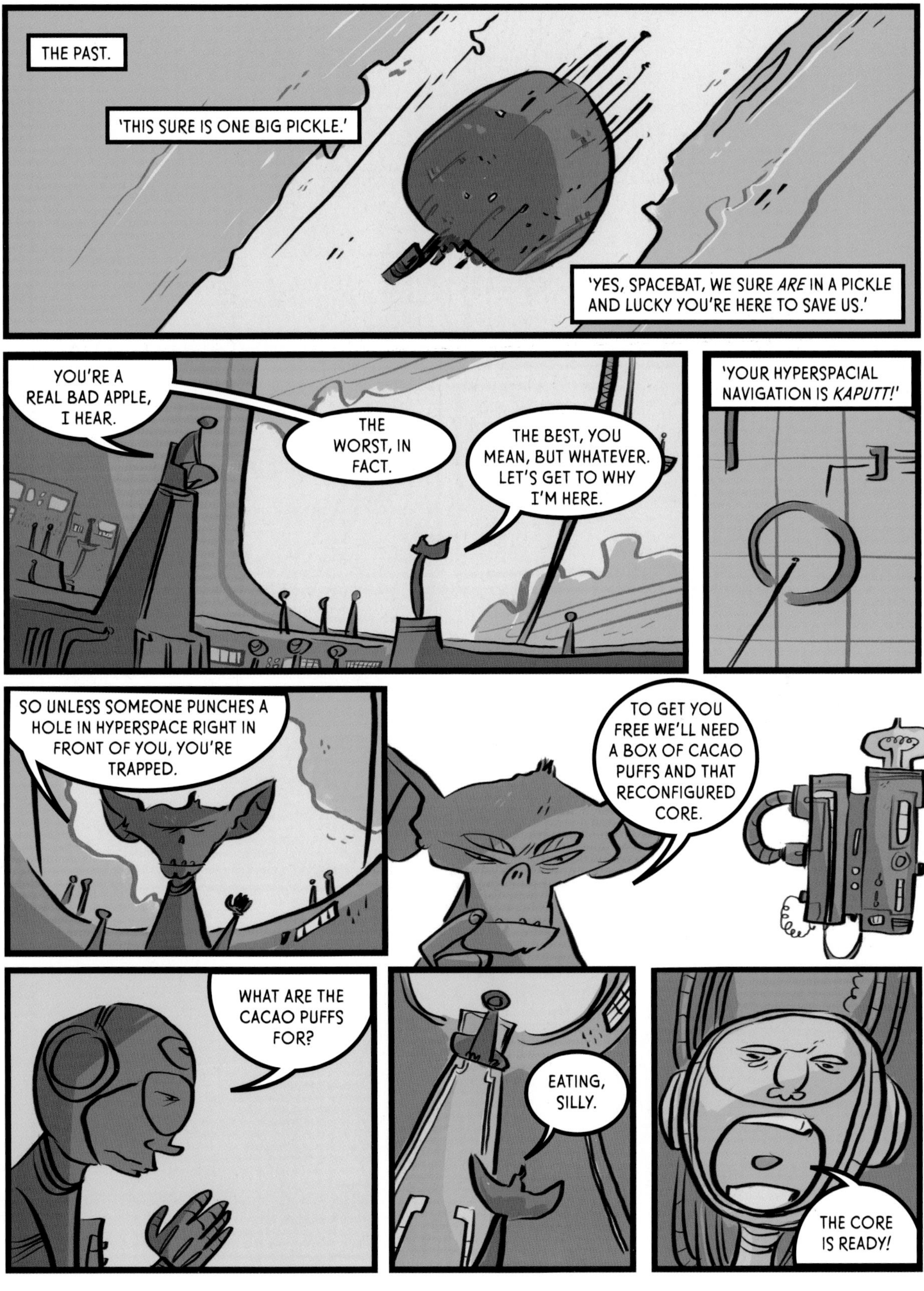

THE PAST.
'THIS SURE IS ONE BIG PICKLE.'
'YES, SPACEBAT, WE SURE *ARE* IN A PICKLE AND LUCKY YOU'RE HERE TO SAVE US.'
YOU'RE A REAL BAD APPLE, I HEAR.
THE WORST, IN FACT.
THE BEST, YOU MEAN, BUT WHATEVER. LET'S GET TO WHY I'M HERE.
'YOUR HYPERSPACIAL NAVIGATION IS *KAPUTT!*'
SO UNLESS SOMEONE PUNCHES A HOLE IN HYPERSPACE RIGHT IN FRONT OF YOU, YOU'RE TRAPPED.
TO GET YOU FREE WE'LL NEED A BOX OF CACAO PUFFS AND THAT RECONFIGURED CORE.
WHAT ARE THE CACAO PUFFS FOR?
EATING, SILLY.
THE CORE IS READY!

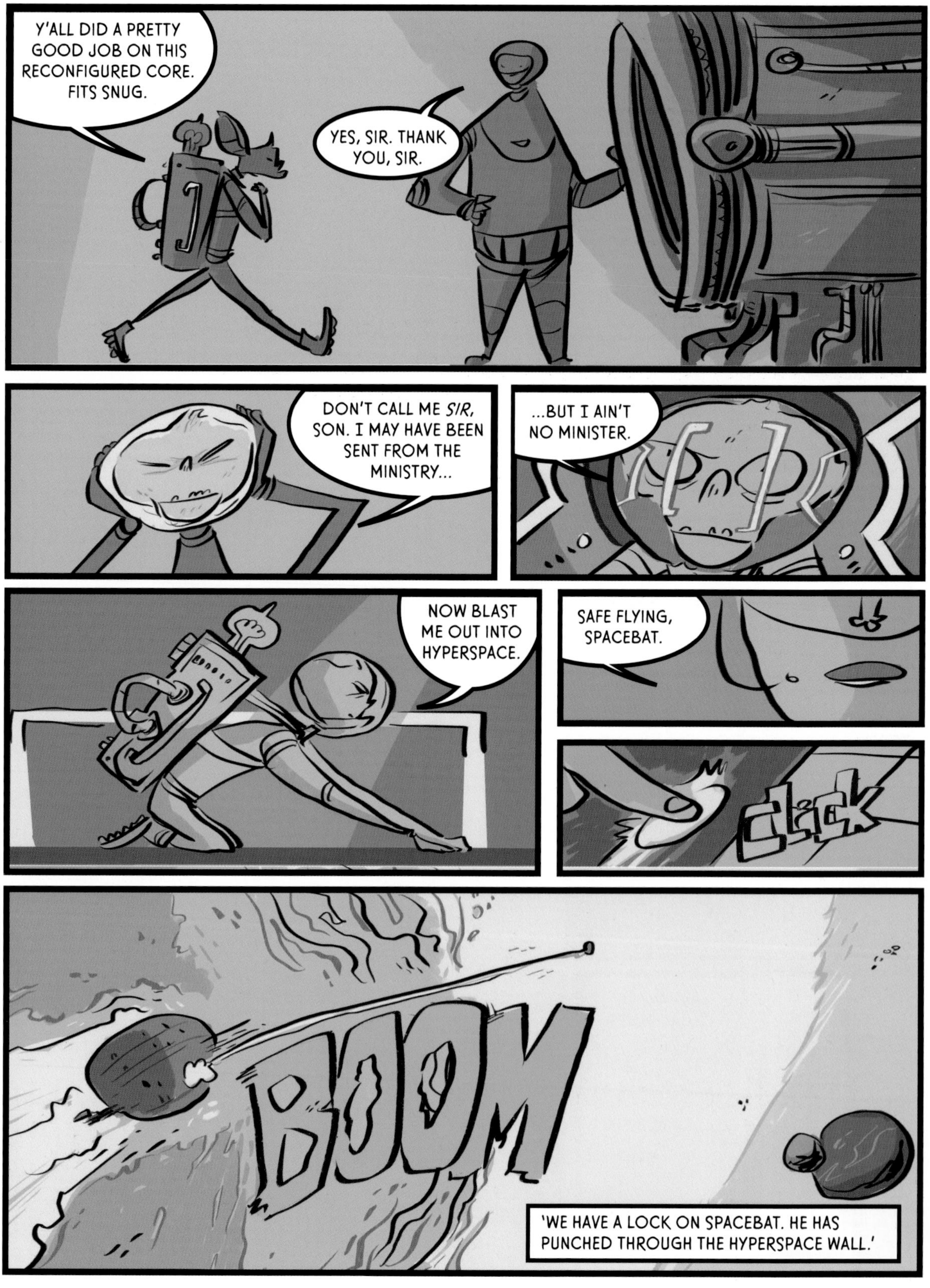
Y'ALL DID A PRETTY GOOD JOB ON THIS RECONFIGURED CORE. FITS SNUG.
YES, SIR. THANK YOU, SIR.
DON'T CALL ME *SIR*, SON. I MAY HAVE BEEN SENT FROM THE MINISTRY...
...BUT I AIN'T NO MINISTER.
NOW BLAST ME OUT INTO HYPERSPACE.
SAFE FLYING, SPACEBAT.
CLICK
BOOM
'WE HAVE A LOCK ON SPACEBAT. HE HAS PUNCHED THROUGH THE HYPERSPACE WALL.'

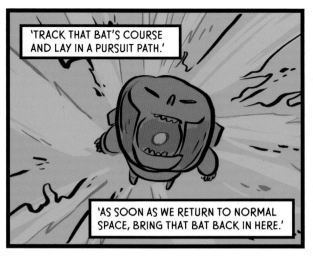

'TRACK THAT BAT'S COURSE AND LAY IN A PURSUIT PATH.'

'AS SOON AS WE RETURN TO NORMAL SPACE, BRING THAT BAT BACK IN HERE.'

'KEEP THAT LOCK ON OUR LITTLE BAT'S TRANSMITTER.'

'THE CORE ON HIS BACK WILL ACT LIKE AN ANCHOR.'

'HYPERSPACE WILL FOLD BACK ON TOP OF HIM.'

'IF THAT HAPPENS, HE'LL BE LOST IN HYPERSPACE. WHO KNOWS WHERE HE WILL END UP?'

'AH...SIR...WE HAVE A PROBLEM.'

'WE'VE SAFELY CROSSED INTO NORMAL SPACE, BUT THERE IS NO SIGN OF HIM.'

'GOOD GRAVY...SPACEBAT IS GONE.'

'LOST...'

'THAT POOR BAT SACRIFICED HIMSELF.'

'HE REALLY WAS ONE *BAD APPLE*.'

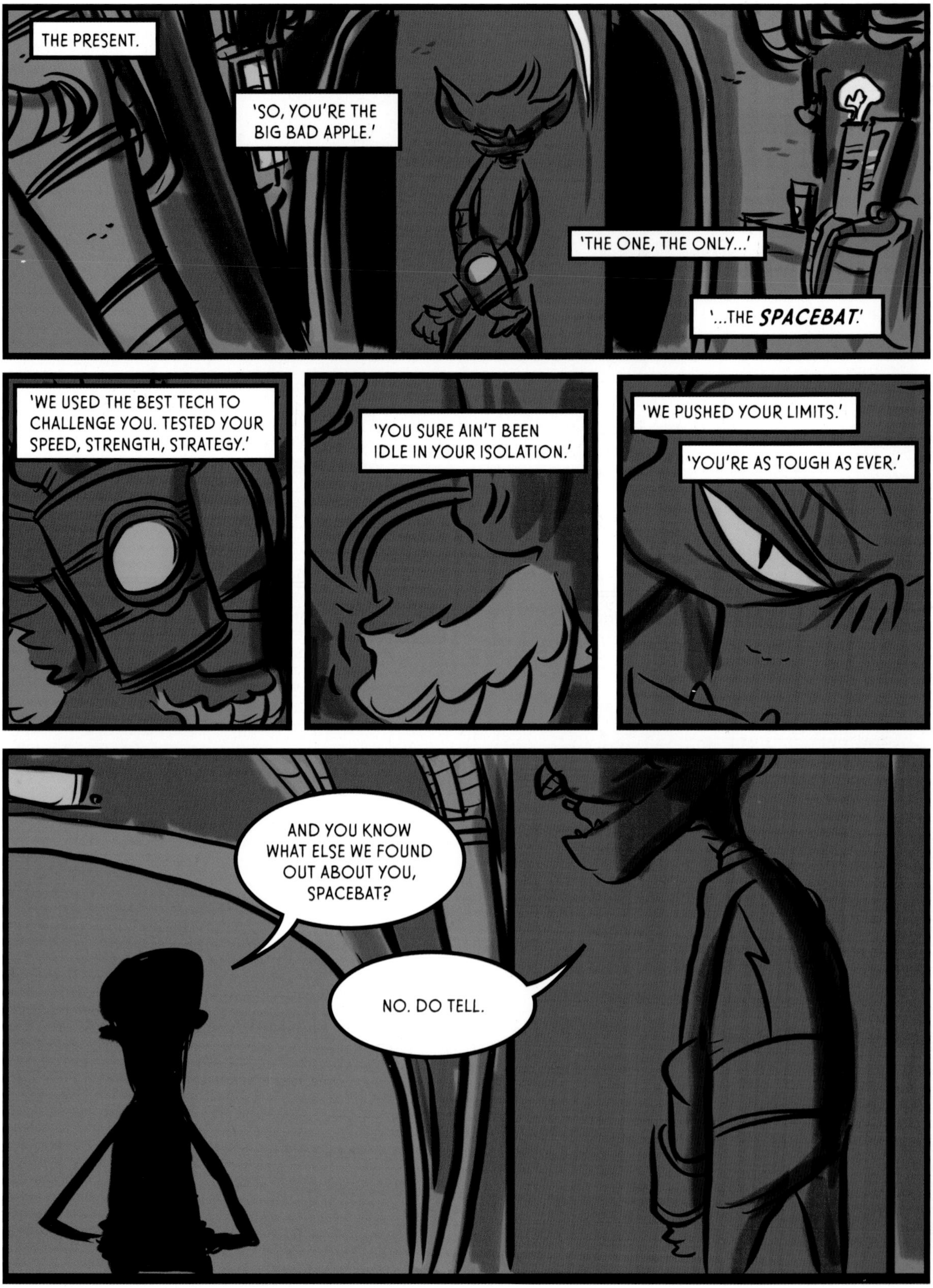
THE PRESENT.
'SO, YOU'RE THE BIG BAD APPLE.'
'THE ONE, THE ONLY...'
'...THE **SPACEBAT**.'
'WE USED THE BEST TECH TO CHALLENGE YOU. TESTED YOUR SPEED, STRENGTH, STRATEGY.'
'YOU SURE AIN'T BEEN IDLE IN YOUR ISOLATION.'
'WE PUSHED YOUR LIMITS.'
'YOU'RE AS TOUGH AS EVER.'
AND YOU KNOW WHAT ELSE WE FOUND OUT ABOUT YOU, SPACEBAT?
NO. DO TELL.

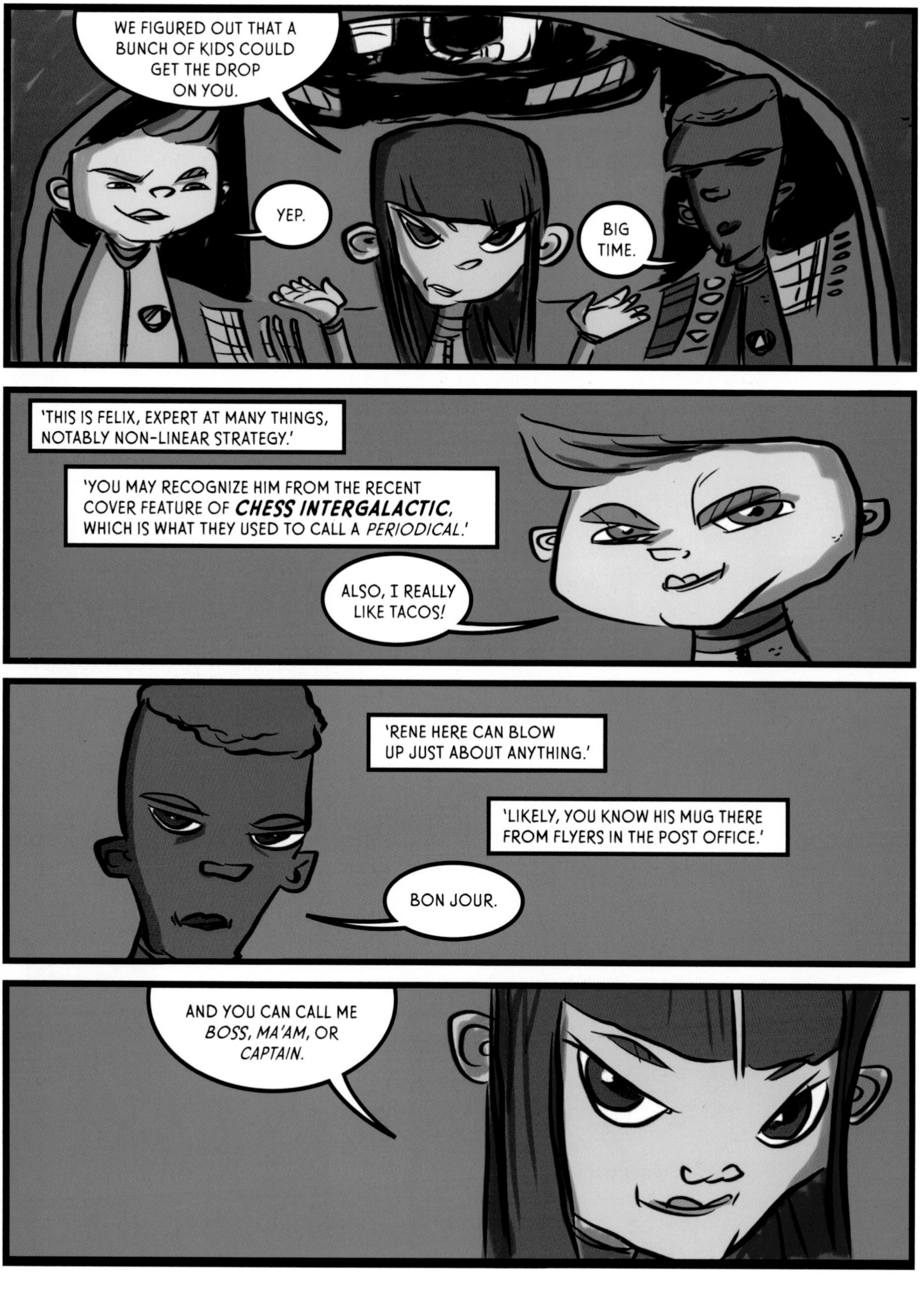
WE FIGURED OUT THAT A BUNCH OF KIDS COULD GET THE DROP ON YOU.
YEP.
BIG TIME.
'THIS IS FELIX, EXPERT AT MANY THINGS, NOTABLY NON-LINEAR STRATEGY.'
'YOU MAY RECOGNIZE HIM FROM THE RECENT COVER FEATURE OF ***CHESS INTERGALACTIC***, WHICH IS WHAT THEY USED TO CALL A *PERIODICAL*.'
ALSO, I REALLY LIKE TACOS!
'RENE HERE CAN BLOW UP JUST ABOUT ANYTHING.'
'LIKELY, YOU KNOW HIS MUG THERE FROM FLYERS IN THE POST OFFICE.'
BON JOUR.
AND YOU CAN CALL ME *BOSS*, *MA'AM*, OR *CAPTAIN*.

WE'RE *THE FUGITIVES.*

WHATEVER YOU SAY, KID. BUT I GOT SOMETHING TO OFFER YOU IN TURN.

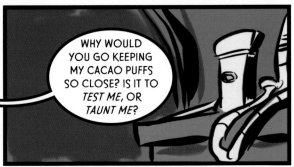

YOU SEEM LIKE A SMART-ISH KIND OF KID. BUT I WONDER...

WHY WOULD YOU GO KEEPING MY CACAO PUFFS SO CLOSE? IS IT TO *TEST ME*, OR *TAUNT ME*?

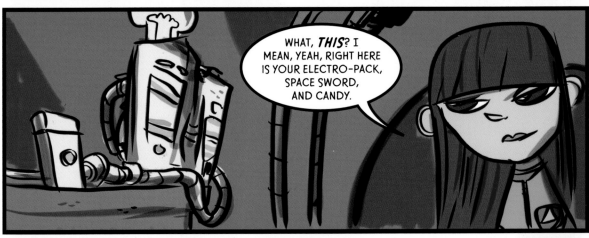

WHAT, *THIS*? I MEAN, YEAH, RIGHT HERE IS YOUR ELECTRO-PACK, SPACE SWORD, AND CANDY.

BUT IT'S NOT LIKE YOU'RE GOING TO BE ABLE TO GET THROUGH THAT SPACE GLASS, RIGHT?

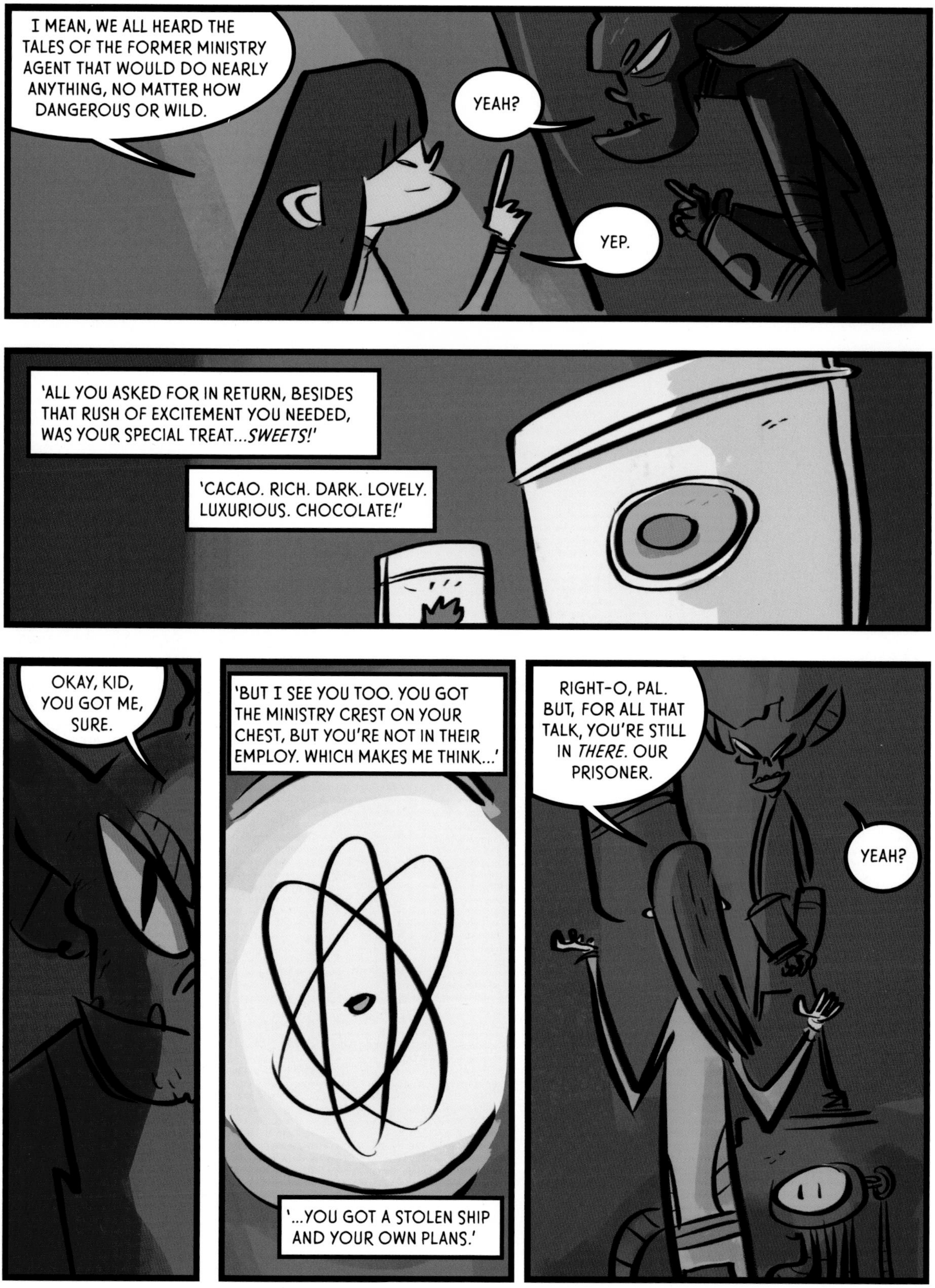

I MEAN, WE ALL HEARD THE TALES OF THE FORMER MINISTRY AGENT THAT WOULD DO NEARLY ANYTHING, NO MATTER HOW DANGEROUS OR WILD.
YEAH?
YEP.
'ALL YOU ASKED FOR IN RETURN, BESIDES THAT RUSH OF EXCITEMENT YOU NEEDED, WAS YOUR SPECIAL TREAT...*SWEETS!*'
'CACAO. RICH. DARK. LOVELY. LUXURIOUS. CHOCOLATE!'
OKAY, KID, YOU GOT ME, SURE.
'BUT I SEE YOU TOO. YOU GOT THE MINISTRY CREST ON YOUR CHEST, BUT YOU'RE NOT IN THEIR EMPLOY. WHICH MAKES ME THINK...'
'...YOU GOT A STOLEN SHIP AND YOUR OWN PLANS.'
RIGHT-O, PAL. BUT, FOR ALL THAT TALK, YOU'RE STILL IN *THERE*. OUR PRISONER.
YEAH?

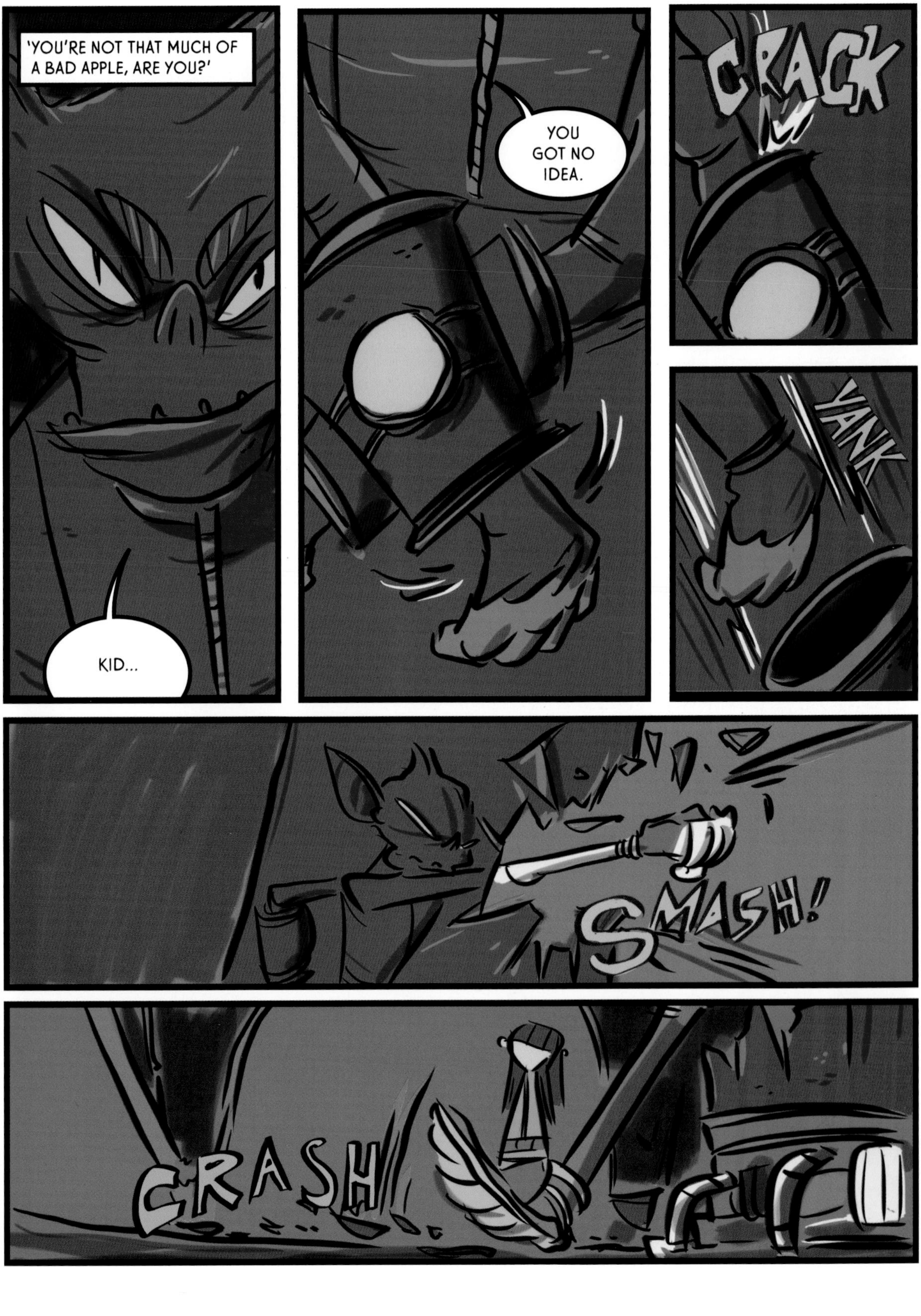
'YOU'RE NOT THAT MUCH OF A BAD APPLE, ARE YOU?'
KID...
YOU GOT NO IDEA.
CRACK
YANK
SMASH!
CRASH

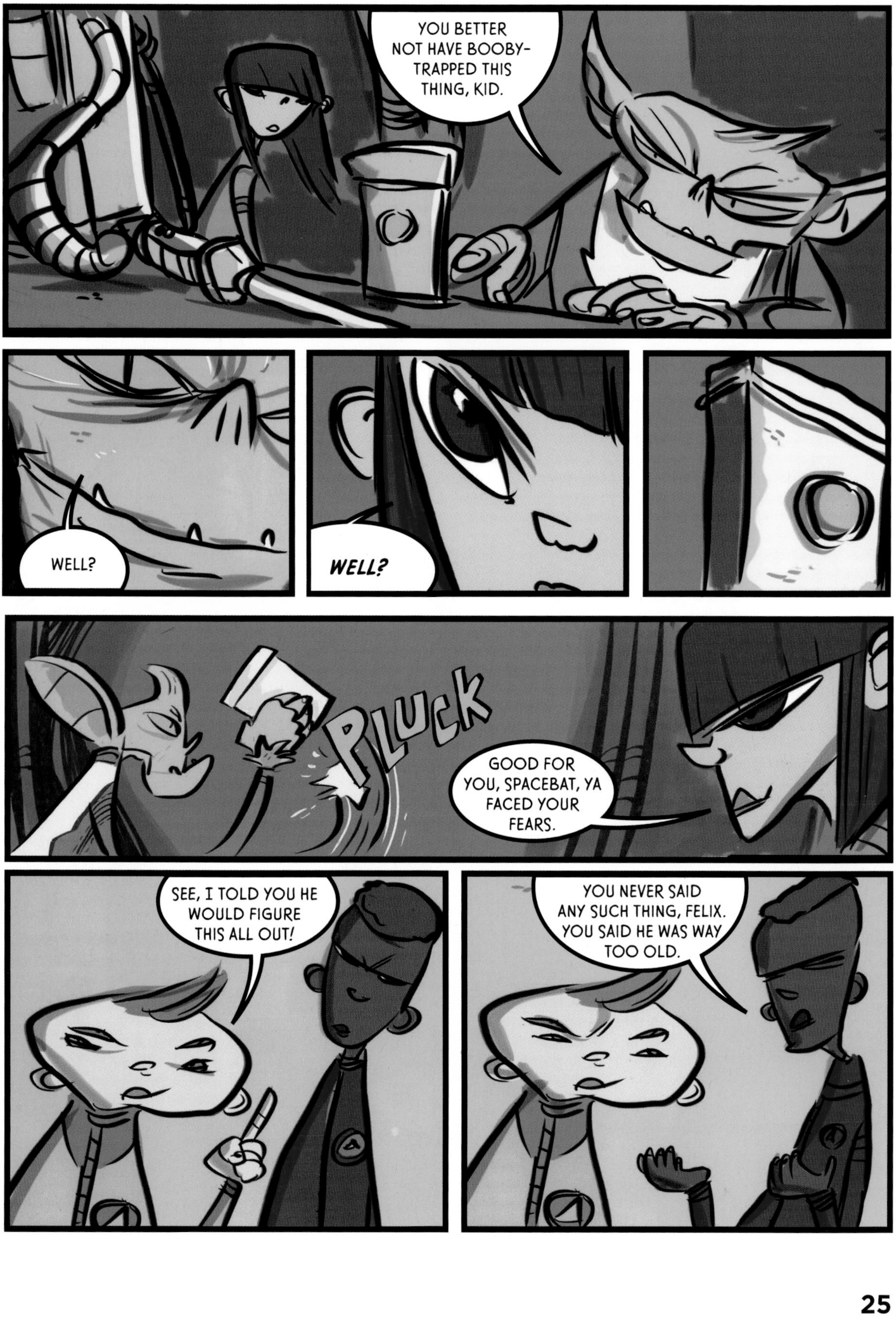
YOU BETTER NOT HAVE BOOBY-TRAPPED THIS THING, KID.
WELL?
WELL?
PLUCK
GOOD FOR YOU, SPACEBAT, YA FACED YOUR FEARS.
SEE, I TOLD YOU HE WOULD FIGURE THIS ALL OUT!
YOU NEVER SAID ANY SUCH THING, FELIX. YOU SAID HE WAS WAY TOO OLD.

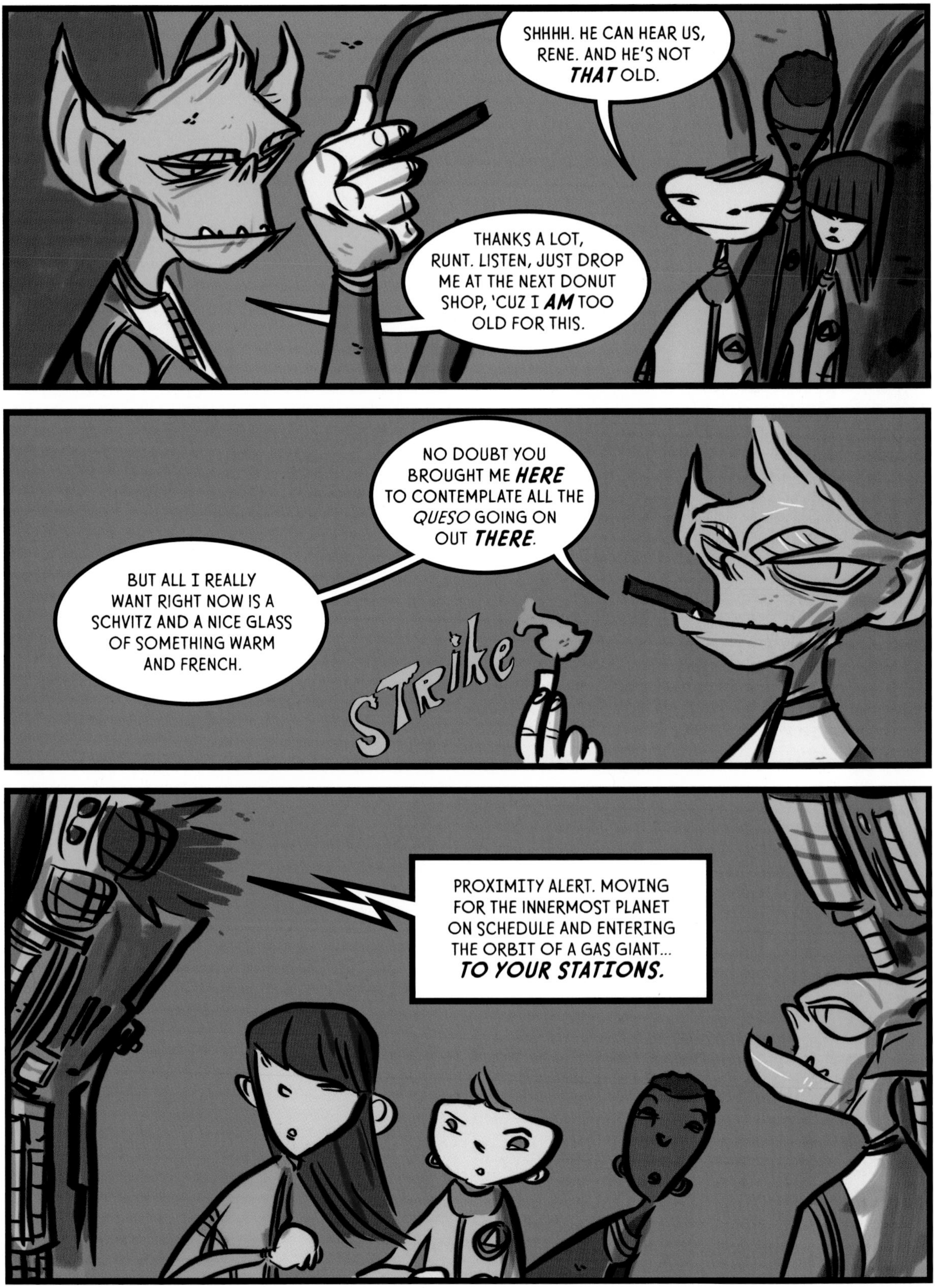
SHHHH. HE CAN HEAR US, RENE. AND HE'S NOT ***THAT*** OLD.
THANKS A LOT, RUNT. LISTEN, JUST DROP ME AT THE NEXT DONUT SHOP, 'CUZ I ***AM*** TOO OLD FOR THIS.
NO DOUBT YOU BROUGHT ME ***HERE*** TO CONTEMPLATE ALL THE *QUESO* GOING ON OUT ***THERE***.
BUT ALL I REALLY WANT RIGHT NOW IS A SCHVITZ AND A NICE GLASS OF SOMETHING WARM AND FRENCH.
STRIKE
PROXIMITY ALERT. MOVING FOR THE INNERMOST PLANET ON SCHEDULE AND ENTERING THE ORBIT OF A GAS GIANT... ***TO YOUR STATIONS.***

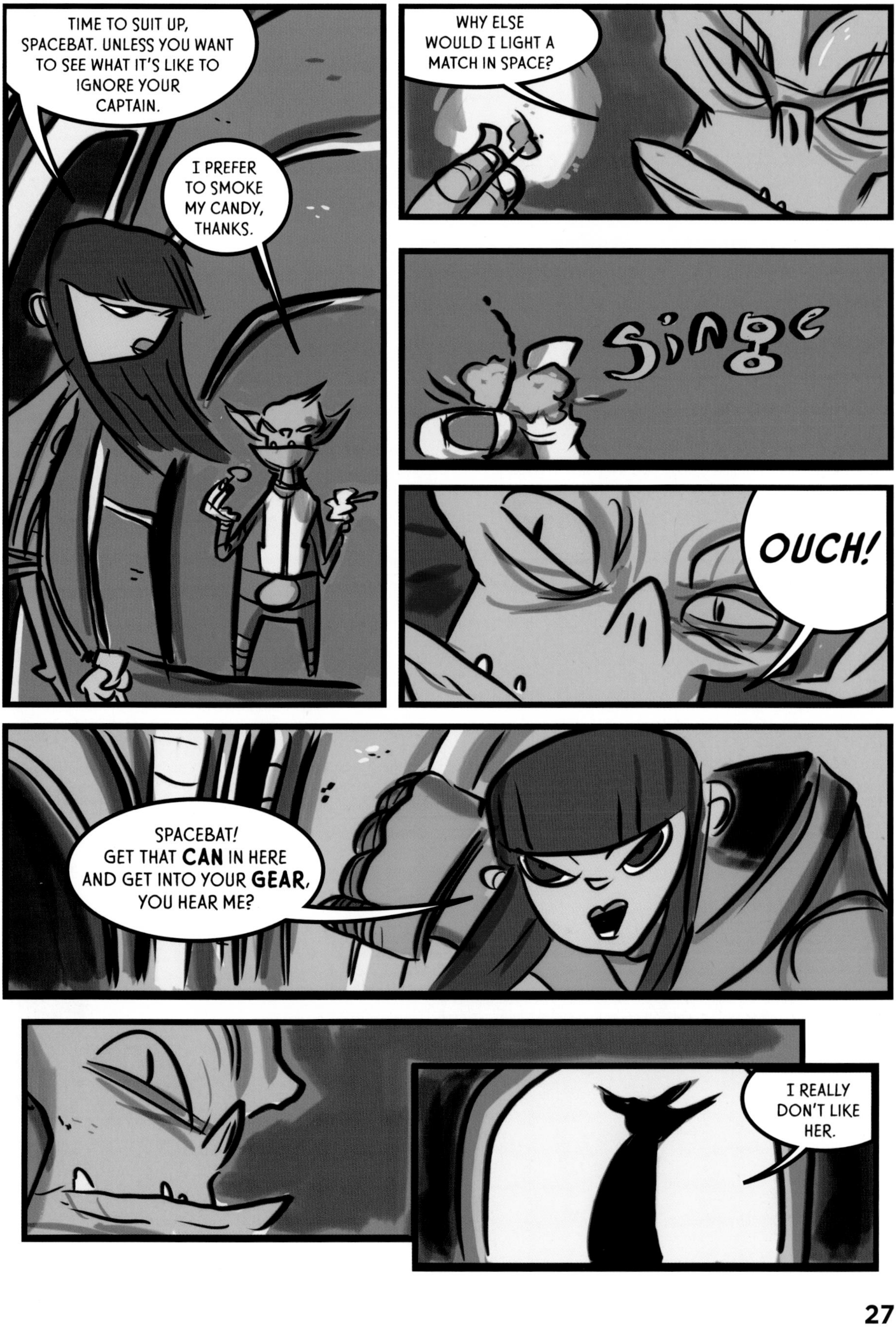
TIME TO SUIT UP, SPACEBAT. UNLESS YOU WANT TO SEE WHAT IT'S LIKE TO IGNORE YOUR CAPTAIN.
I PREFER TO SMOKE MY CANDY, THANKS.
WHY ELSE WOULD I LIGHT A MATCH IN SPACE?
SINGE
OUCH!
SPACEBAT! GET THAT CAN IN HERE AND GET INTO YOUR GEAR, YOU HEAR ME?
I REALLY DON'T LIKE HER.

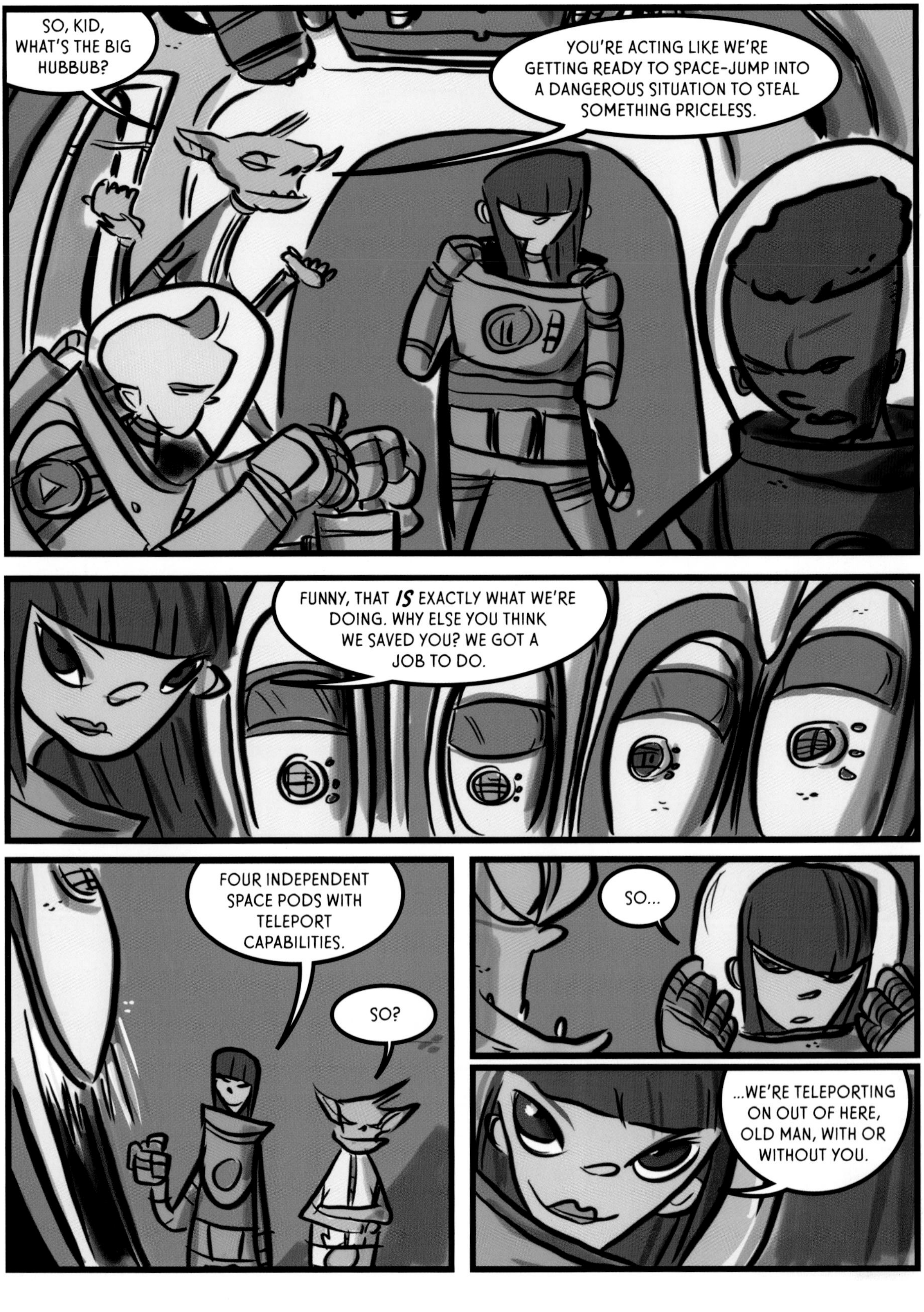
SO, KID, WHAT'S THE BIG HUBBUB?
YOU'RE ACTING LIKE WE'RE GETTING READY TO SPACE-JUMP INTO A DANGEROUS SITUATION TO STEAL SOMETHING PRICELESS.
FUNNY, THAT *IS* EXACTLY WHAT WE'RE DOING. WHY ELSE YOU THINK WE SAVED YOU? WE GOT A JOB TO DO.
FOUR INDEPENDENT SPACE PODS WITH TELEPORT CAPABILITIES.
SO?
SO...
...WE'RE TELEPORTING ON OUT OF HERE, OLD MAN, WITH OR WITHOUT YOU.

YOU IN OR NOT?

YOU MENTIONED *QUESO* BEFORE? WELL, THAT'S WHAT *THIS* IS ALL ABOUT.

tink

'THE QUESO'S ABOUT TO GO UP IN SMOKE.'

CLANG

'BUT WE'RE GOING TO SAVE THE DAY.'

CLink

WE WERE BEHIND THE CHICAGO THING IN SEVENTY-TWO, WE SAVED CHRISTMAS LAST WINTER, AND NOW WE'RE GOING TO SAVE THE UNIVERSE.

YOU SHOULD KNOW, WE ARE ON A COLLISION COURSE WITH THAT PLANET.

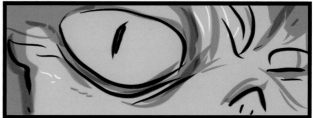

DANGE

29

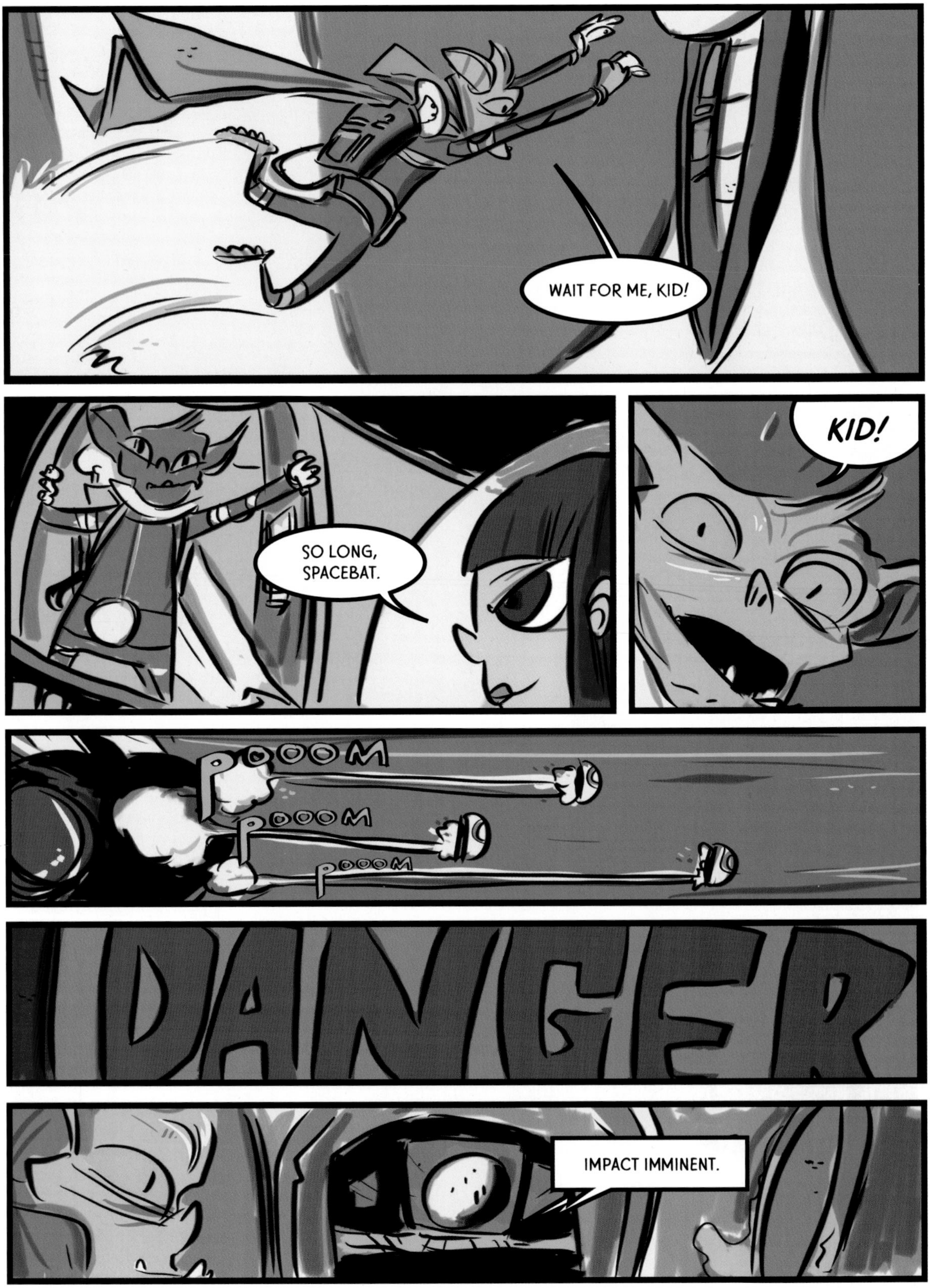
WAIT FOR ME, KID!
SO LONG, SPACEBAT.
KID!
POOOM
POOOM
POOOM
DANGER
IMPACT IMMINENT.

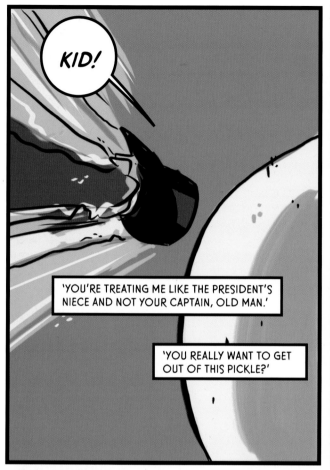

KID!

'YOU'RE TREATING ME LIKE THE PRESIDENT'S NIECE AND NOT YOUR CAPTAIN, OLD MAN.'

'YOU REALLY WANT TO GET OUT OF THIS PICKLE?'

PLEASE!

DON'T CALL ME KID.

tink

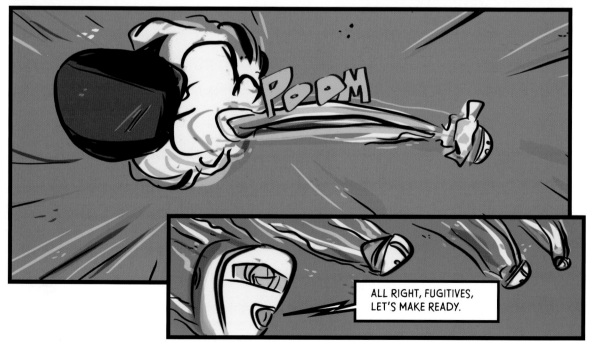

POOM

ALL RIGHT, FUGITIVES, LET'S MAKE READY.

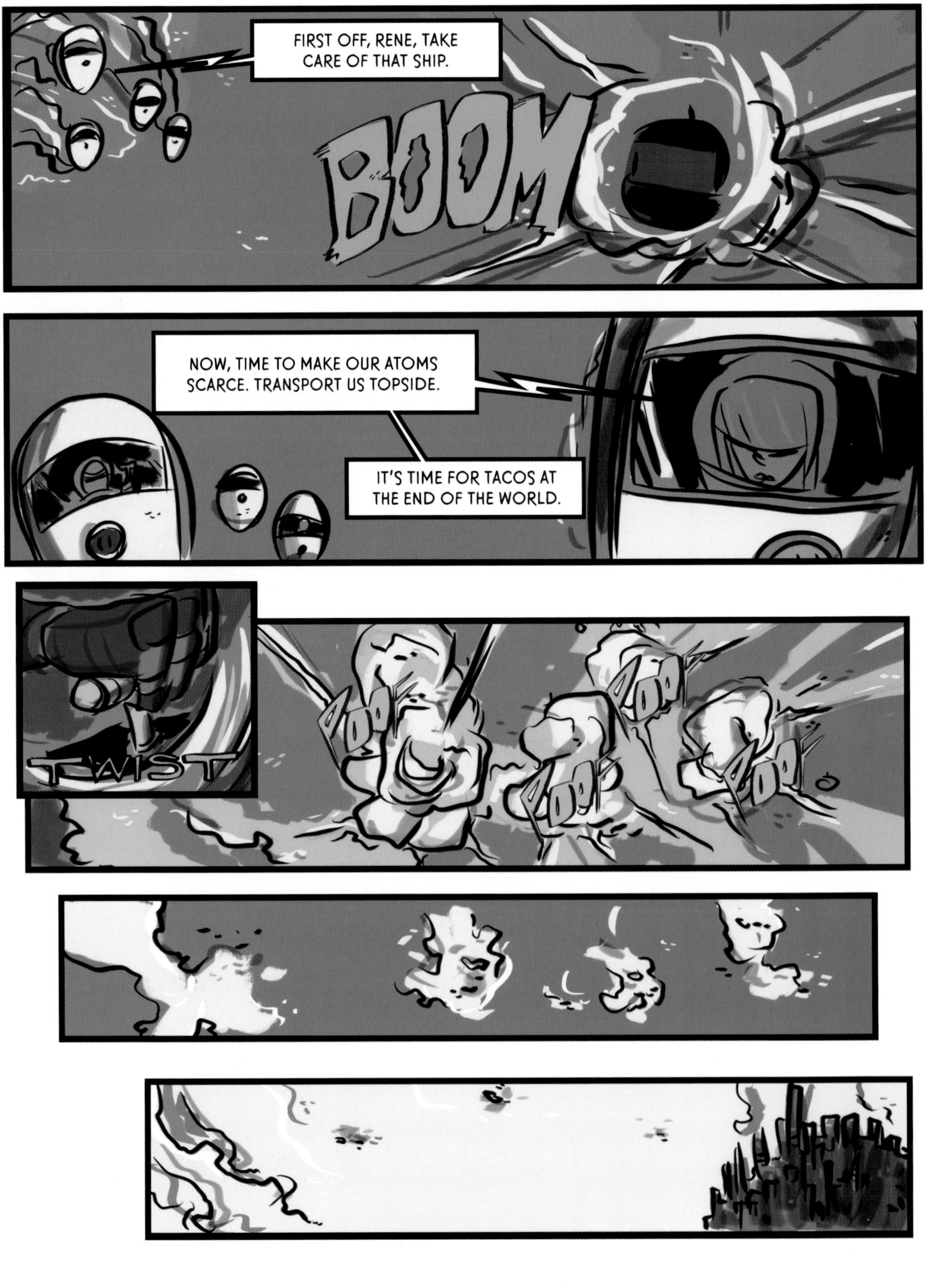
FIRST OFF, RENE, TAKE CARE OF THAT SHIP.
BOOM
NOW, TIME TO MAKE OUR ATOMS SCARCE. TRANSPORT US TOPSIDE.
IT'S TIME FOR TACOS AT THE END OF THE WORLD.
TWIST

NEXT: TACOS AT THE END OF THE WORLD

ISSUE TWO:
TACOS AT THE END OF THE WORLD

SMILE:
To smile is to register the absurdity of the universe, thus, no doubt, one should always be smiling.

-STEPHEN HAWKING

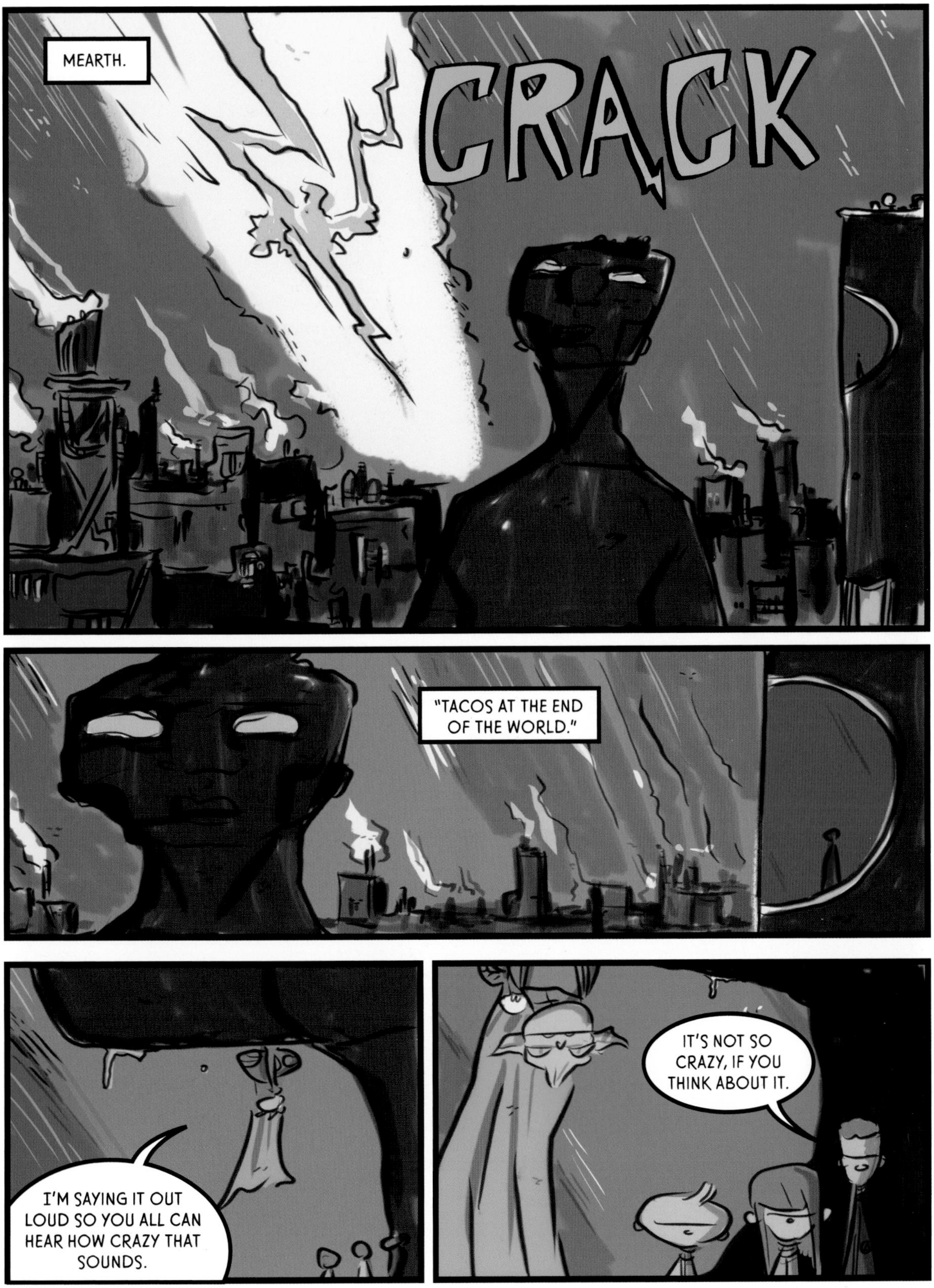
MEARTH.
CRACK
"TACOS AT THE END OF THE WORLD."
I'M SAYING IT OUT LOUD SO YOU ALL CAN HEAR HOW CRAZY THAT SOUNDS.
IT'S NOT SO CRAZY, IF YOU THINK ABOUT IT.

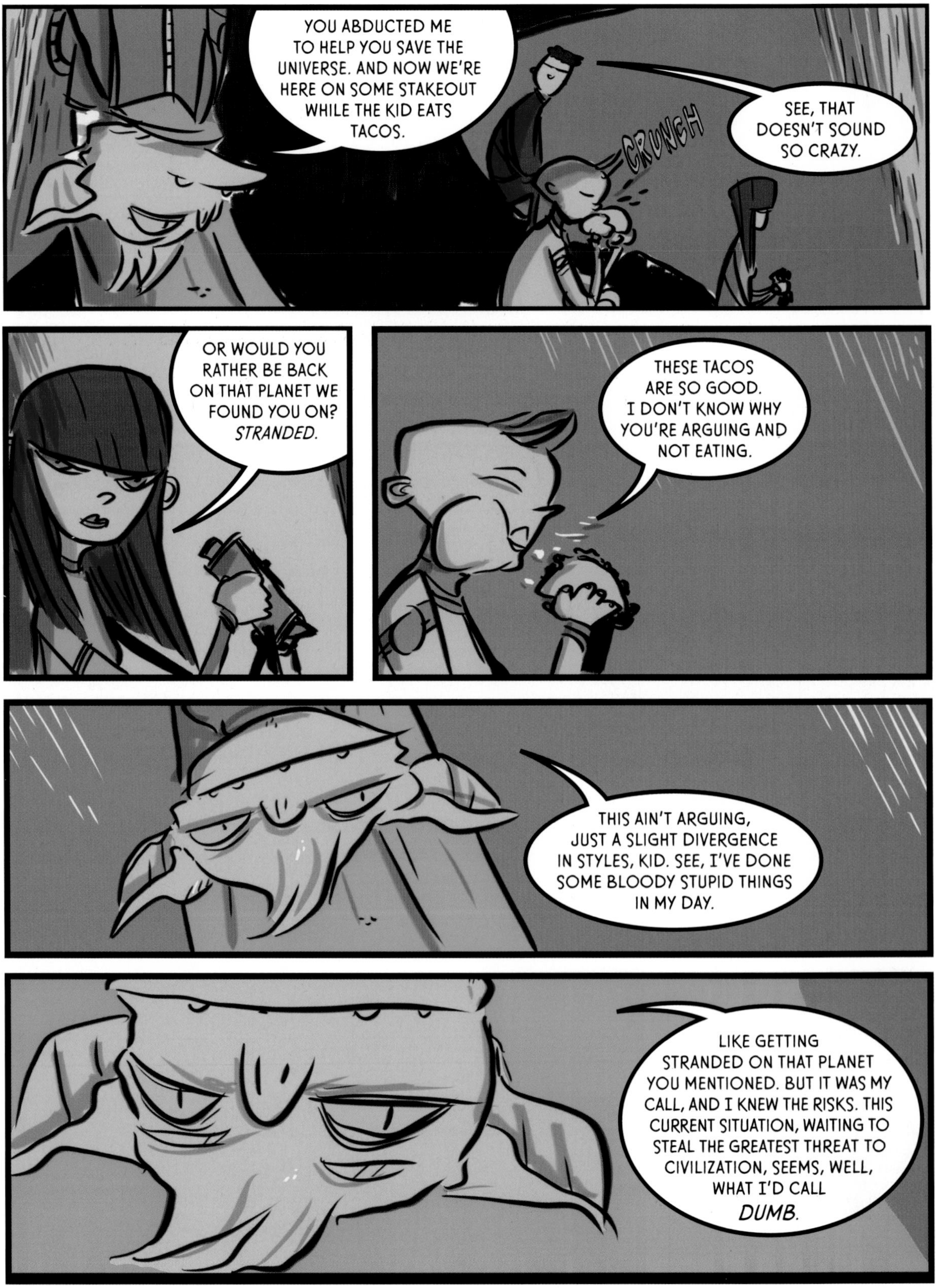
YOU ABDUCTED ME TO HELP YOU SAVE THE UNIVERSE. AND NOW WE'RE HERE ON SOME STAKEOUT WHILE THE KID EATS TACOS.
CRUNCH
SEE, THAT DOESN'T SOUND SO CRAZY.
OR WOULD YOU RATHER BE BACK ON THAT PLANET WE FOUND YOU ON? *STRANDED.*
THESE TACOS ARE SO GOOD. I DON'T KNOW WHY YOU'RE ARGUING AND NOT EATING.
THIS AIN'T ARGUING, JUST A SLIGHT DIVERGENCE IN STYLES, KID. SEE, I'VE DONE SOME BLOODY STUPID THINGS IN MY DAY.
LIKE GETTING STRANDED ON THAT PLANET YOU MENTIONED. BUT IT WAS MY CALL, AND I KNEW THE RISKS. THIS CURRENT SITUATION, WAITING TO STEAL THE GREATEST THREAT TO CIVILIZATION, SEEMS, WELL, WHAT I'D CALL *DUMB.*

CALL IT WHAT YOU WANT, BUT WE'RE HERE AND WE'RE DOING THIS. END OF DISCUSSION.

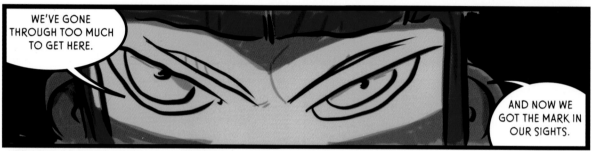

WE'VE GONE THROUGH TOO MUCH TO GET HERE.

AND NOW WE GOT THE MARK IN OUR SIGHTS.

'THAT GOON IS SITTING A HUNDRED YARDS AWAY DRINKING MOJITOS OUT OF A TEA CUP.'

'HE IS JUST WAITING FOR A CALL TO TELL HIM WHERE TO PICK UP THIS DOOMSDAY DEVICE.'

'THE MAN FROM *SICILY*.'

'HE HAS NO IDEA WE'RE GOING TO PIGGY-BACK THAT TRANSMISSION AND BEAT HIM TO THE DROP SITE.'

'EVERYTHING IS SET.'

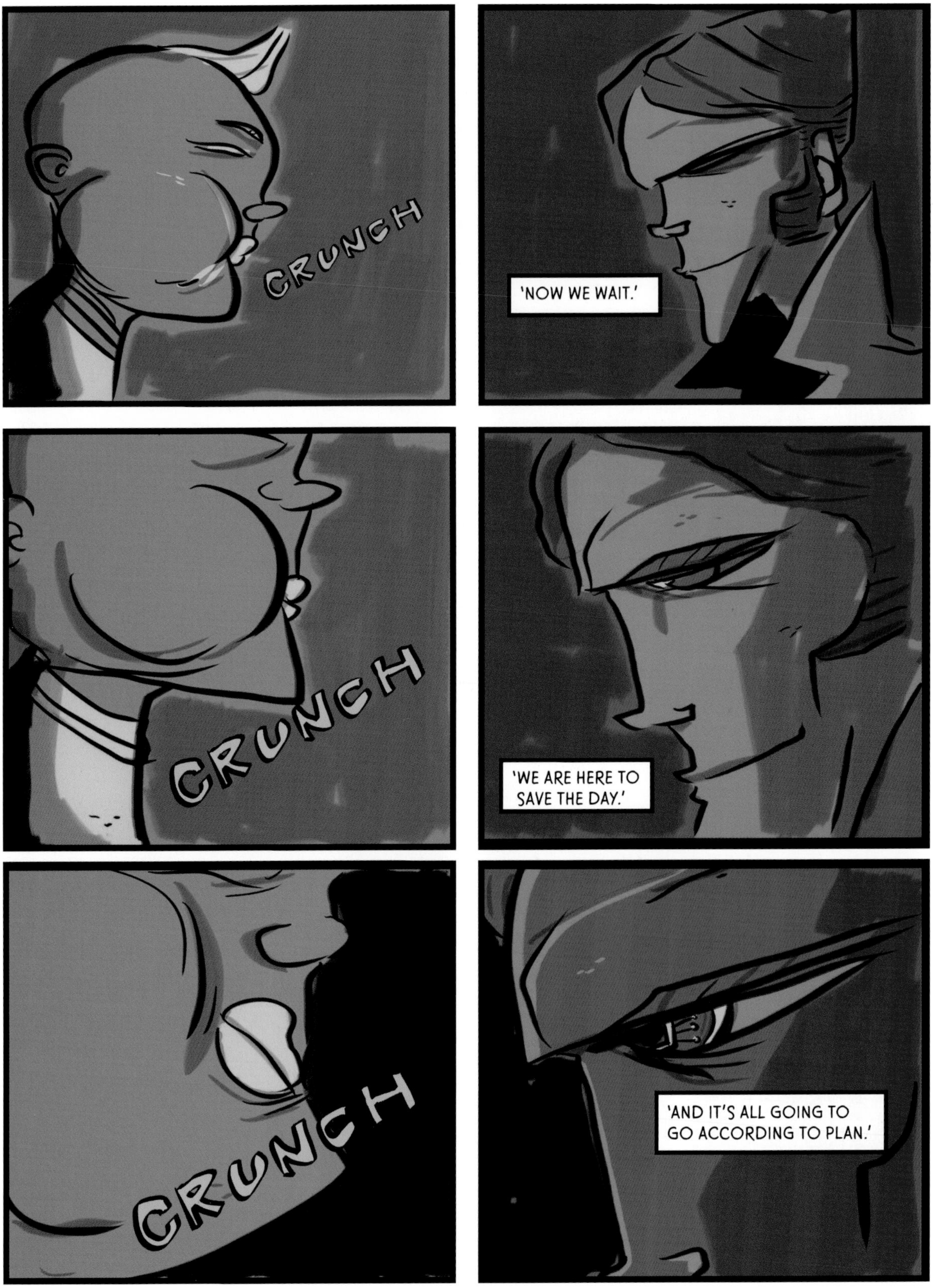
CRUNCH
'NOW WE WAIT.'
CRUNCH
'WE ARE HERE TO SAVE THE DAY.'
CRUNCH
'AND IT'S ALL GOING TO GO ACCORDING TO PLAN.'

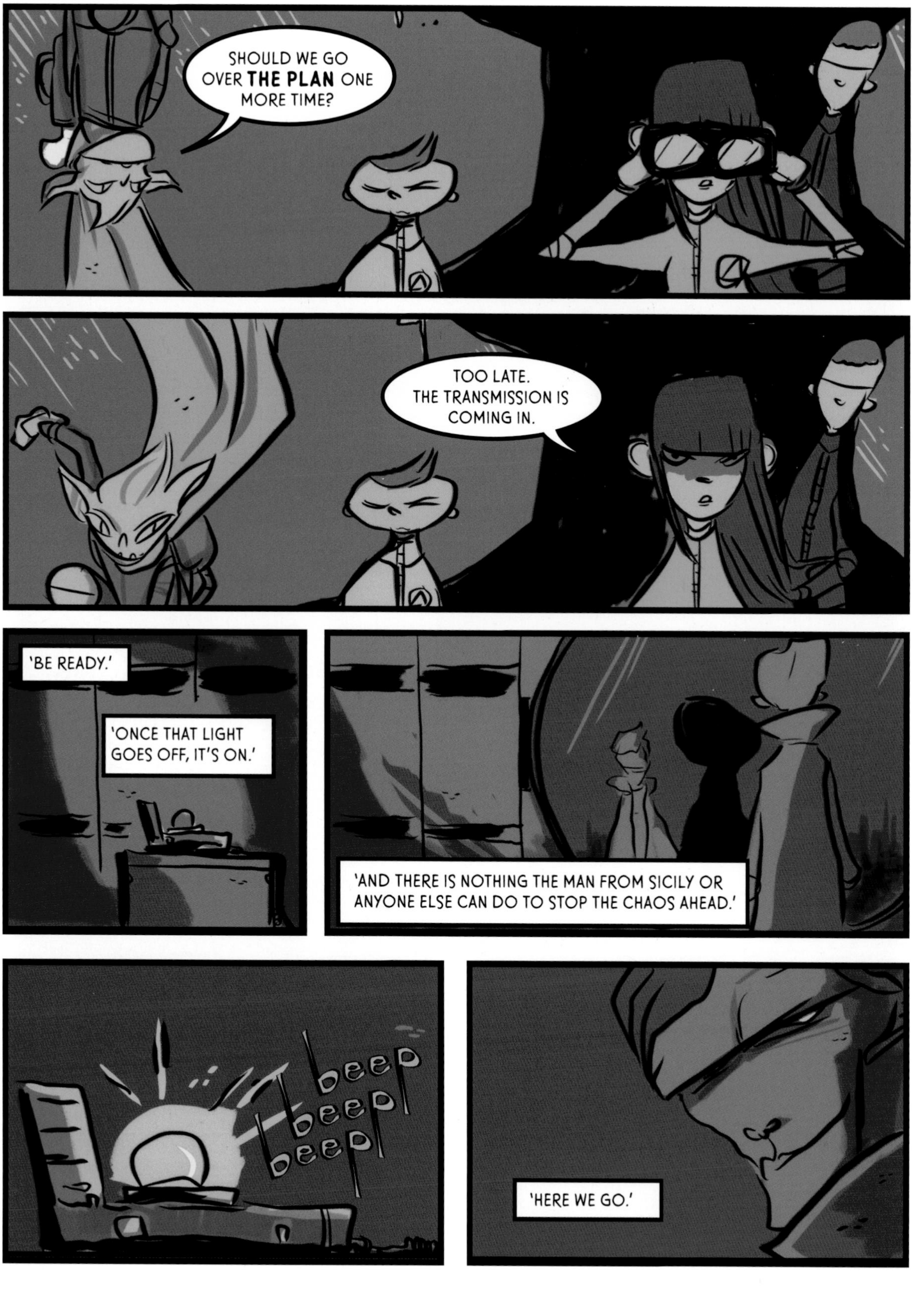
SHOULD WE GO OVER **THE PLAN** ONE MORE TIME?
TOO LATE. THE TRANSMISSION IS COMING IN.
'BE READY.'
'ONCE THAT LIGHT GOES OFF, IT'S ON.'
'AND THERE IS NOTHING THE MAN FROM SICILY OR ANYONE ELSE CAN DO TO STOP THE CHAOS AHEAD.'
beep beep beep
'HERE WE GO.'

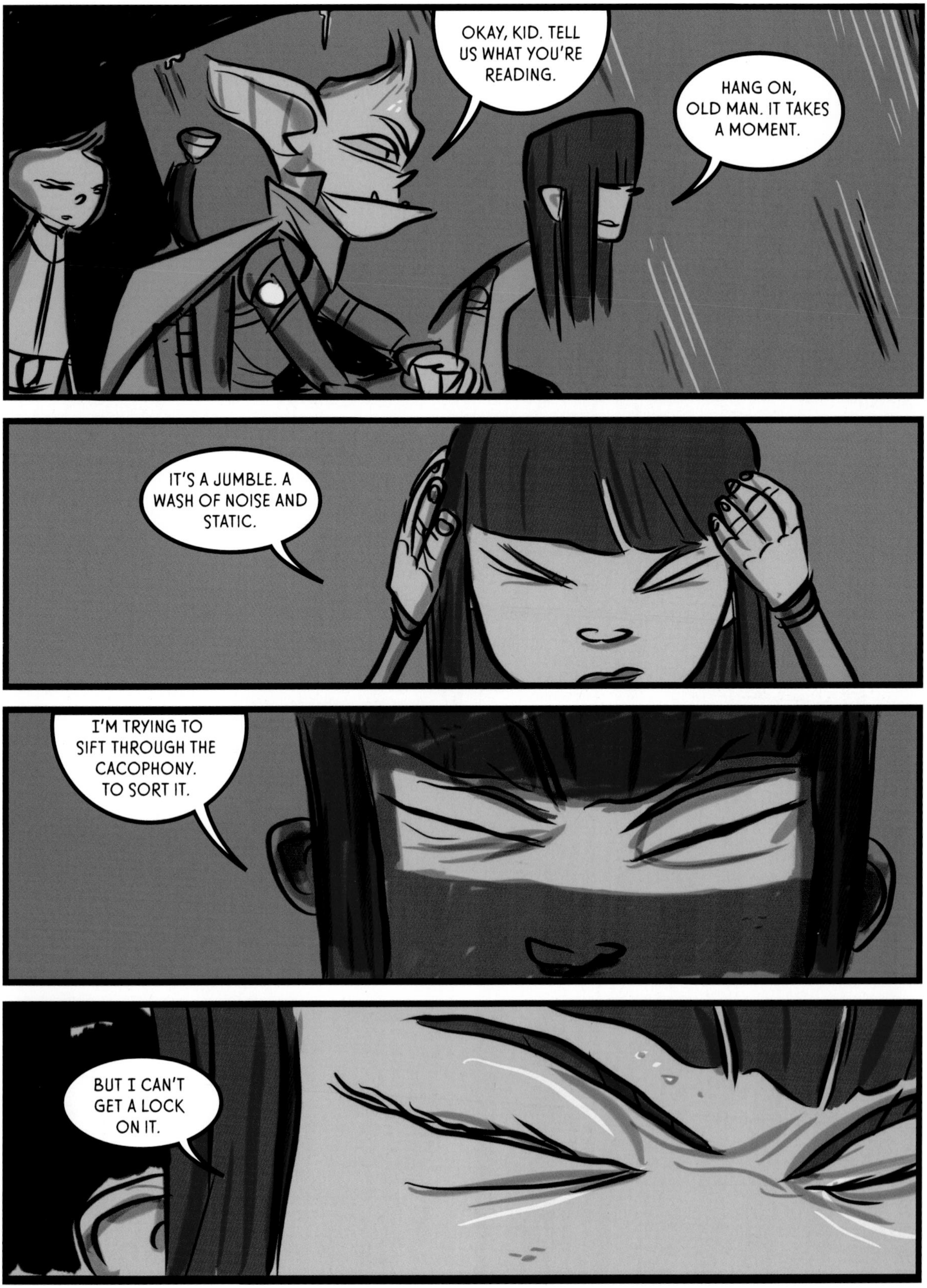
OKAY, KID. TELL US WHAT YOU'RE READING.
HANG ON, OLD MAN. IT TAKES A MOMENT.
IT'S A JUMBLE. A WASH OF NOISE AND STATIC.
I'M TRYING TO SIFT THROUGH THE CACOPHONY. TO SORT IT.
BUT I CAN'T GET A LOCK ON IT.

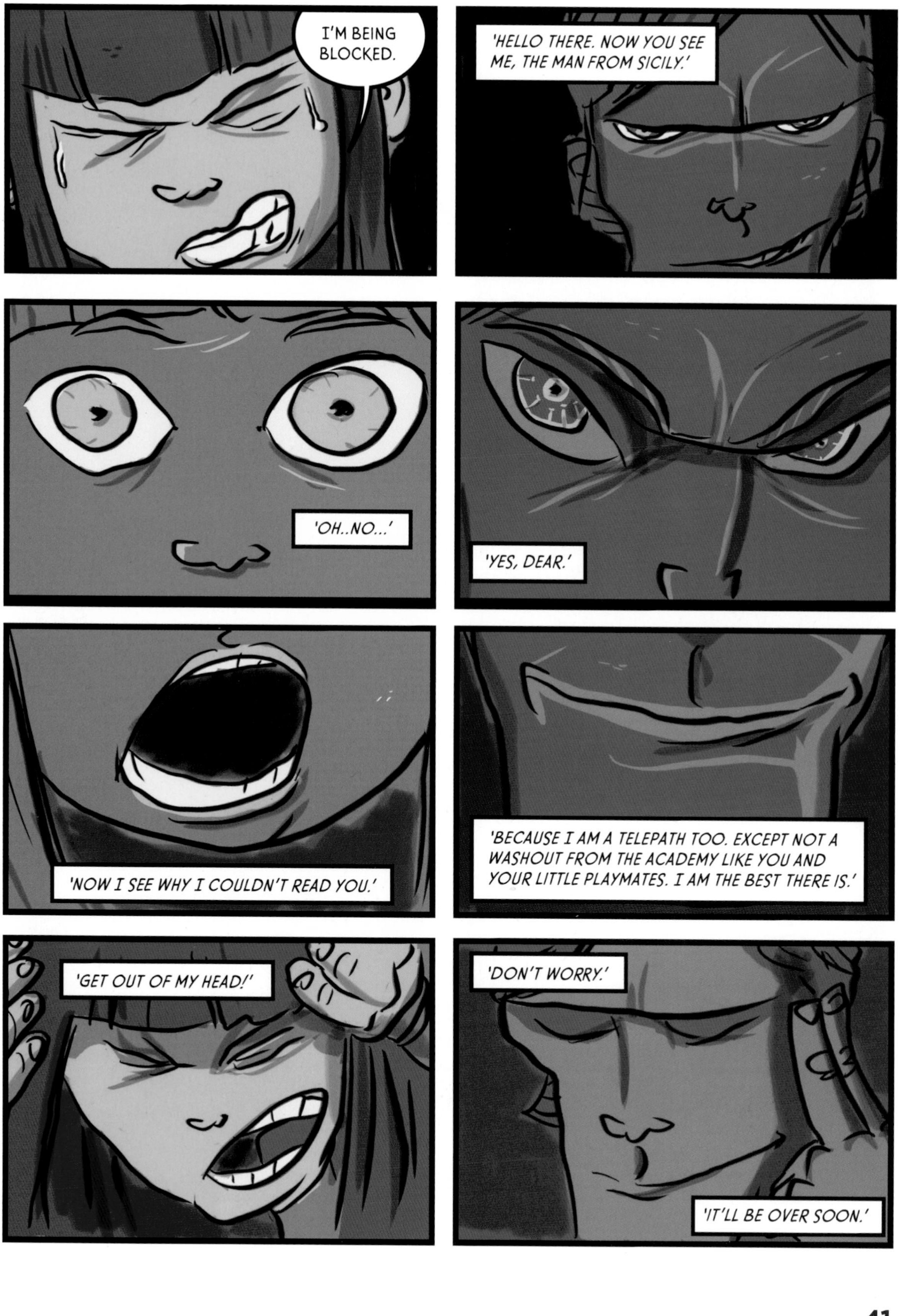
I'M BEING BLOCKED.
'HELLO THERE. NOW YOU SEE ME, THE MAN FROM SICILY.'
'OH..NO...'
'YES, DEAR.'
'NOW I SEE WHY I COULDN'T READ YOU.'
'BECAUSE I AM A TELEPATH TOO. EXCEPT NOT A WASHOUT FROM THE ACADEMY LIKE YOU AND YOUR LITTLE PLAYMATES. I AM THE BEST THERE IS.'
'GET OUT OF MY HEAD!'
'DON'T WORRY.'
'IT'LL BE OVER SOON.'

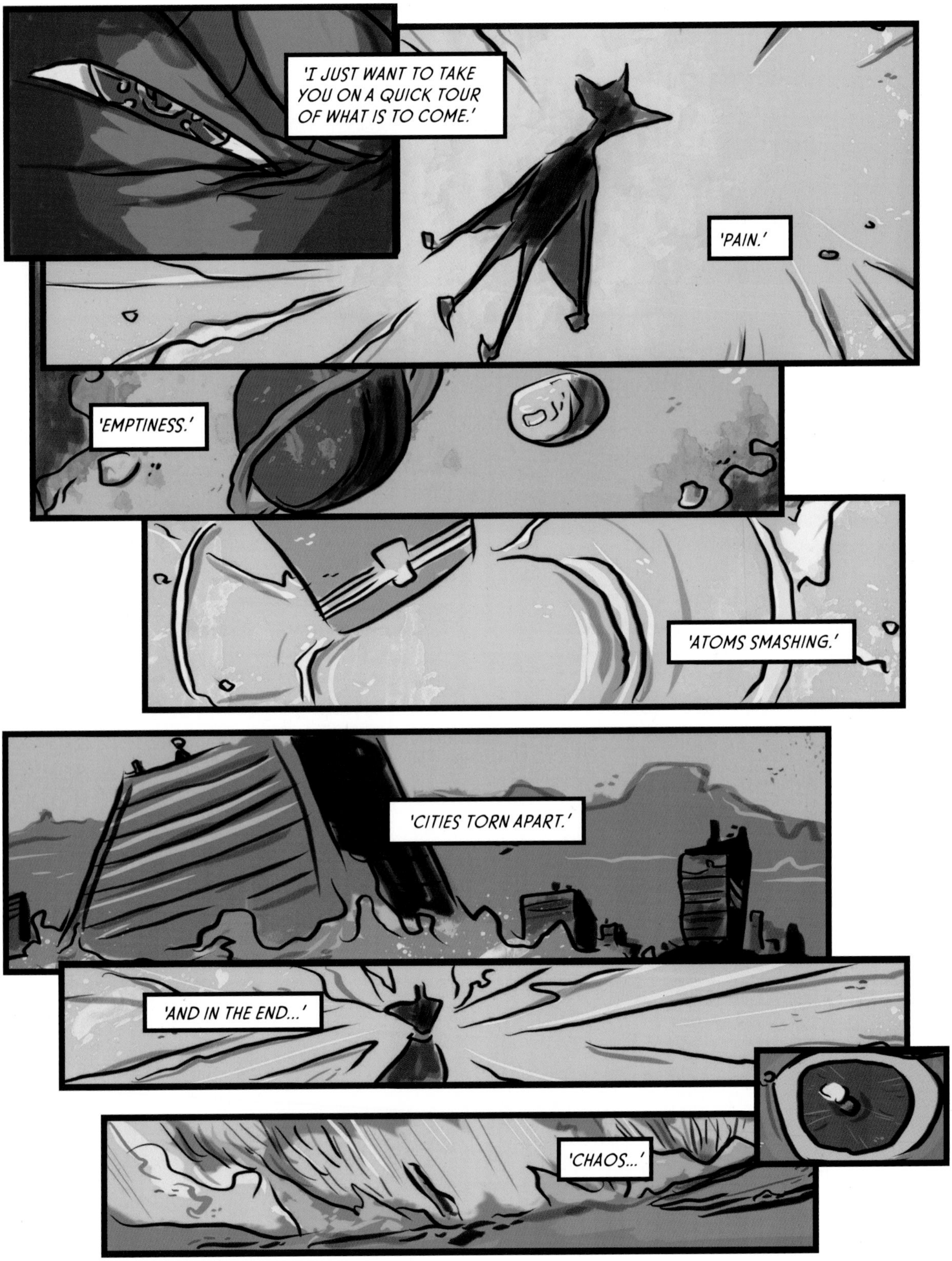
'I JUST WANT TO TAKE YOU ON A QUICK TOUR OF WHAT IS TO COME.'
'PAIN.'
'EMPTINESS.'
'ATOMS SMASHING.'
'CITIES TORN APART.'
'AND IN THE END...'
'CHAOS...'

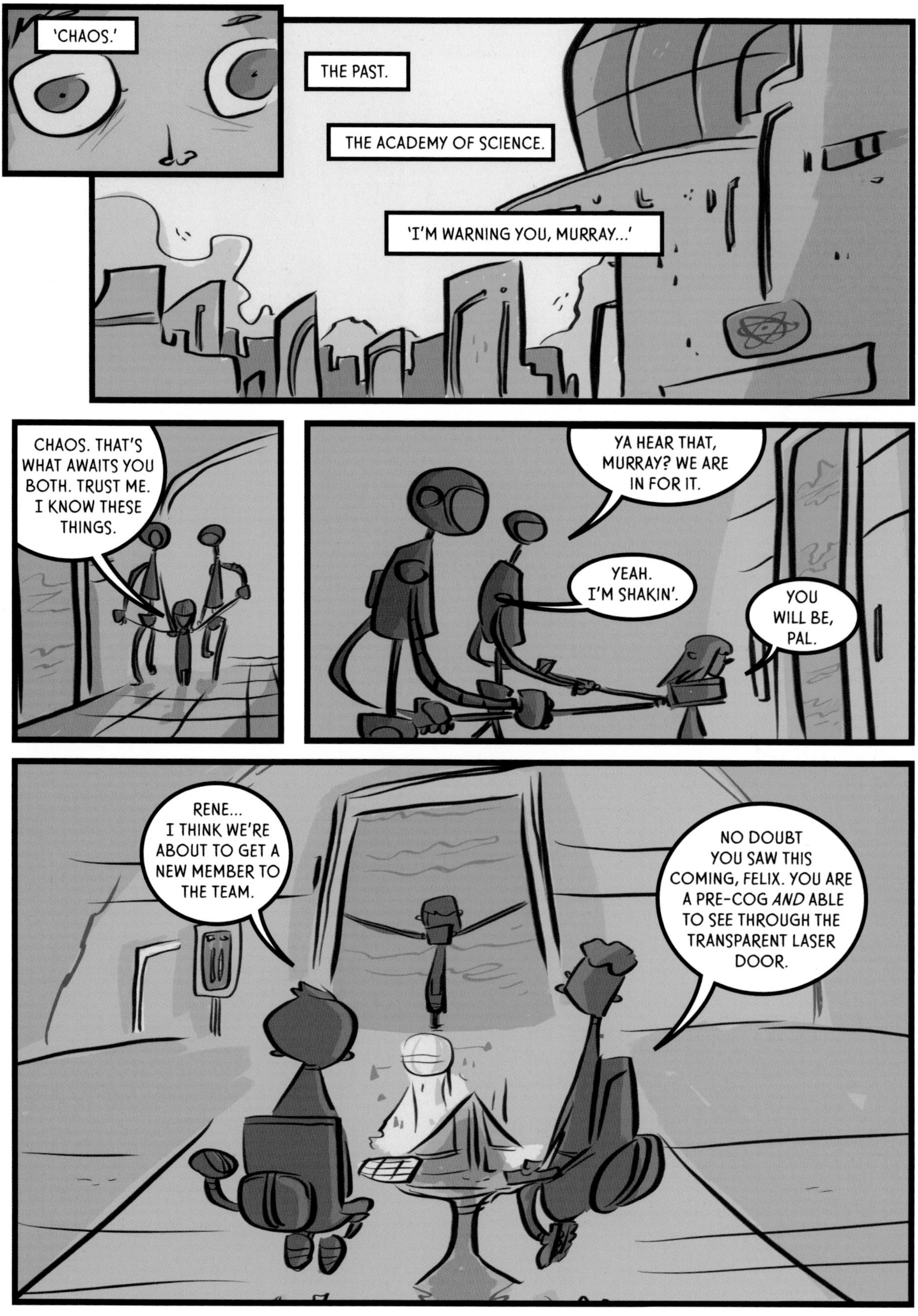
'CHAOS.'
THE PAST.
THE ACADEMY OF SCIENCE.
'I'M WARNING YOU, MURRAY...'
CHAOS. THAT'S WHAT AWAITS YOU BOTH. TRUST ME. I KNOW THESE THINGS.
YA HEAR THAT, MURRAY? WE ARE IN FOR IT.
YEAH. I'M SHAKIN'.
YOU WILL BE, PAL.
RENE... I THINK WE'RE ABOUT TO GET A NEW MEMBER TO THE TEAM.
NO DOUBT YOU SAW THIS COMING, FELIX. YOU ARE A PRE-COG *AND* ABLE TO SEE THROUGH THE TRANSPARENT LASER DOOR.

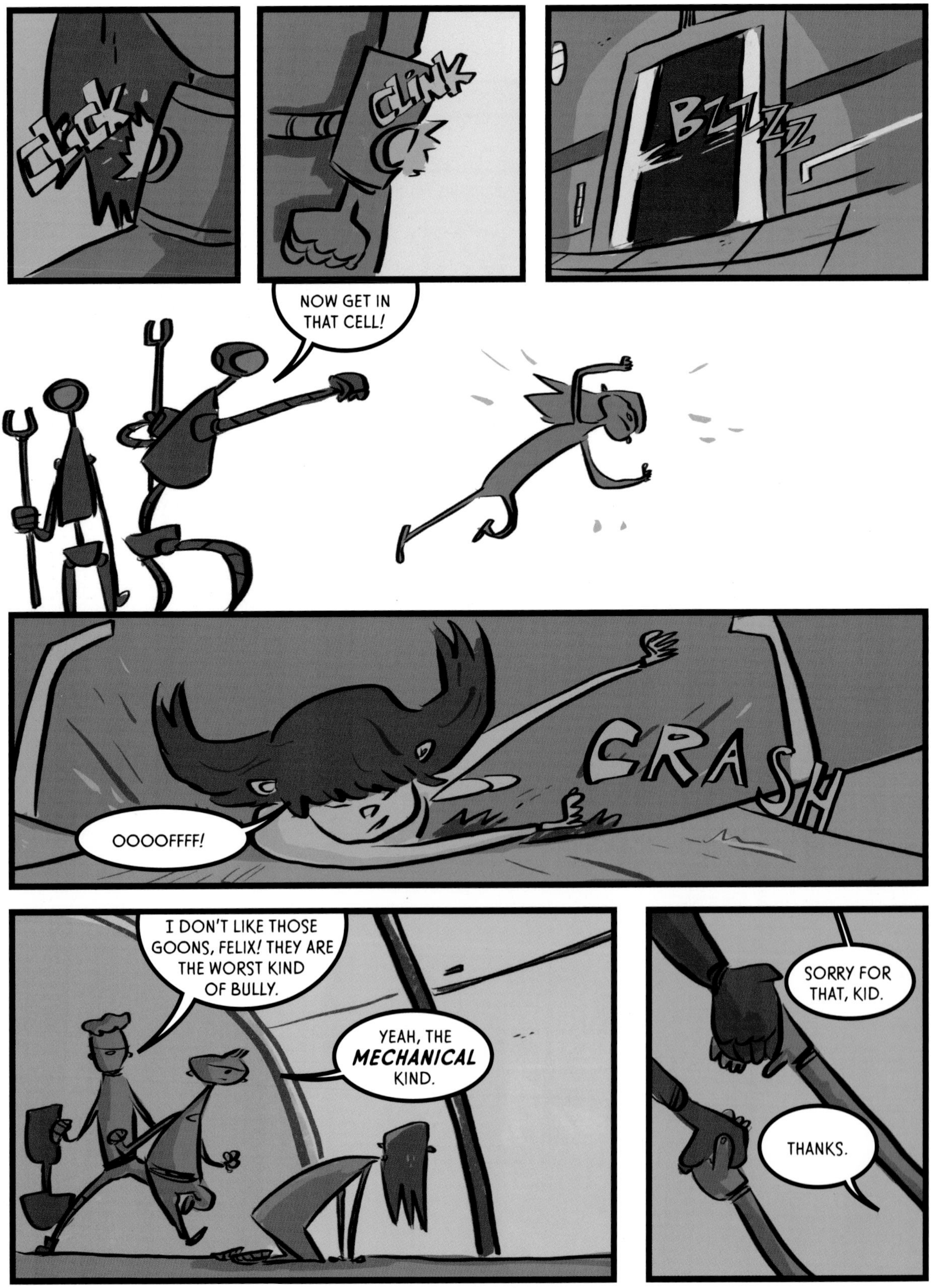
CLICK
CLINK
BZZZZ
NOW GET IN THAT CELL!
CRASH
OOOOFFFF!
I DON'T LIKE THOSE GOONS, FELIX! THEY ARE THE WORST KIND OF BULLY.
YEAH, THE ***MECHANICAL*** KIND.
SORRY FOR THAT, KID.
THANKS.

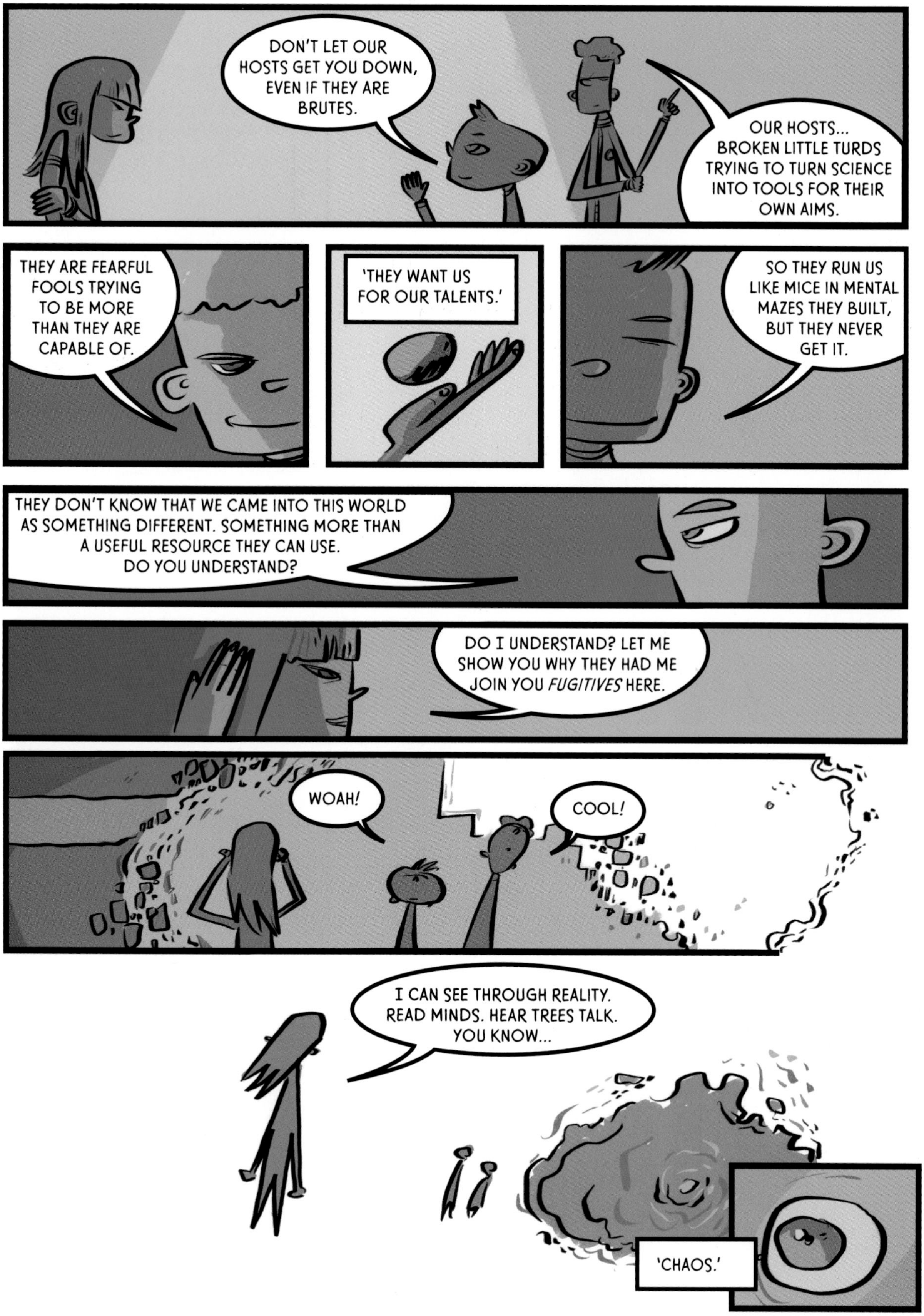
DON'T LET OUR HOSTS GET YOU DOWN, EVEN IF THEY ARE BRUTES.
OUR HOSTS... BROKEN LITTLE TURDS TRYING TO TURN SCIENCE INTO TOOLS FOR THEIR OWN AIMS.
THEY ARE FEARFUL FOOLS TRYING TO BE MORE THAN THEY ARE CAPABLE OF.
'THEY WANT US FOR OUR TALENTS.'
SO THEY RUN US LIKE MICE IN MENTAL MAZES THEY BUILT, BUT THEY NEVER GET IT.
THEY DON'T KNOW THAT WE CAME INTO THIS WORLD AS SOMETHING DIFFERENT. SOMETHING MORE THAN A USEFUL RESOURCE THEY CAN USE. DO YOU UNDERSTAND?
DO I UNDERSTAND? LET ME SHOW YOU WHY THEY HAD ME JOIN YOU *FUGITIVES* HERE.
WOAH!
COOL!
I CAN SEE THROUGH REALITY. READ MINDS. HEAR TREES TALK. YOU KNOW...
'CHAOS.'

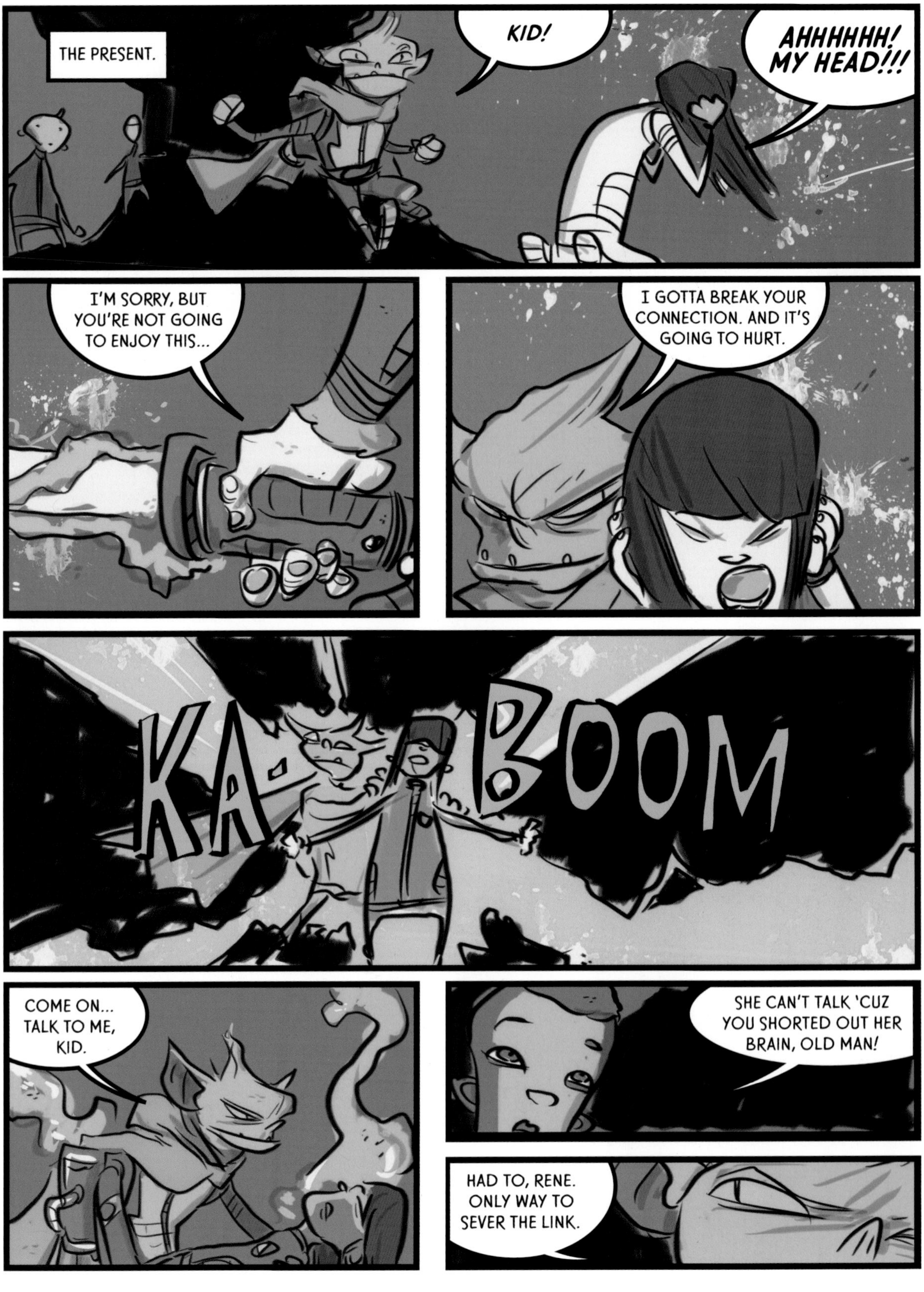
THE PRESENT.
KID!
AHHHHHH! MY HEAD!!!
I'M SORRY, BUT YOU'RE NOT GOING TO ENJOY THIS...
I GOTTA BREAK YOUR CONNECTION. AND IT'S GOING TO HURT.
KA-BOOM
COME ON... TALK TO ME, KID.
SHE CAN'T TALK 'CUZ YOU SHORTED OUT HER BRAIN, OLD MAN!
HAD TO, RENE. ONLY WAY TO SEVER THE LINK.

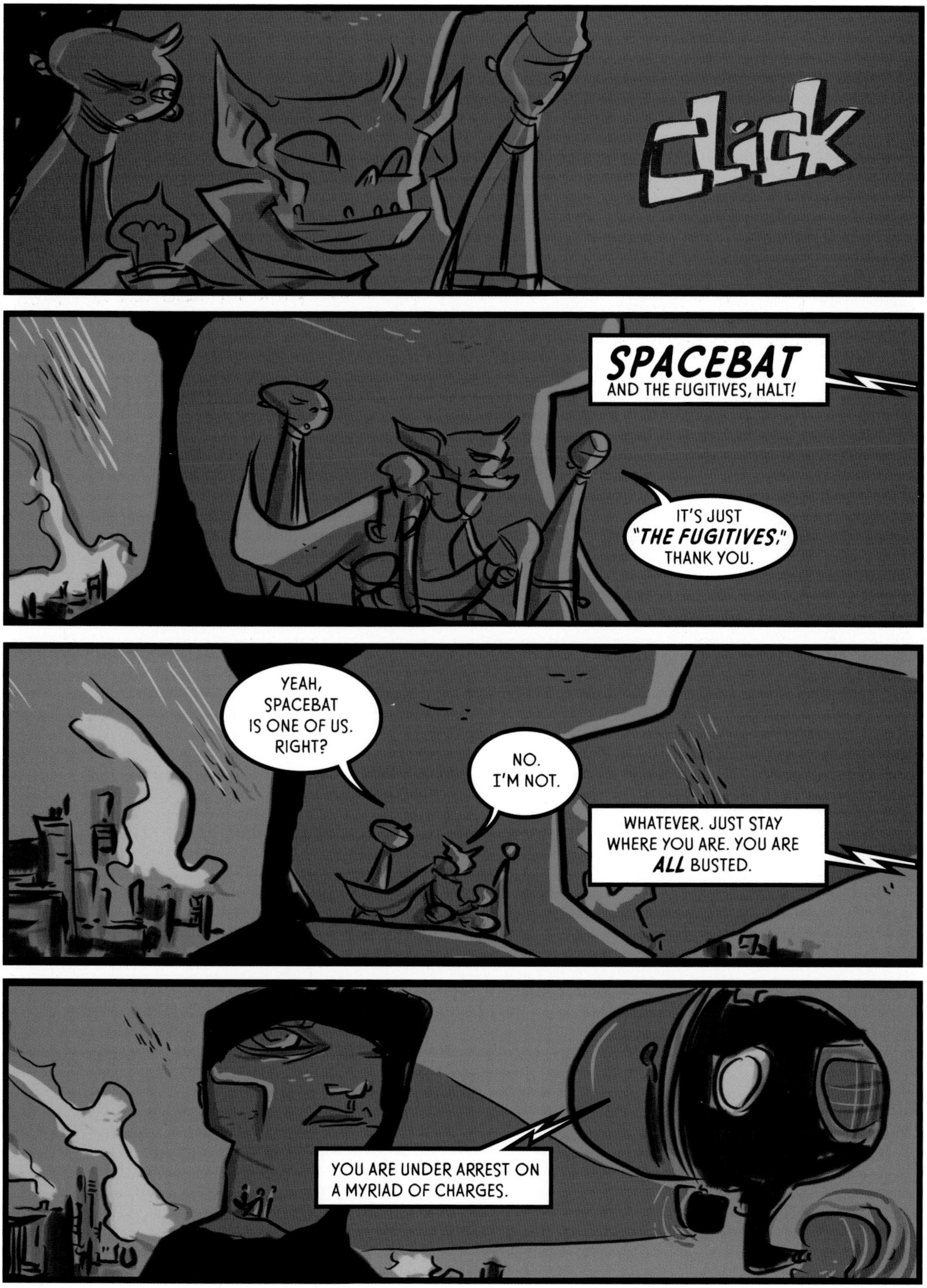
CLICK
SPACEBAT AND THE FUGITIVES, HALT!
IT'S JUST "THE FUGITIVES," THANK YOU.
YEAH, SPACEBAT IS ONE OF US. RIGHT?
NO. I'M NOT.
WHATEVER. JUST STAY WHERE YOU ARE. YOU ARE ALL BUSTED.
YOU ARE UNDER ARREST ON A MYRIAD OF CHARGES.

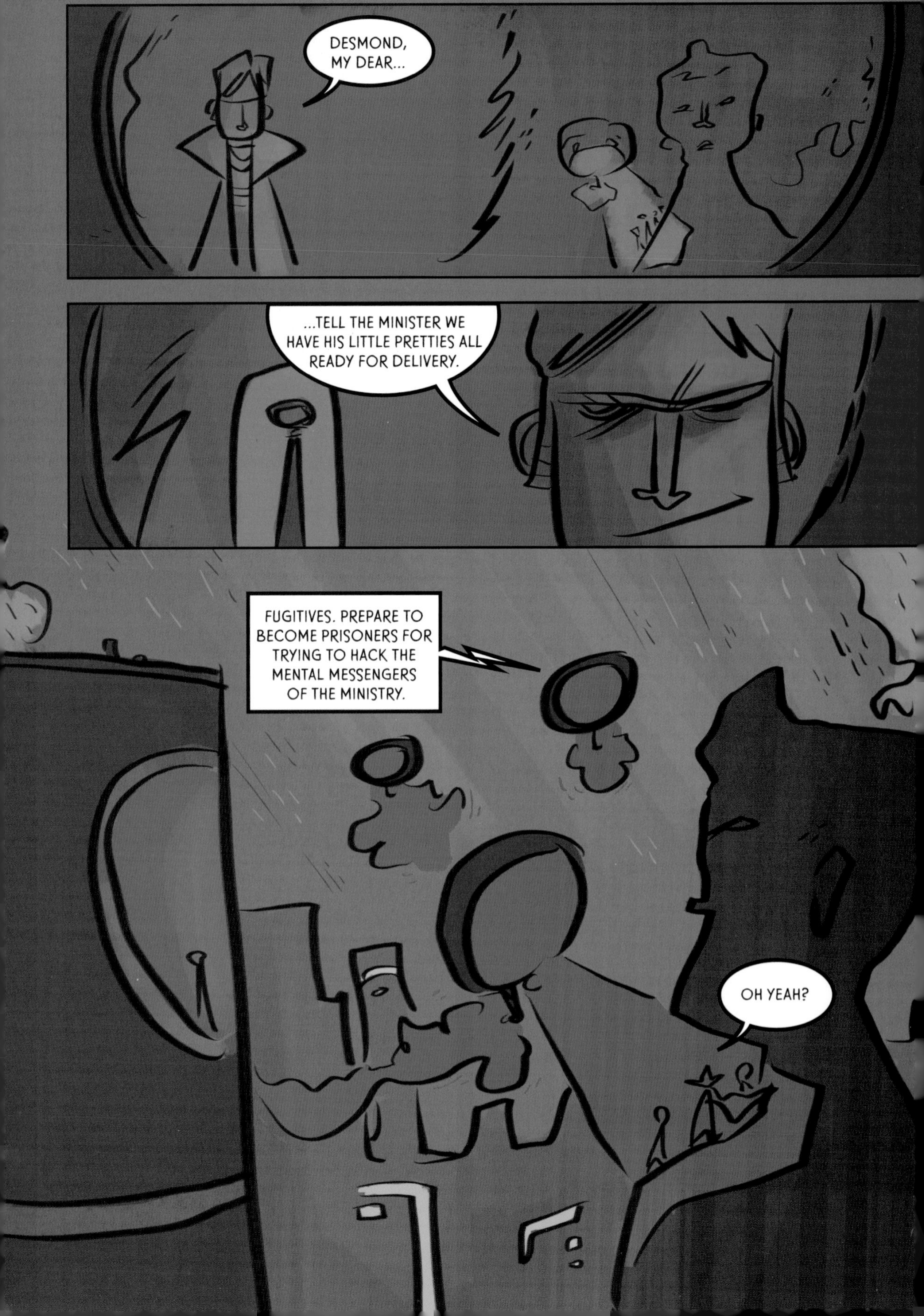
DESMOND, MY DEAR...
...TELL THE MINISTER WE HAVE HIS LITTLE PRETTIES ALL READY FOR DELIVERY.
FUGITIVES. PREPARE TO BECOME PRISONERS FOR TRYING TO HACK THE MENTAL MESSENGERS OF THE MINISTRY.
OH YEAH?

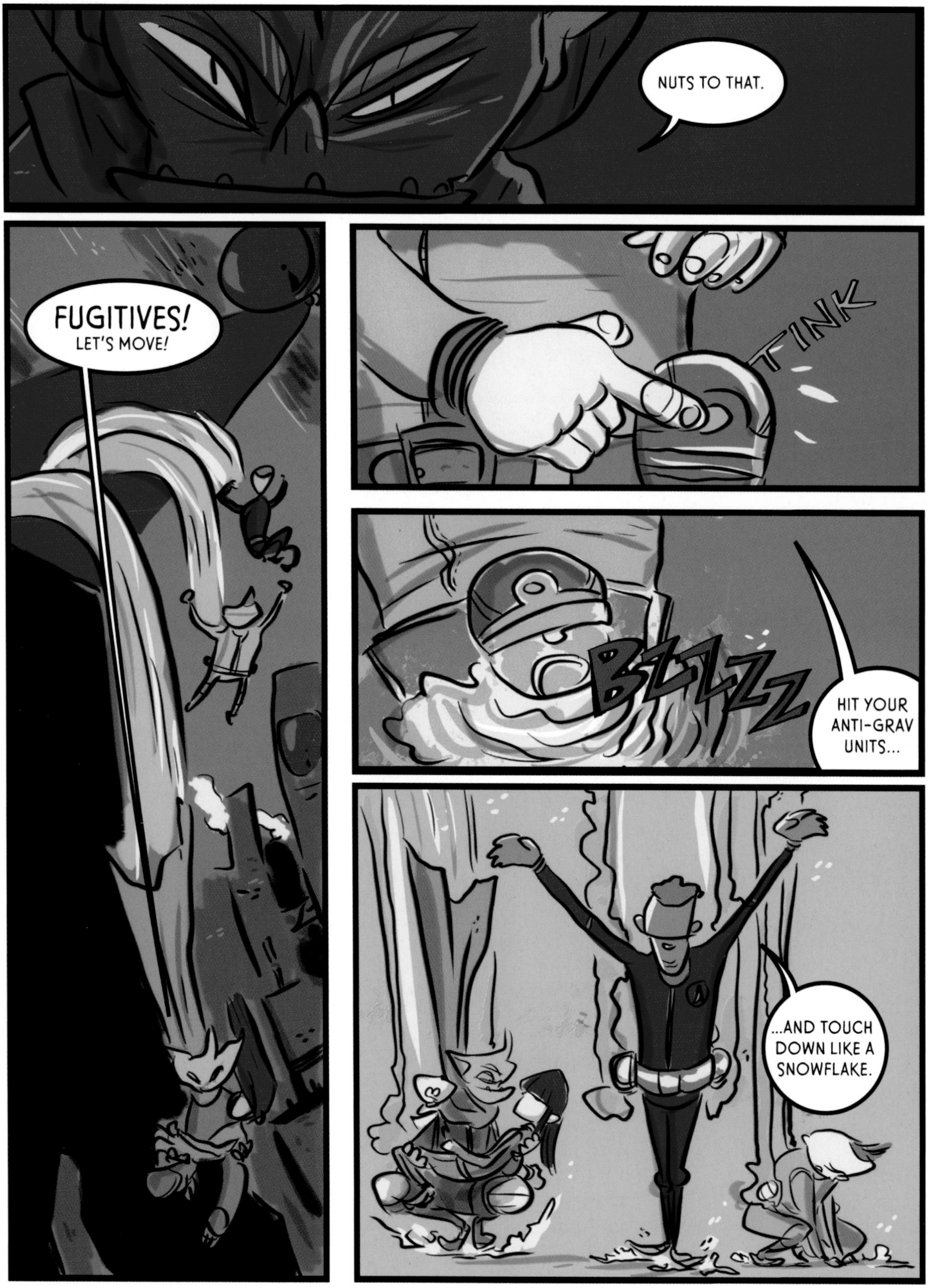
NUTS TO THAT.
FUGITIVES! LET'S MOVE!
TINK
BZZZZZ
HIT YOUR ANTI-GRAV UNITS...
...AND TOUCH DOWN LIKE A SNOWFLAKE.

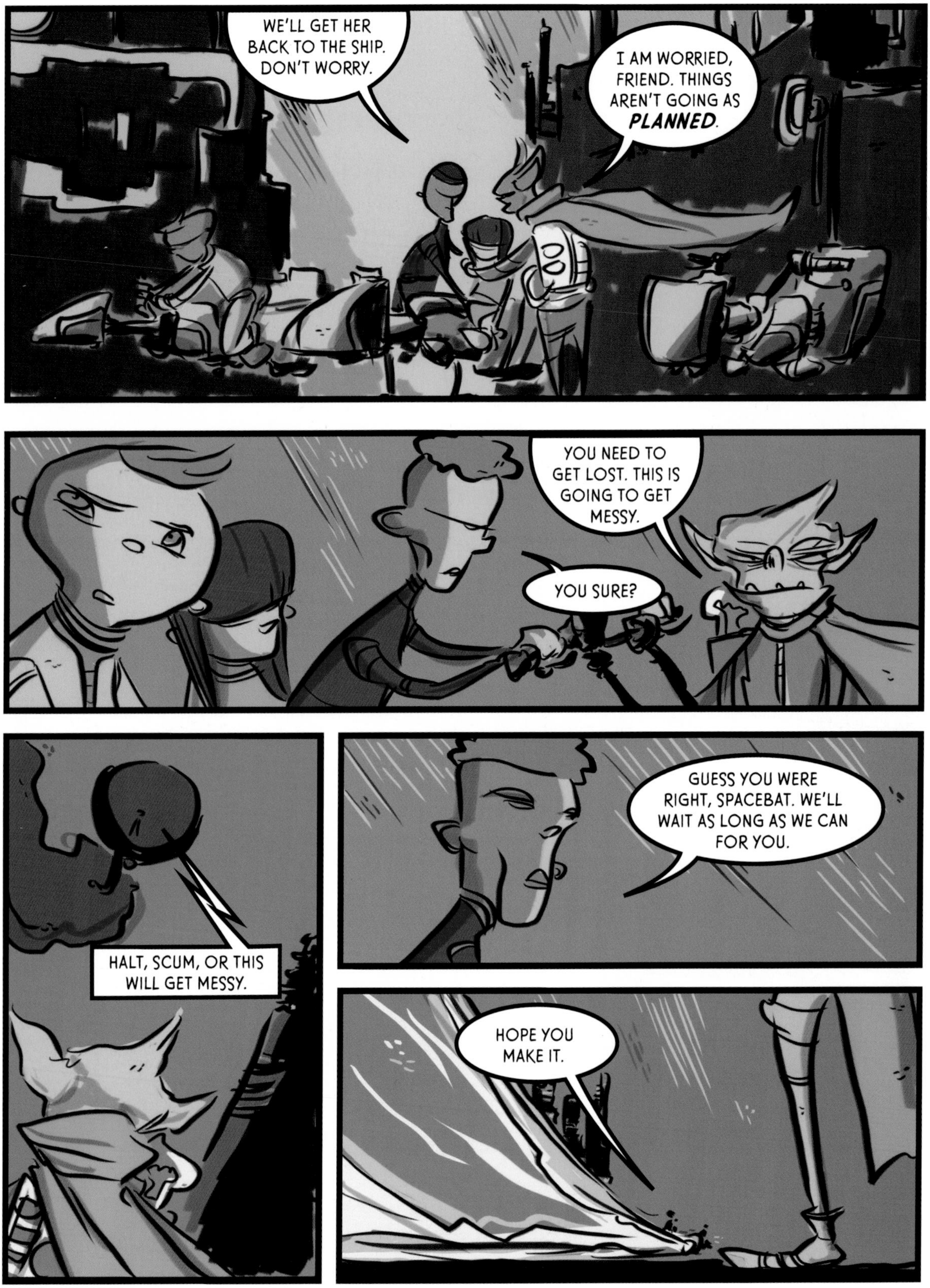
WE'LL GET HER BACK TO THE SHIP. DON'T WORRY.
I AM WORRIED, FRIEND. THINGS AREN'T GOING AS ***PLANNED***.
YOU NEED TO GET LOST. THIS IS GOING TO GET MESSY.
YOU SURE?
HALT, SCUM, OR THIS WILL GET MESSY.
GUESS YOU WERE RIGHT, SPACEBAT. WE'LL WAIT AS LONG AS WE CAN FOR YOU.
HOPE YOU MAKE IT.

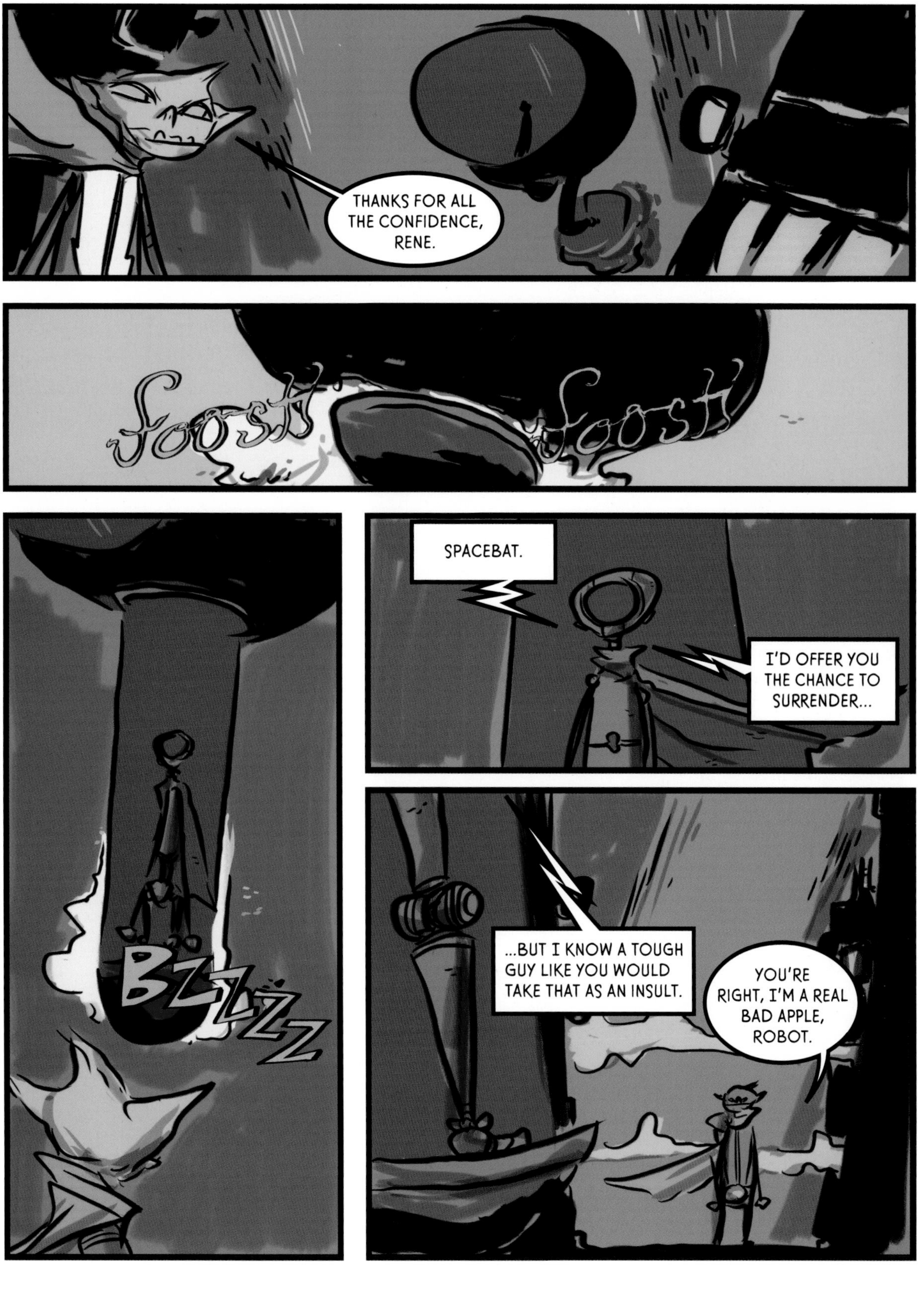
THANKS FOR ALL THE CONFIDENCE, RENE.
FOOSH
FOOSH
BZZZZZ
SPACEBAT.
I'D OFFER YOU THE CHANCE TO SURRENDER...
...BUT I KNOW A TOUGH GUY LIKE YOU WOULD TAKE THAT AS AN INSULT.
YOU'RE RIGHT, I'M A REAL BAD APPLE, ROBOT.

AND NO PLEASANTRIES OR COURTESIES WILL KEEP YOU FROM GETTING A SOCK IN THE JAW OR KNOCKED ON YOUR METAL KEISTER, MATE.

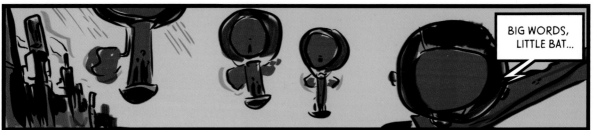

BIG WORDS, LITTLE BAT...

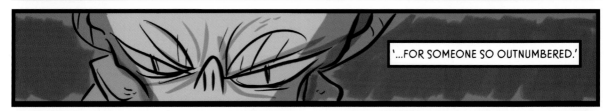

'...FOR SOMEONE SO OUTNUMBERED.'

KEISTER-KICKING TIME HAS ARRIVED.

KICK IT!

I MAY BE *BAD*...

...BUT I SURE AIN'T NUTS.

GIVEN THE ODDS, TIME TO MAKE AN EXIT!

THIS MAY BE HASTY, BUT I'M NOT RUNNING.

'IT'S A TACTIC.'

'IT'S STRATEGIC.'

BOOM

'SEE IF YOU CAN KEEP UP!'

X-71, PLOT A COURSE TO THE CITY CENTER.

CITY CENTER?

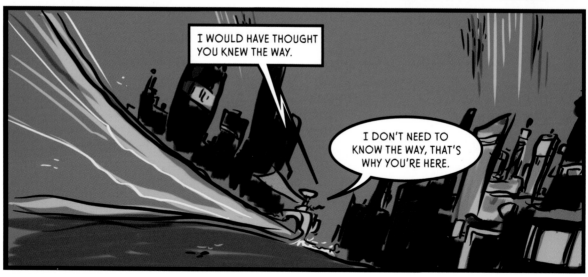

I WOULD HAVE THOUGHT YOU KNEW THE WAY.

I DON'T NEED TO KNOW THE WAY, THAT'S WHY YOU'RE HERE.

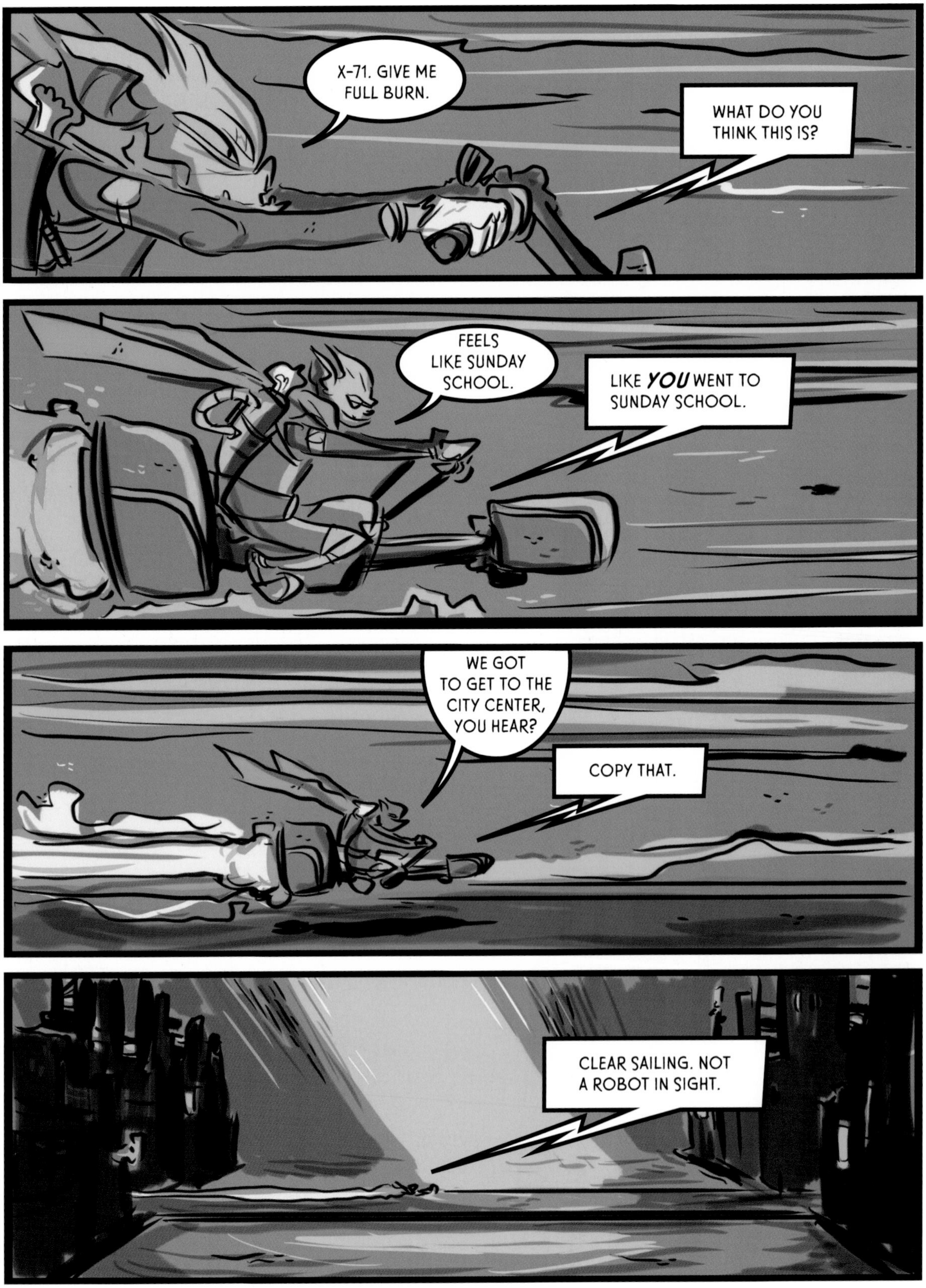
X-71. GIVE ME FULL BURN.
WHAT DO YOU THINK THIS IS?
FEELS LIKE SUNDAY SCHOOL.
LIKE *YOU* WENT TO SUNDAY SCHOOL.
WE GOT TO GET TO THE CITY CENTER, YOU HEAR?
COPY THAT.
CLEAR SAILING. NOT A ROBOT IN SIGHT.

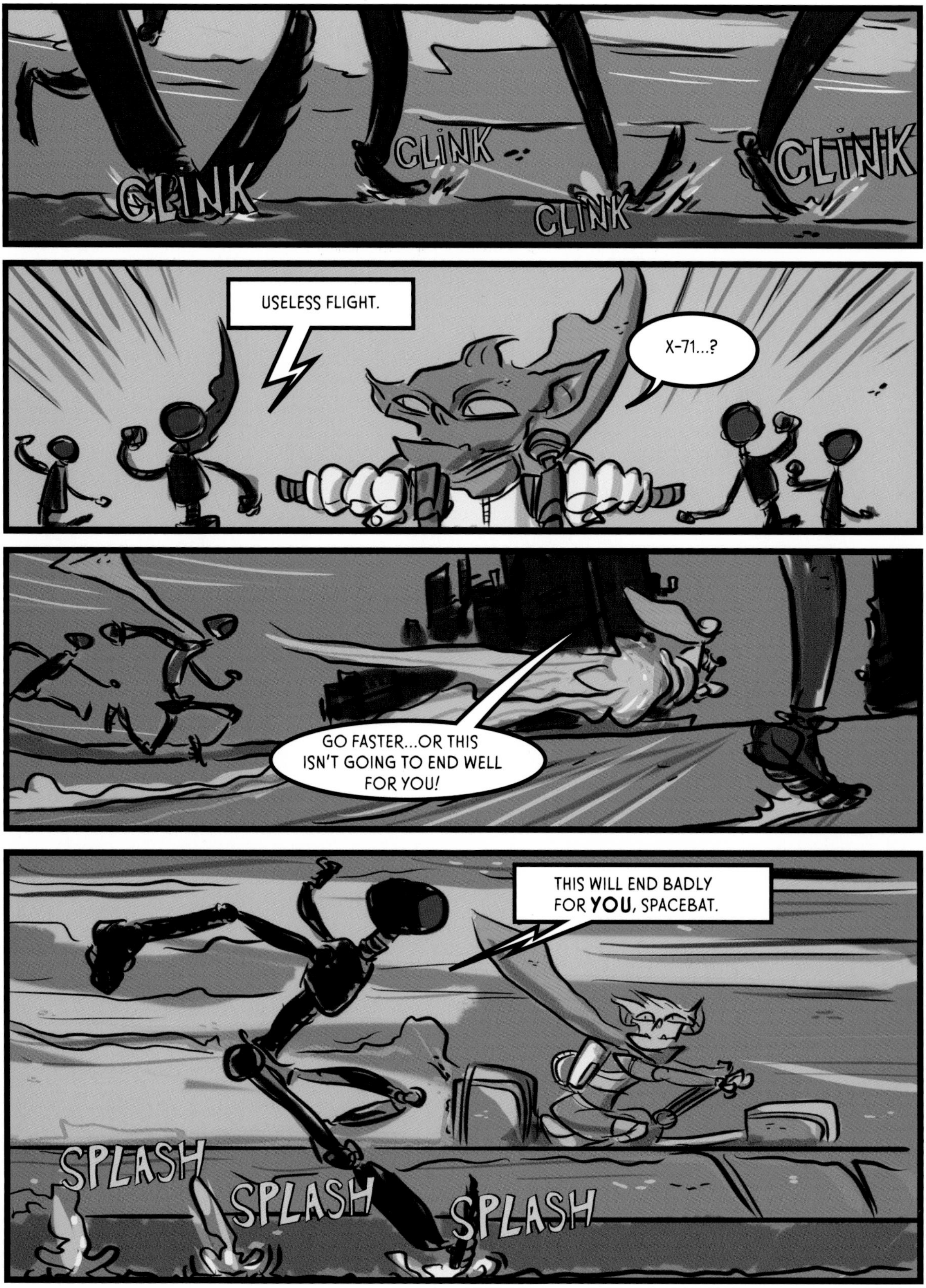
CLINK
CLINK
CLINK
CLINK
USELESS FLIGHT.
X-71...?
GO FASTER...OR THIS ISN'T GOING TO END WELL FOR YOU!
THIS WILL END BADLY FOR **YOU**, SPACEBAT.
SPLASH
SPLASH
SPLASH

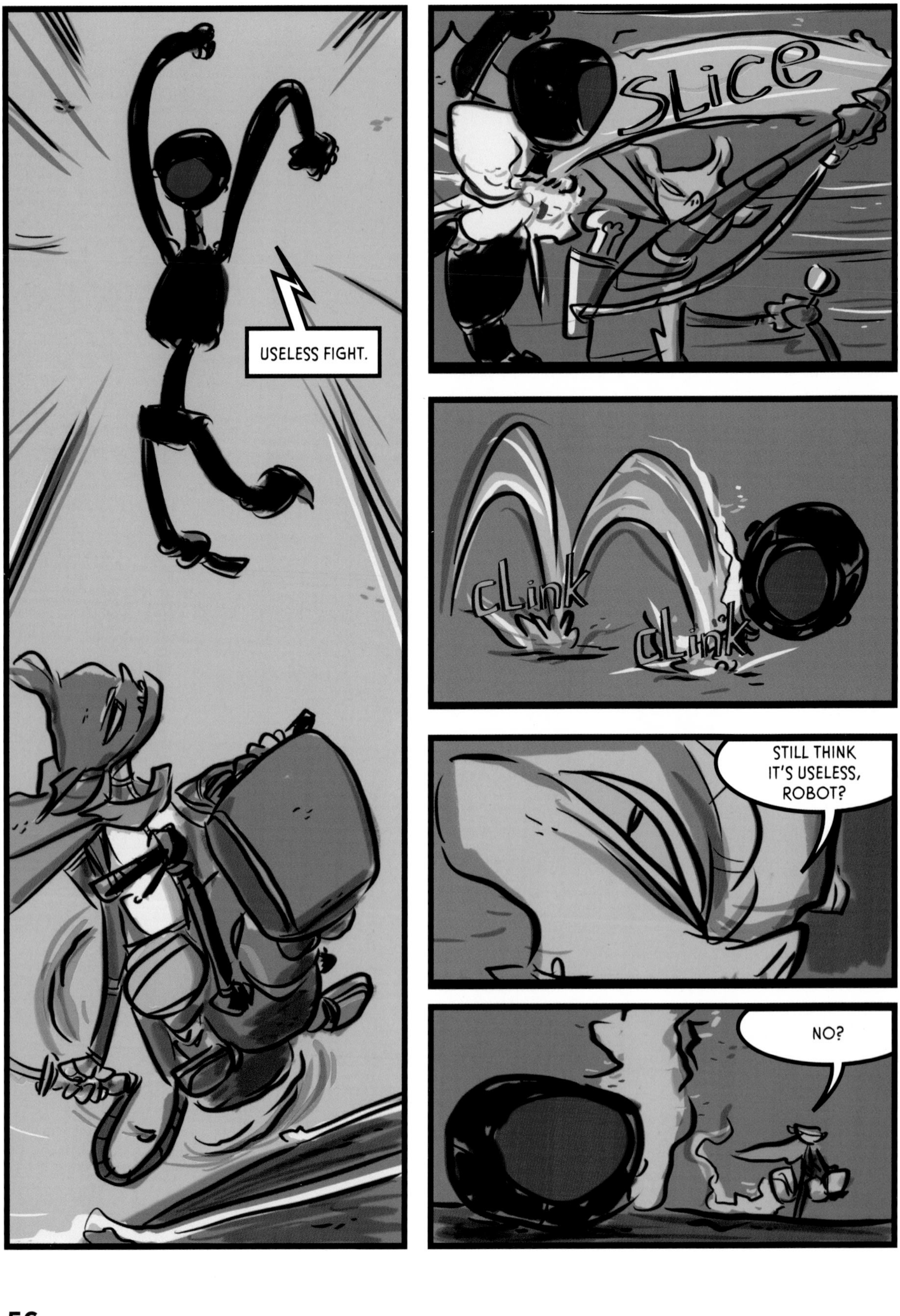
USELESS FIGHT.
SLICE
CLINK
CLINK
STILL THINK IT'S USELESS, ROBOT?
NO?

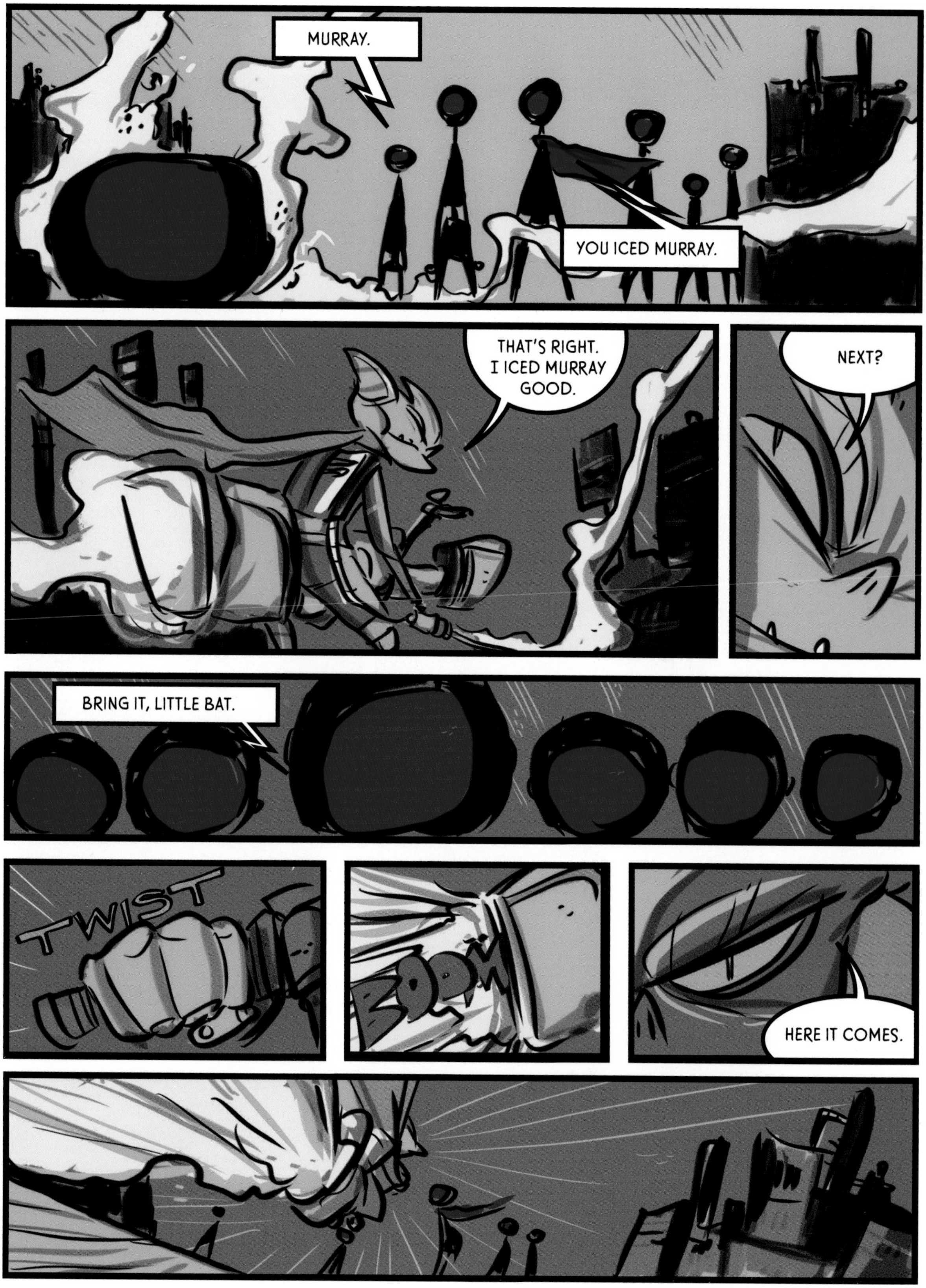
MURRAY.
YOU ICED MURRAY.
THAT'S RIGHT. I ICED MURRAY GOOD.
NEXT?
BRING IT, LITTLE BAT.
TWIST
BOOM
HERE IT COMES.

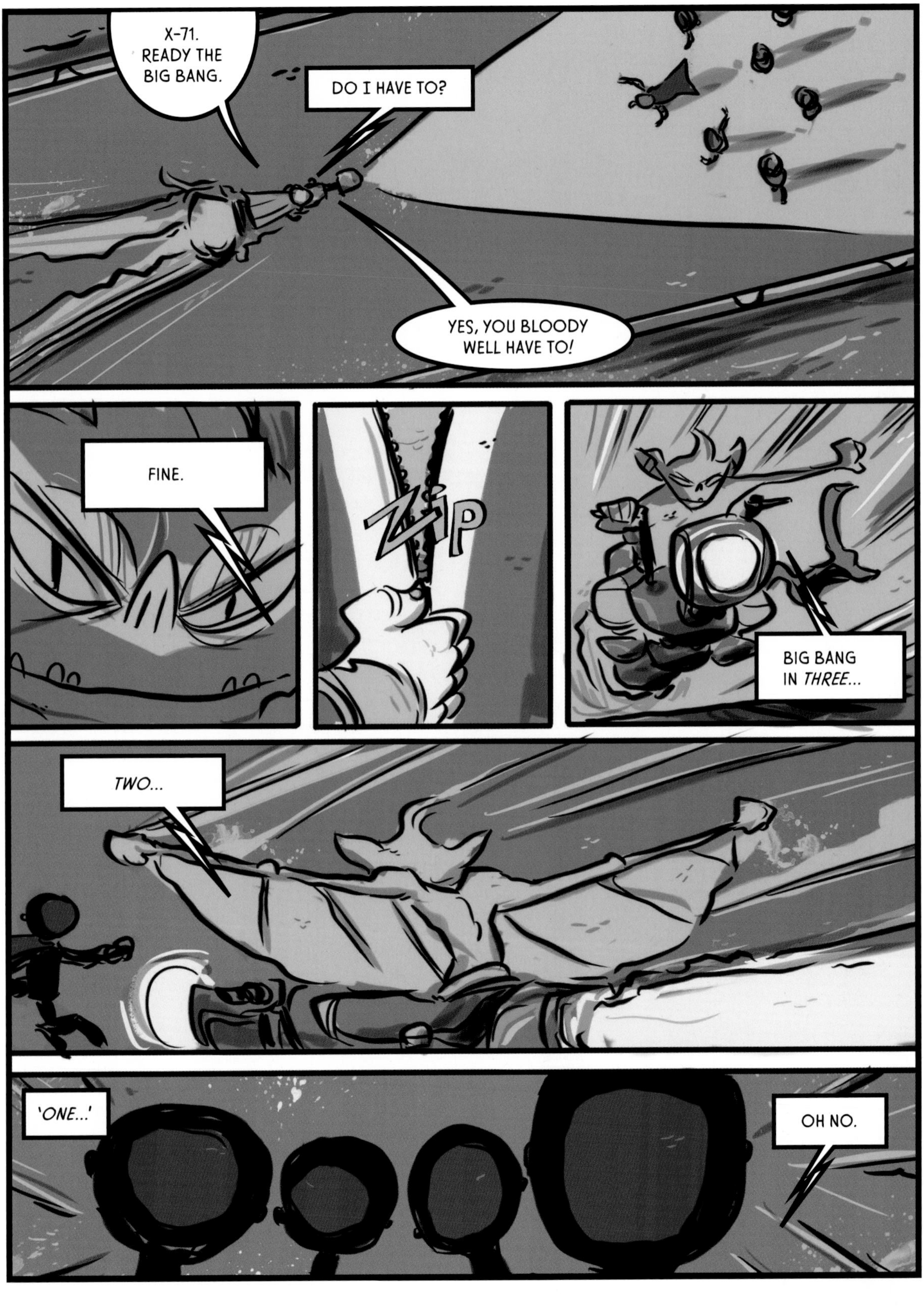
X-71. READY THE BIG BANG.
DO I HAVE TO?
YES, YOU BLOODY WELL HAVE TO!
FINE.
ZIP
BIG BANG IN *THREE...*
TWO...
'ONE...'
OH NO.

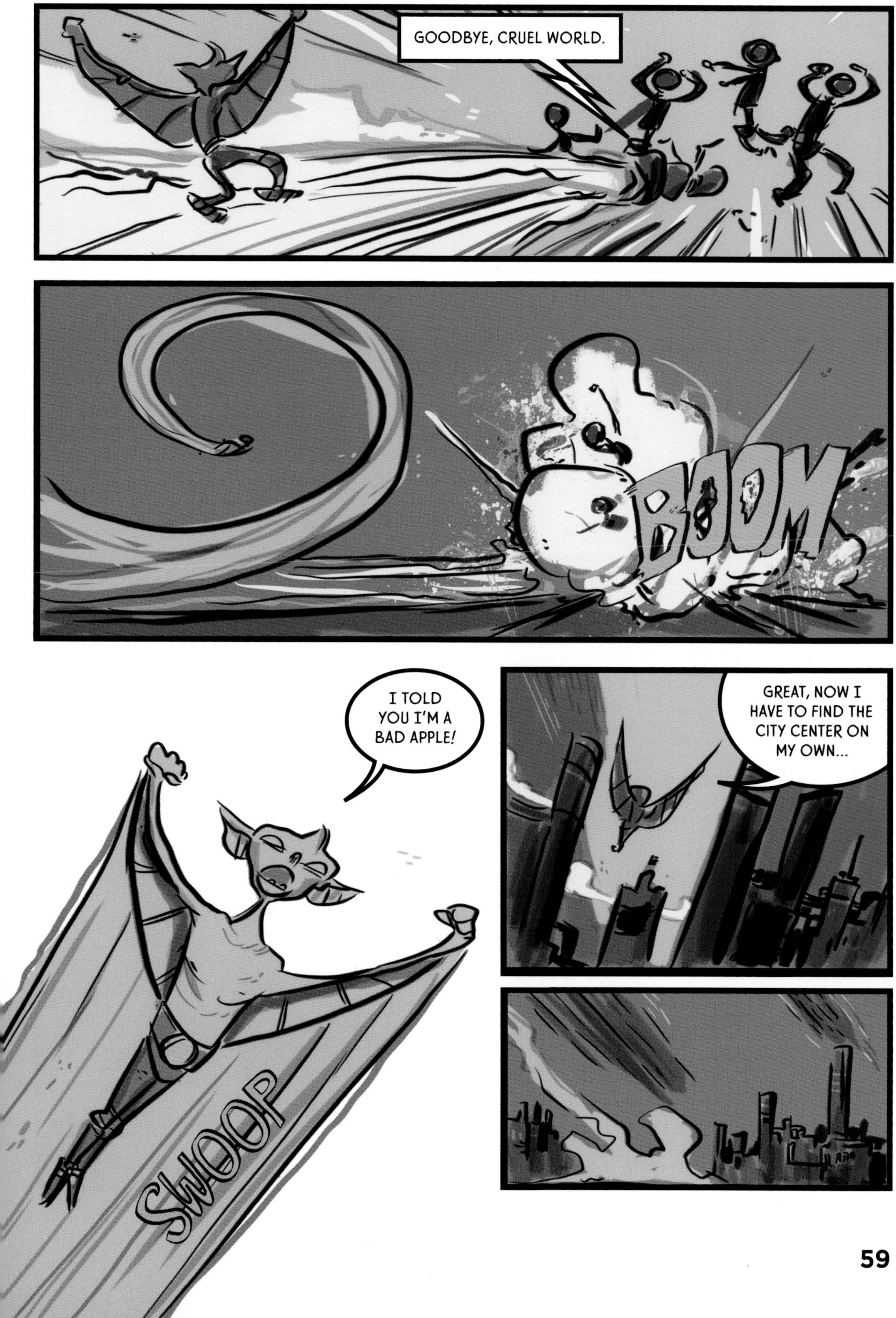
GOODBYE, CRUEL WORLD.
BOOM
I TOLD YOU I'M A BAD APPLE!
SWOOP
GREAT, NOW I HAVE TO FIND THE CITY CENTER ON MY OWN...

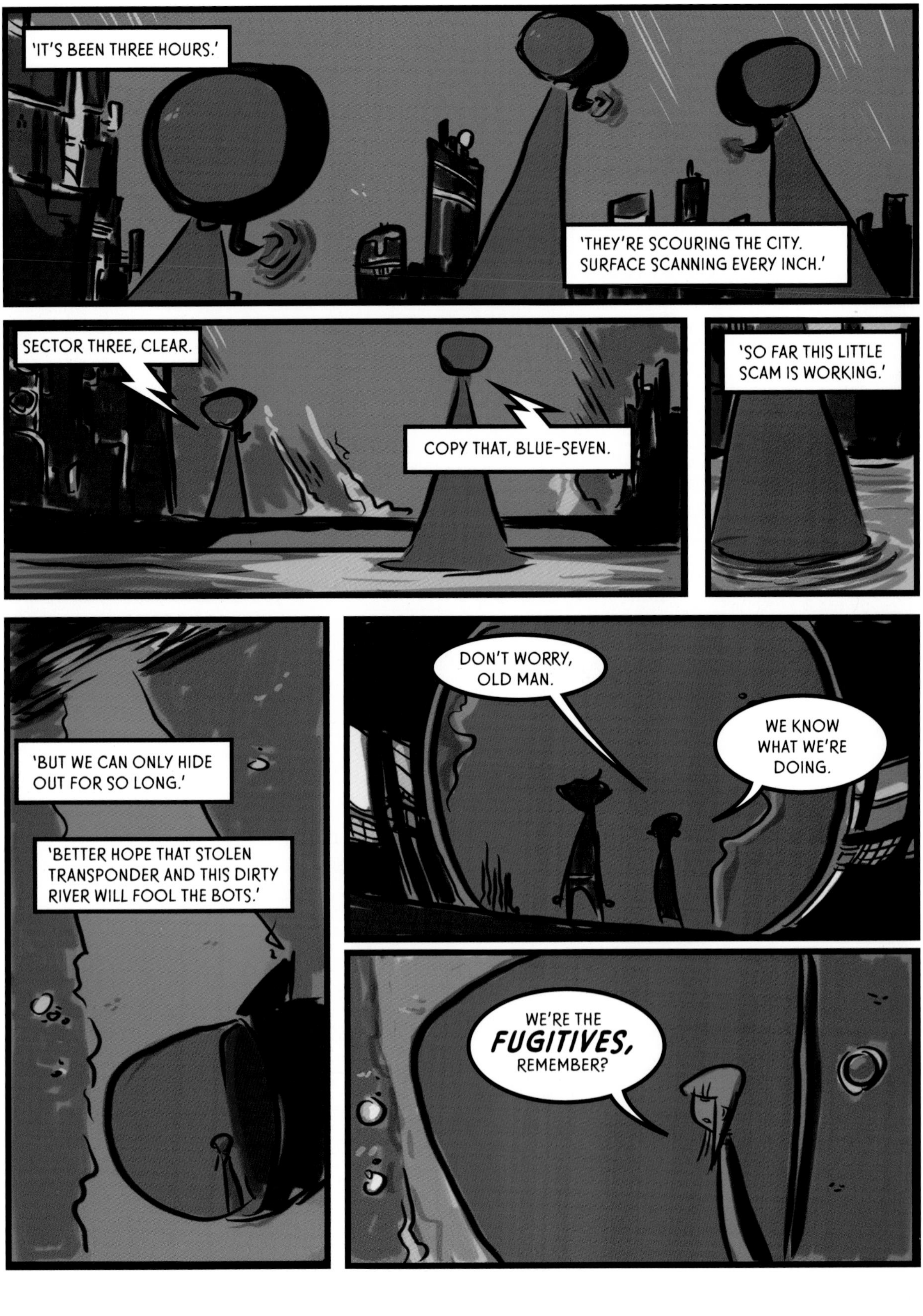
'IT'S BEEN THREE HOURS.'
'THEY'RE SCOURING THE CITY. SURFACE SCANNING EVERY INCH.'
SECTOR THREE, CLEAR.
COPY THAT, BLUE-SEVEN.
'SO FAR THIS LITTLE SCAM IS WORKING.'
'BUT WE CAN ONLY HIDE OUT FOR SO LONG.'
'BETTER HOPE THAT STOLEN TRANSPONDER AND THIS DIRTY RIVER WILL FOOL THE BOTS.'
DON'T WORRY, OLD MAN.
WE KNOW WHAT WE'RE DOING.
WE'RE THE *FUGITIVES,* REMEMBER?

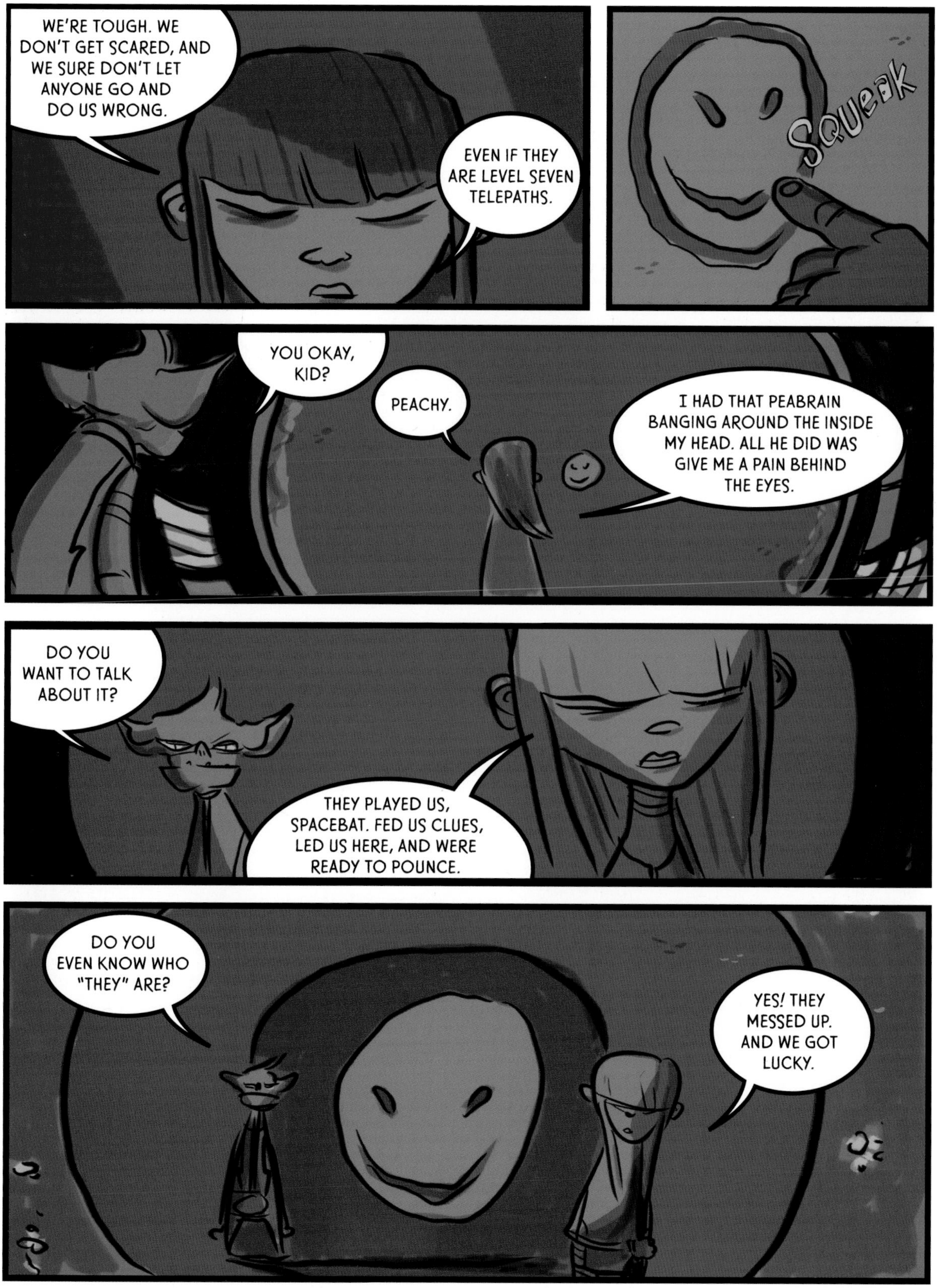
WE'RE TOUGH. WE DON'T GET SCARED, AND WE SURE DON'T LET ANYONE GO AND DO US WRONG.
EVEN IF THEY ARE LEVEL SEVEN TELEPATHS.
SQUEAK
YOU OKAY, KID?
PEACHY.
I HAD THAT PEABRAIN BANGING AROUND THE INSIDE MY HEAD. ALL HE DID WAS GIVE ME A PAIN BEHIND THE EYES.
DO YOU WANT TO TALK ABOUT IT?
THEY PLAYED US, SPACEBAT. FED US CLUES, LED US HERE, AND WERE READY TO POUNCE.
DO YOU EVEN KNOW WHO "THEY" ARE?
YES! THEY MESSED UP. AND WE GOT LUCKY.

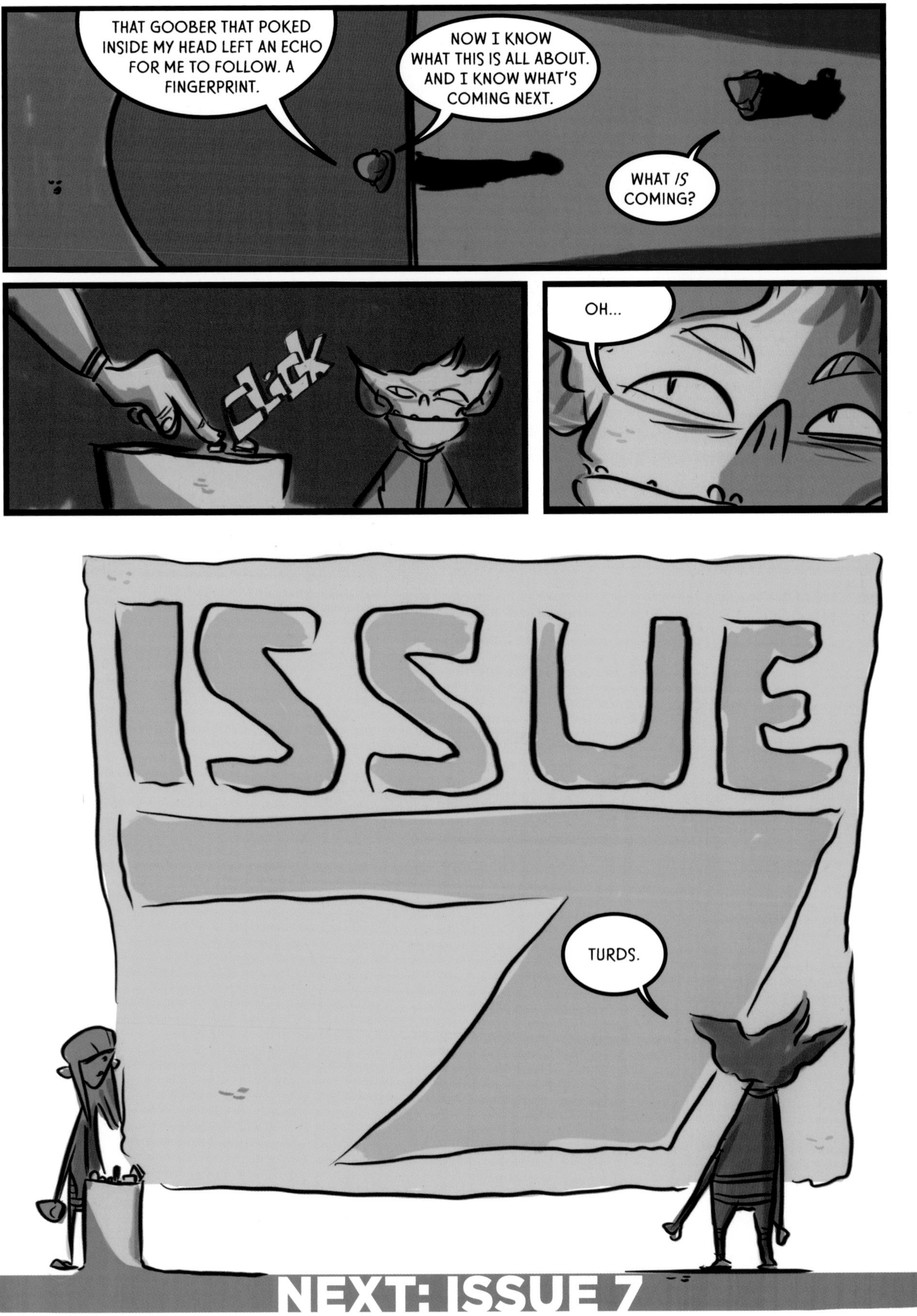
THAT GOOBER THAT POKED INSIDE MY HEAD LEFT AN ECHO FOR ME TO FOLLOW. A FINGERPRINT.
NOW I KNOW WHAT THIS IS ALL ABOUT. AND I KNOW WHAT'S COMING NEXT.
WHAT *IS* COMING?
CLICK
OH...
ISSUE 7
TURDS.
NEXT: ISSUE 7

ISSUE THREE:
ISSUE SEVEN

SPACE PIG:

The space pig is the only creature known that, presented with alternatives, will still choose to rut in its own filth. Therefore, one cannot, in good conscience, extend to them an invitation to a respectable dinner.

-PENELOPE WINTWORTH the THIRD
Excerpted from *Matriarch of Manners*

I WATCHED IT ALL UNFOLD, LIKE AN OLD PICTURE SHOW.

'I CAN SEE IT IN SINGLE SNAPSHOTS, EVEN NOW.'

'THE STORM, THE FIRE, AND YOU, FLOATING THROUGH SPACE.'

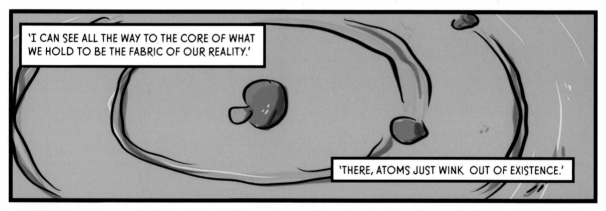

'I CAN SEE ALL THE WAY TO THE CORE OF WHAT WE HOLD TO BE THE FABRIC OF OUR REALITY.'

'THERE, ATOMS JUST WINK OUT OF EXISTENCE.'

'AND FINALLY I SEE IT ALL COME UNDONE.'

'POOF.'

'THE END.'

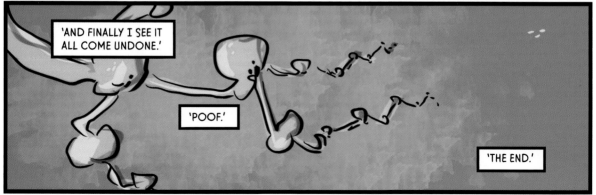

THAT'S ISSUE 7. IT'S WHAT LIES AHEAD. AND NO MATTER HOW FAR I DIG INTO WHAT I SAW, IT NEVER CHANGES, OR GETS BETTER.

WE'RE GOING AFTER ISSUE 7, AND THIS DOESN'T END WELL, SPACEBAT. FOR ANY OF US.

KID, I'VE BEEN AROUND LONG ENOUGH TO SEE A THING OR TWO. THE TELEPATH THAT TINKERED IN YOUR BRAIN MAY HAVE BEEN A MIND READER, BUT HE AIN'T A SOOTHSAYER. I MAKE MY OWN FUTURE.

IT'S NO JOKE, SPACEBAT. I'VE SEEN THE FUTURE.

'THE FUTURE IS BLEAK.'

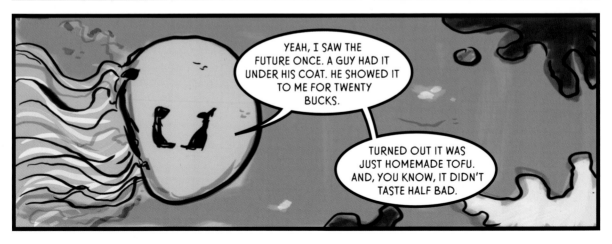

YEAH, I SAW THE FUTURE ONCE. A GUY HAD IT UNDER HIS COAT. HE SHOWED IT TO ME FOR TWENTY BUCKS.

TURNED OUT IT WAS JUST HOMEMADE TOFU. AND, YOU KNOW, IT DIDN'T TASTE HALF BAD.

THE POINT IS, NOTHING IS **INEVITABLE**. ESPECIALLY NOT WHEN IT COMES TO THE FOOD SERVICE INDUSTRY. AND *CERTAINLY NOT* WHEN IT COMES FROM A TELEPATH THAT SET US UP.

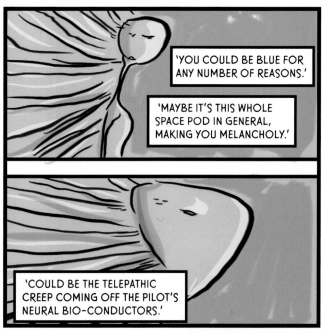

'YOU COULD BE BLUE FOR ANY NUMBER OF REASONS.'

'MAYBE IT'S THIS WHOLE SPACE POD IN GENERAL, MAKING YOU MELANCHOLY.'

'COULD BE THE TELEPATHIC CREEP COMING OFF THE PILOT'S NEURAL BIO-CONDUCTORS.'

'WHATEVER IT IS, BUCK UP, WILL YA?'

'WE'RE GOING AFTER *ISSUE 7.*'

'THIS AIIN'T SOME FAMILY VACATION! WE'RE ON A MISSION TO SAVE THE UNIVERSE, AND WE NEED YOU, KID.'

NOW THAT WE HAD OUR MINUTE ALONE, KID, EXCUSE ME AS I TURN THE COMMS BACK ON AS WE'RE GONNA LAND.

OH, YEAH. THANKS FOR THE PEP TALK.

67

HOWDY, FUGITIVES. THOUGHT YOU SHOULD KNOW, WE'RE ABOUT TO PASS THROUGH THE MANIFOLD DISTURBANCE OF THE OUTER ATMOSPHERE. IT'S GOING TO TINGLE A BIT, DESPITE THE NICE SPACE-SEAWEED SUITS WE'RE WEARING. THIS WORLD IS POISON TO INORGANIC COMPOUNDS, SO ENJOY YOUR NIFTY NEW PAJAMAS.

FUGITIVES, THIS IS IT. THIS IS THE BIG BURRITO.

'THIS IS PLANET Z-973, SAID TO BE THE MOST INHOSPITABLE PLACE IN THE BIG, COLD UNIVERSE.'

RUMORED HOME OF ISSUE 7. COOL!

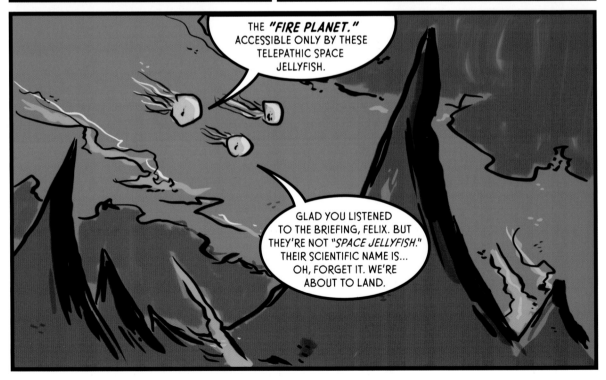

THE *"FIRE PLANET."* ACCESSIBLE ONLY BY THESE TELEPATHIC SPACE JELLYFISH.

GLAD YOU LISTENED TO THE BRIEFING, FELIX. BUT THEY'RE NOT *"SPACE JELLYFISH."* THEIR SCIENTIFIC NAME IS... OH, FORGET IT. WE'RE ABOUT TO LAND.

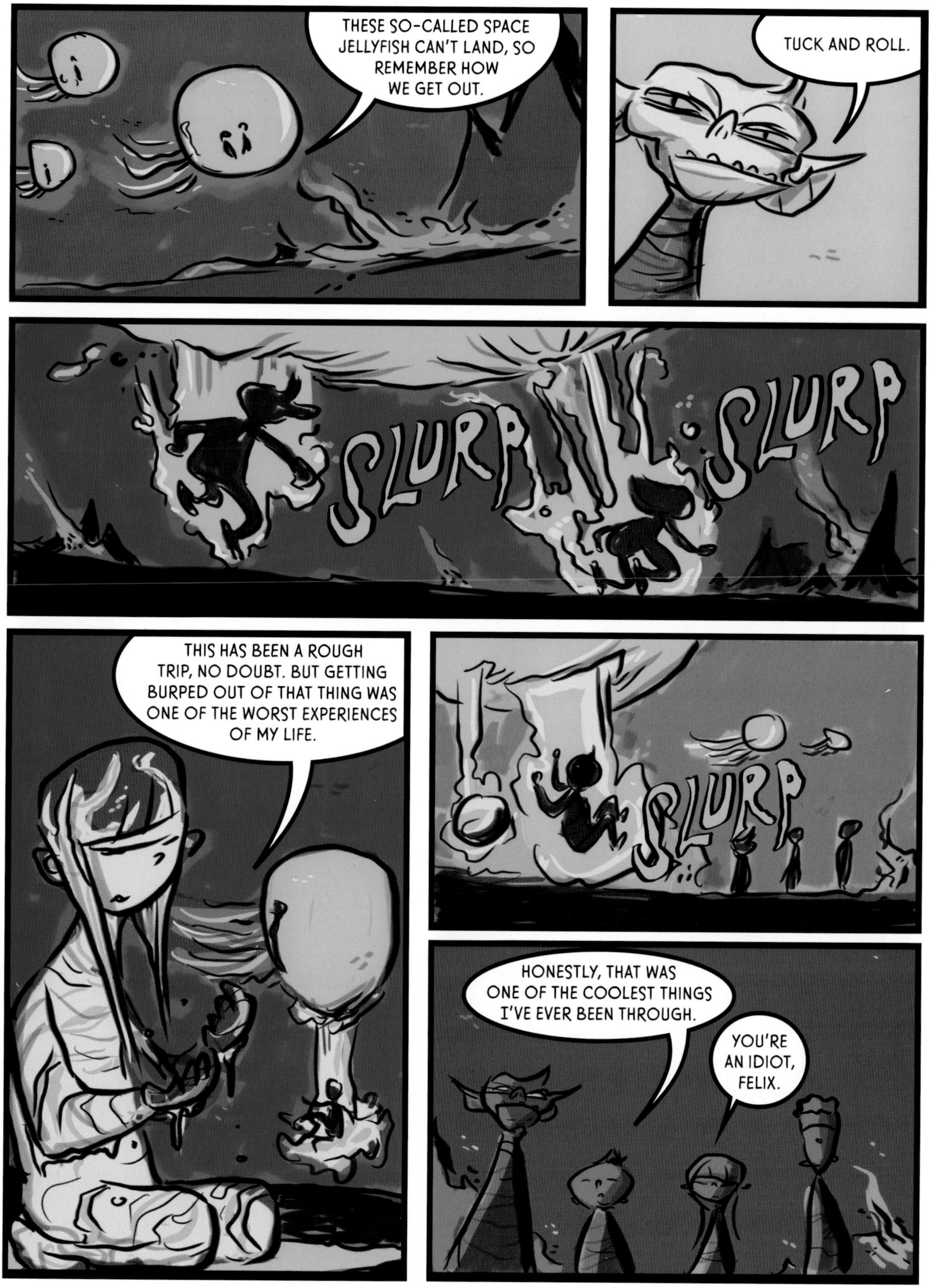
THESE SO-CALLED SPACE JELLYFISH CAN'T LAND, SO REMEMBER HOW WE GET OUT.
TUCK AND ROLL.
SLURP
SLURP
THIS HAS BEEN A ROUGH TRIP, NO DOUBT. BUT GETTING BURPED OUT OF THAT THING WAS ONE OF THE WORST EXPERIENCES OF MY LIFE.
SLURP
HONESTLY, THAT WAS ONE OF THE COOLEST THINGS I'VE EVER BEEN THROUGH.
YOU'RE AN IDIOT, FELIX.

NO, I'M NOT. THIS ORGANIC SUIT IS AMAZING.

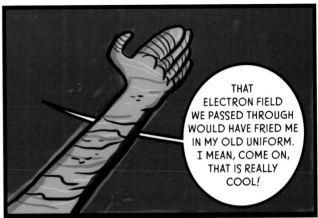

THAT ELECTRON FIELD WE PASSED THROUGH WOULD HAVE FRIED ME IN MY OLD UNIFORM. I MEAN, COME ON, THAT IS REALLY COOL!

RIGHT?

RIGHT, NOW *CAN IT*. WE GOT WORK TO DO.

IT'S UP TO YOU NOW, KID.

CRACK

BLINK BLINK

'DON'T LOOK AT IT IN THE EYE. IT REALLY DOESN'T LIKE THAT.'

FINE.

BUT, LET ME JUST SAY AGAIN, THIS IS REALLY, REALLY, NASTY.

SLURP

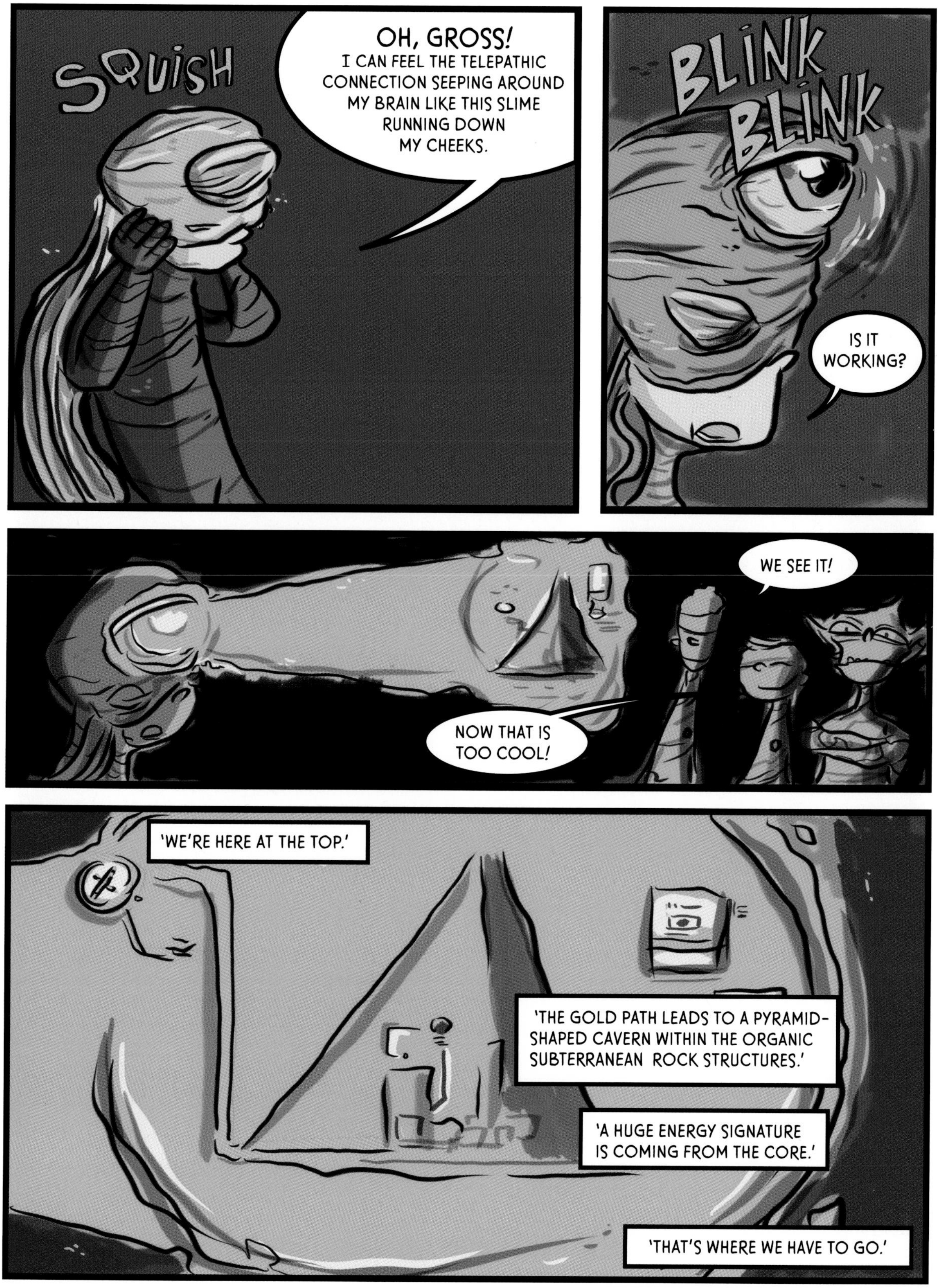
SQUISH
OH, GROSS! I CAN FEEL THE TELEPATHIC CONNECTION SEEPING AROUND MY BRAIN LIKE THIS SLIME RUNNING DOWN MY CHEEKS.
BLINK BLINK
IS IT WORKING?
WE SEE IT!
NOW THAT IS TOO COOL!
'WE'RE HERE AT THE TOP.'
'THE GOLD PATH LEADS TO A PYRAMID-SHAPED CAVERN WITHIN THE ORGANIC SUBTERRANEAN ROCK STRUCTURES.'
'A HUGE ENERGY SIGNATURE IS COMING FROM THE CORE.'
'THAT'S WHERE WE HAVE TO GO.'

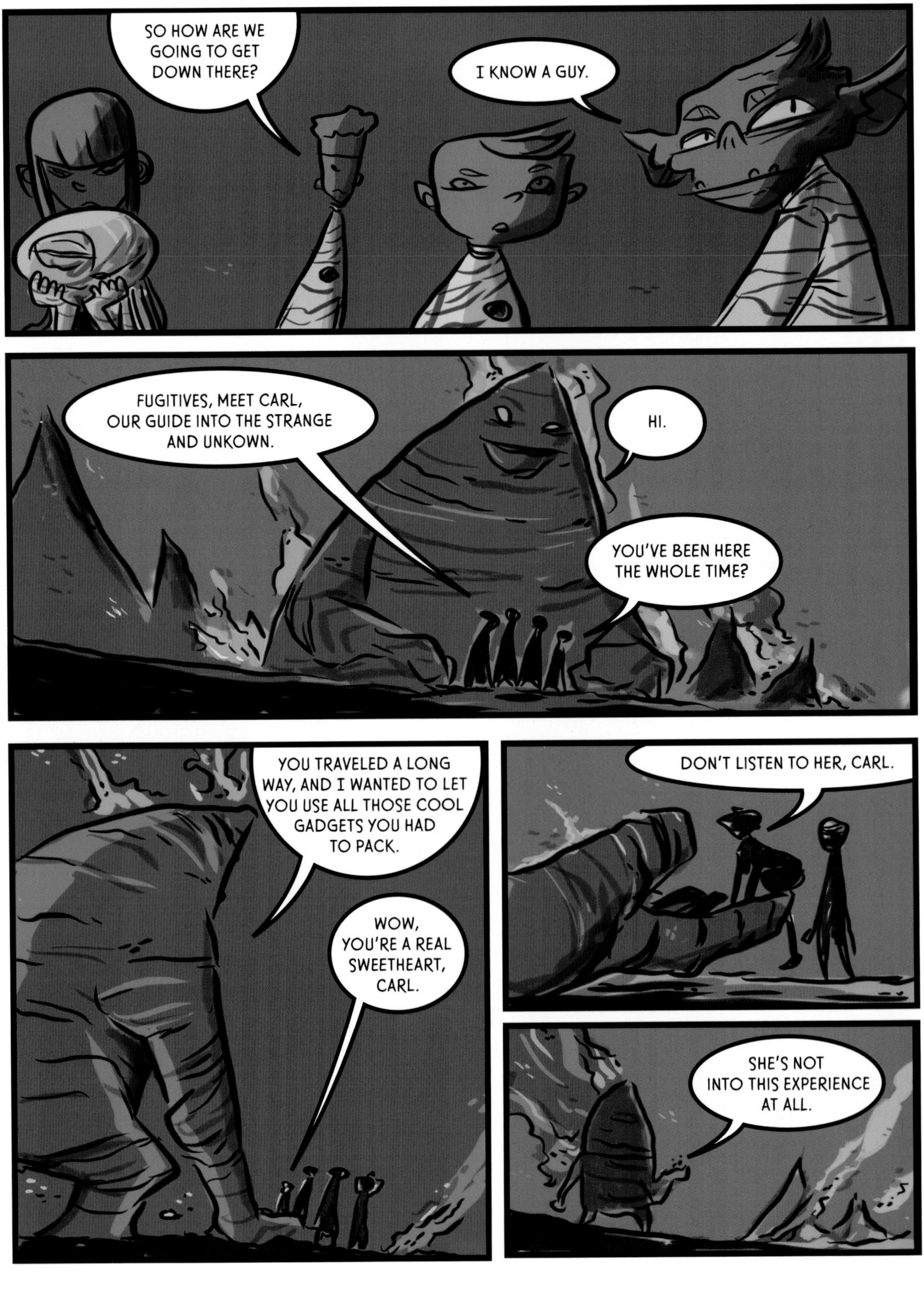
SO HOW ARE WE GOING TO GET DOWN THERE?
I KNOW A GUY.
FUGITIVES, MEET CARL, OUR GUIDE INTO THE STRANGE AND UNKOWN.
HI.
YOU'VE BEEN HERE THE WHOLE TIME?
YOU TRAVELED A LONG WAY, AND I WANTED TO LET YOU USE ALL THOSE COOL GADGETS YOU HAD TO PACK.
WOW, YOU'RE A REAL SWEETHEART, CARL.
DON'T LISTEN TO HER, CARL.
SHE'S NOT INTO THIS EXPERIENCE AT ALL.

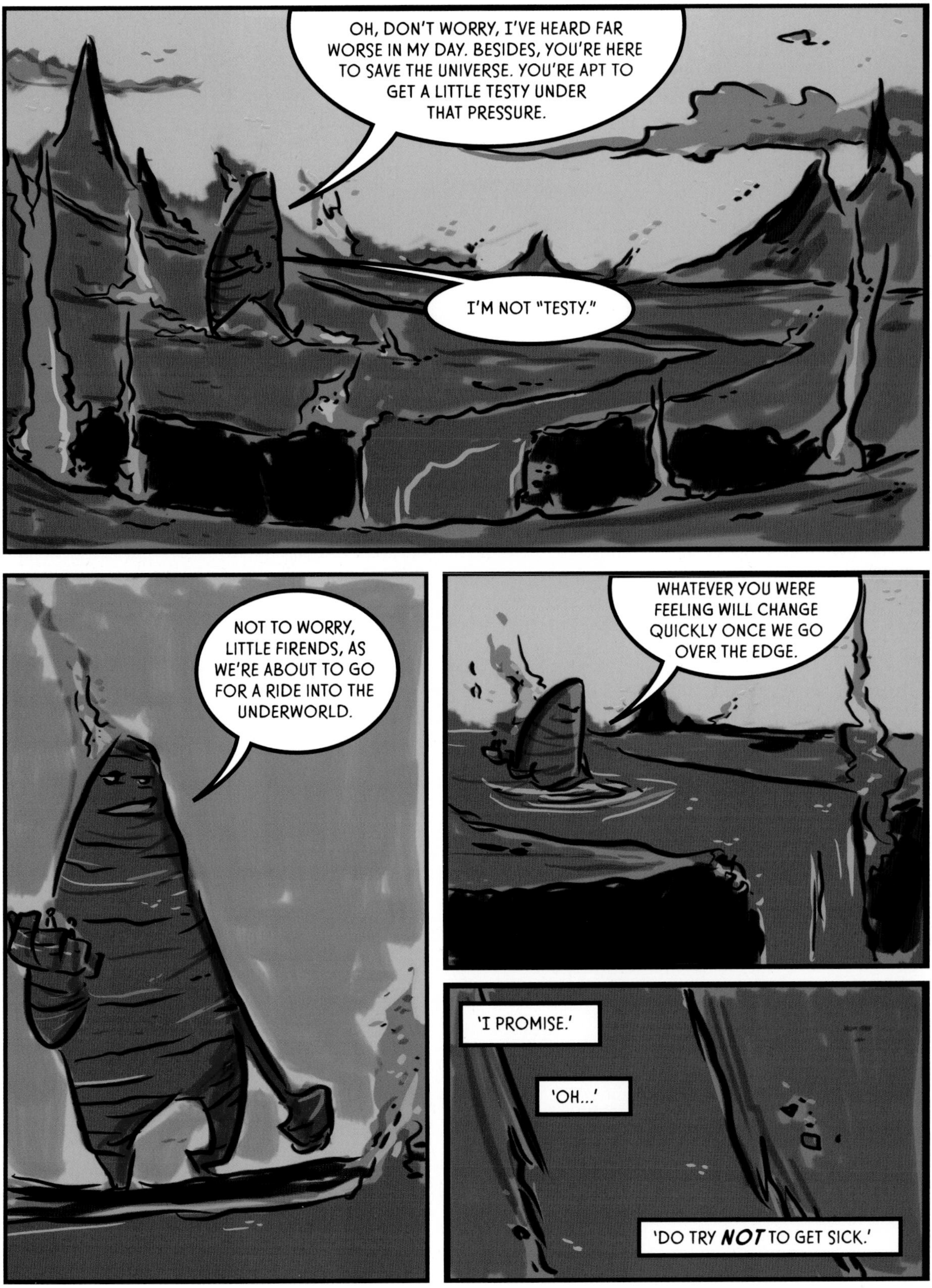
OH, DON'T WORRY, I'VE HEARD FAR WORSE IN MY DAY. BESIDES, YOU'RE HERE TO SAVE THE UNIVERSE. YOU'RE APT TO GET A LITTLE TESTY UNDER THAT PRESSURE.
I'M NOT "TESTY."
NOT TO WORRY, LITTLE FIRENDS, AS WE'RE ABOUT TO GO FOR A RIDE INTO THE UNDERWORLD.
WHATEVER YOU WERE FEELING WILL CHANGE QUICKLY ONCE WE GO OVER THE EDGE.
'I PROMISE.'
'OH...'
'DO TRY **NOT** TO GET SICK.'

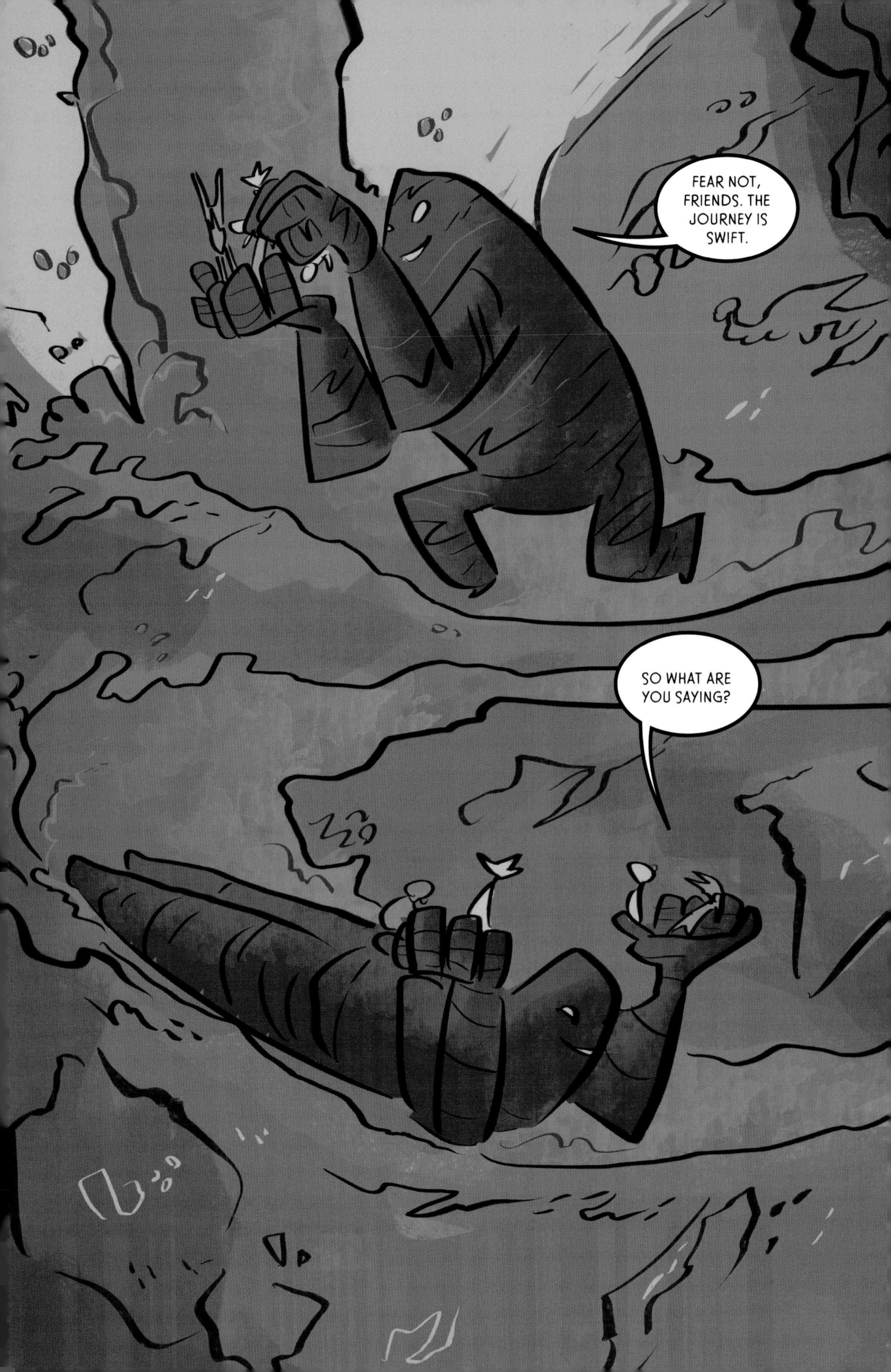
FEAR NOT, FRIENDS. THE JOURNEY IS SWIFT.
SO WHAT ARE YOU SAYING?

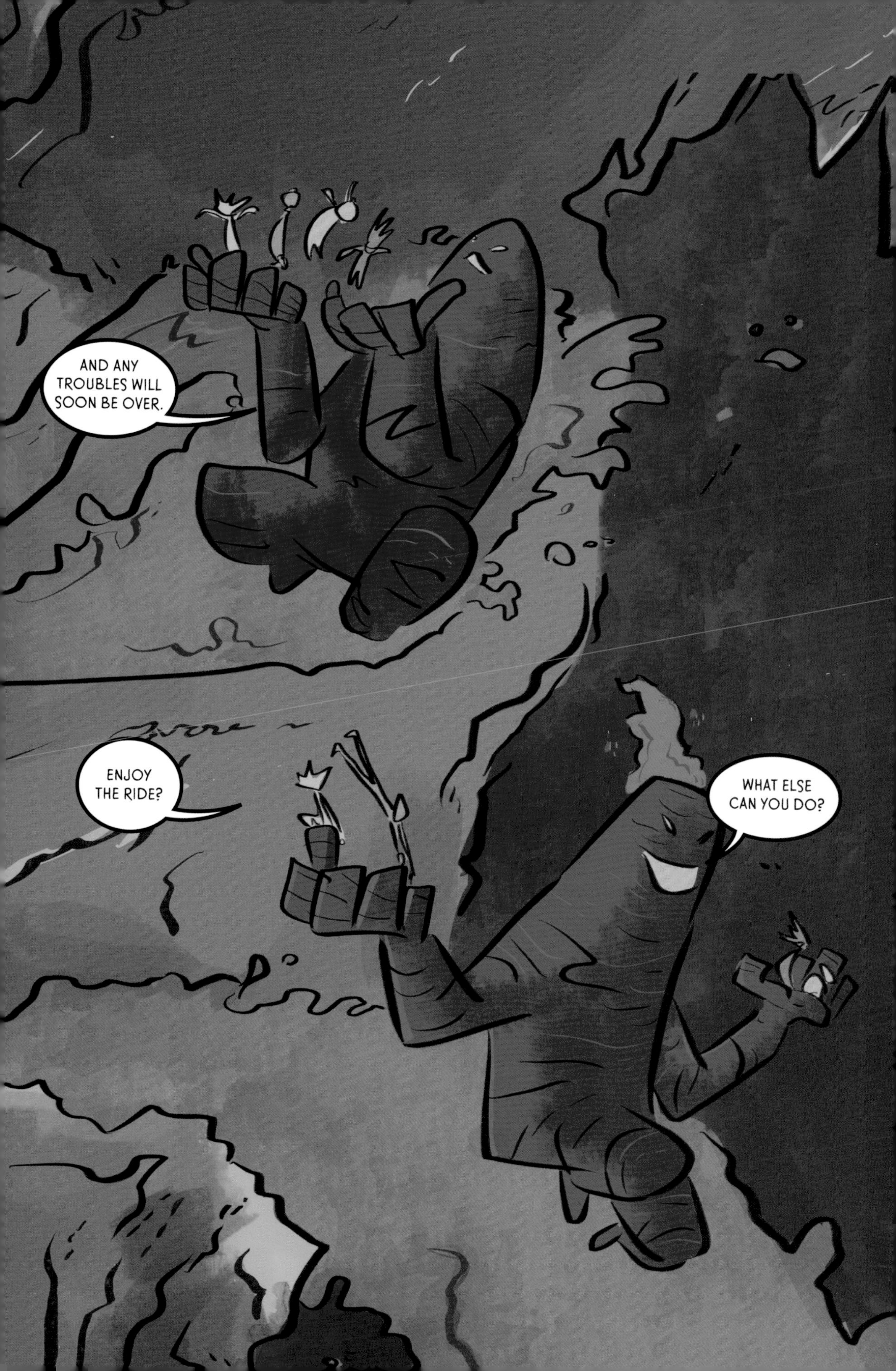
AND ANY TROUBLES WILL SOON BE OVER.
ENJOY THE RIDE?
WHAT ELSE CAN YOU DO?

THE PAST.

'WHAT ELSE CAN YOU DO?'

WE'RE JUST STEALING THE FULLY SOUPED-UP SHIP OF THE MINISTER OF SCIENCE. AND IF WE'RE CAUGHT, WE'RE SURE TO GET MORE THAN A *GROUNDING*.

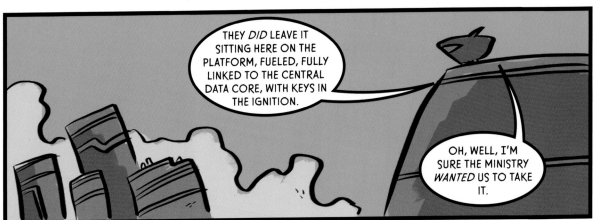

THEY *DID* LEAVE IT SITTING HERE ON THE PLATFORM, FUELED, FULLY LINKED TO THE CENTRAL DATA CORE, WITH KEYS IN THE IGNITION.

OH, WELL, I'M SURE THE MINISTRY *WANTED* US TO TAKE IT.

WELL, WE CAN ALL AGREE THE PRESSURE IS ON. WE ARE ABOUT TO FLEE THE DEPARTMENT OF SCIENCE IN A STOLEN SHIP ON A MISSION TO SAVE THE UNIVERSE.

YEP. WE CAN FEEL THE WEIGHT OF OUR IMPOSSIBLE TASK, BUT, LIKE FELIX SAID, WE GOT THIS COOL SHIP.

I JUST WISH THEY HAD LEFT US SOME TACOS, 'CUZ I CAN HEAR FELIX'S STOMACH GRUMBLING.

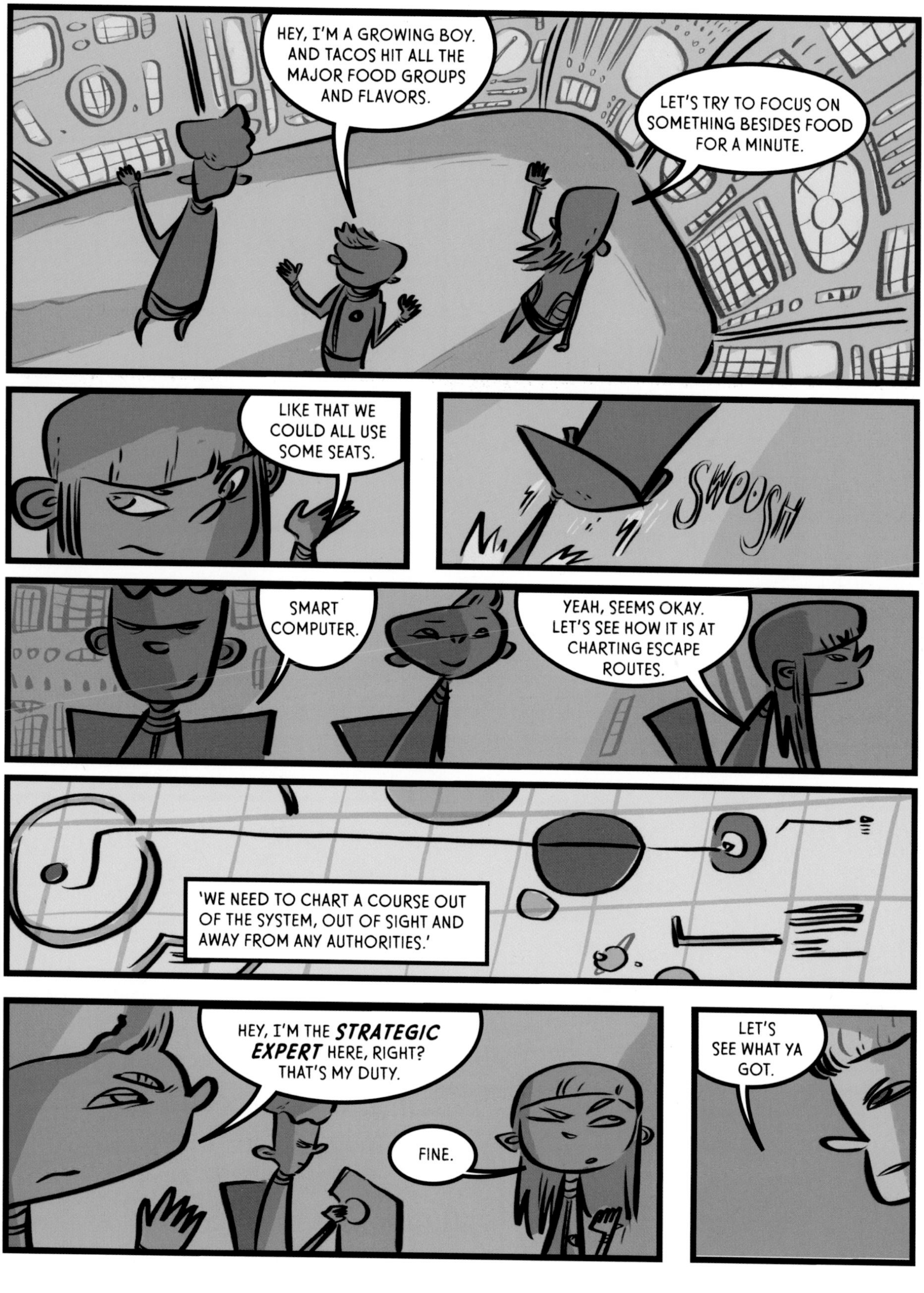
HEY, I'M A GROWING BOY. AND TACOS HIT ALL THE MAJOR FOOD GROUPS AND FLAVORS.
LET'S TRY TO FOCUS ON SOMETHING BESIDES FOOD FOR A MINUTE.
LIKE THAT WE COULD ALL USE SOME SEATS.
SWOOSH
SMART COMPUTER.
YEAH, SEEMS OKAY. LET'S SEE HOW IT IS AT CHARTING ESCAPE ROUTES.
'WE NEED TO CHART A COURSE OUT OF THE SYSTEM, OUT OF SIGHT AND AWAY FROM ANY AUTHORITIES.'
HEY, I'M THE ***STRATEGIC EXPERT*** HERE, RIGHT? THAT'S MY DUTY.
FINE.
LET'S SEE WHAT YA GOT.

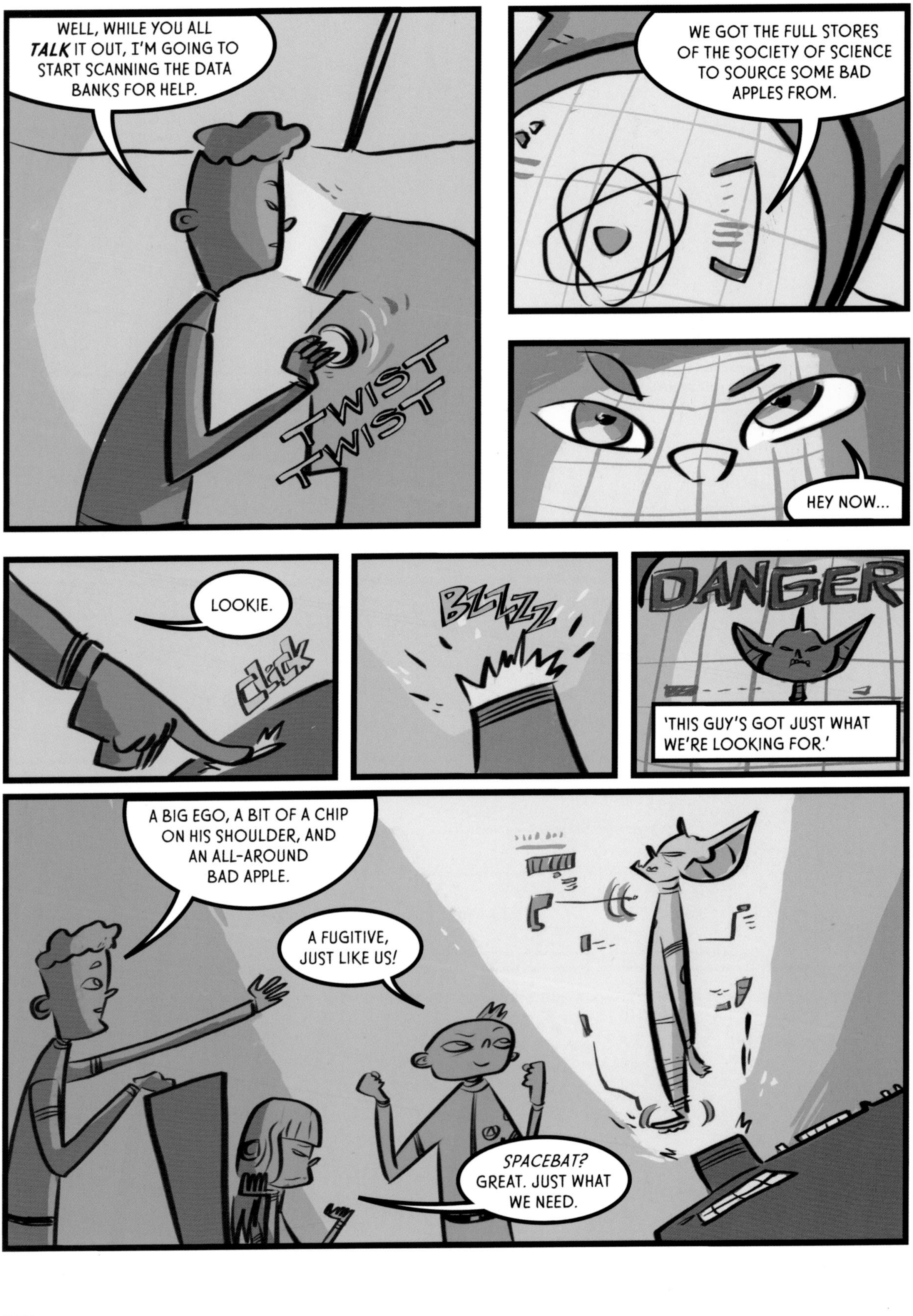
WELL, WHILE YOU ALL *TALK* IT OUT, I'M GOING TO START SCANNING THE DATA BANKS FOR HELP.
TWIST TWIST
WE GOT THE FULL STORES OF THE SOCIETY OF SCIENCE TO SOURCE SOME BAD APPLES FROM.
HEY NOW...
LOOKIE.
click
BZZZZ
DANGER
'THIS GUY'S GOT JUST WHAT WE'RE LOOKING FOR.'
A BIG EGO, A BIT OF A CHIP ON HIS SHOULDER, AND AN ALL-AROUND BAD APPLE.
A FUGITIVE, JUST LIKE US!
SPACEBAT? GREAT. JUST WHAT WE NEED.

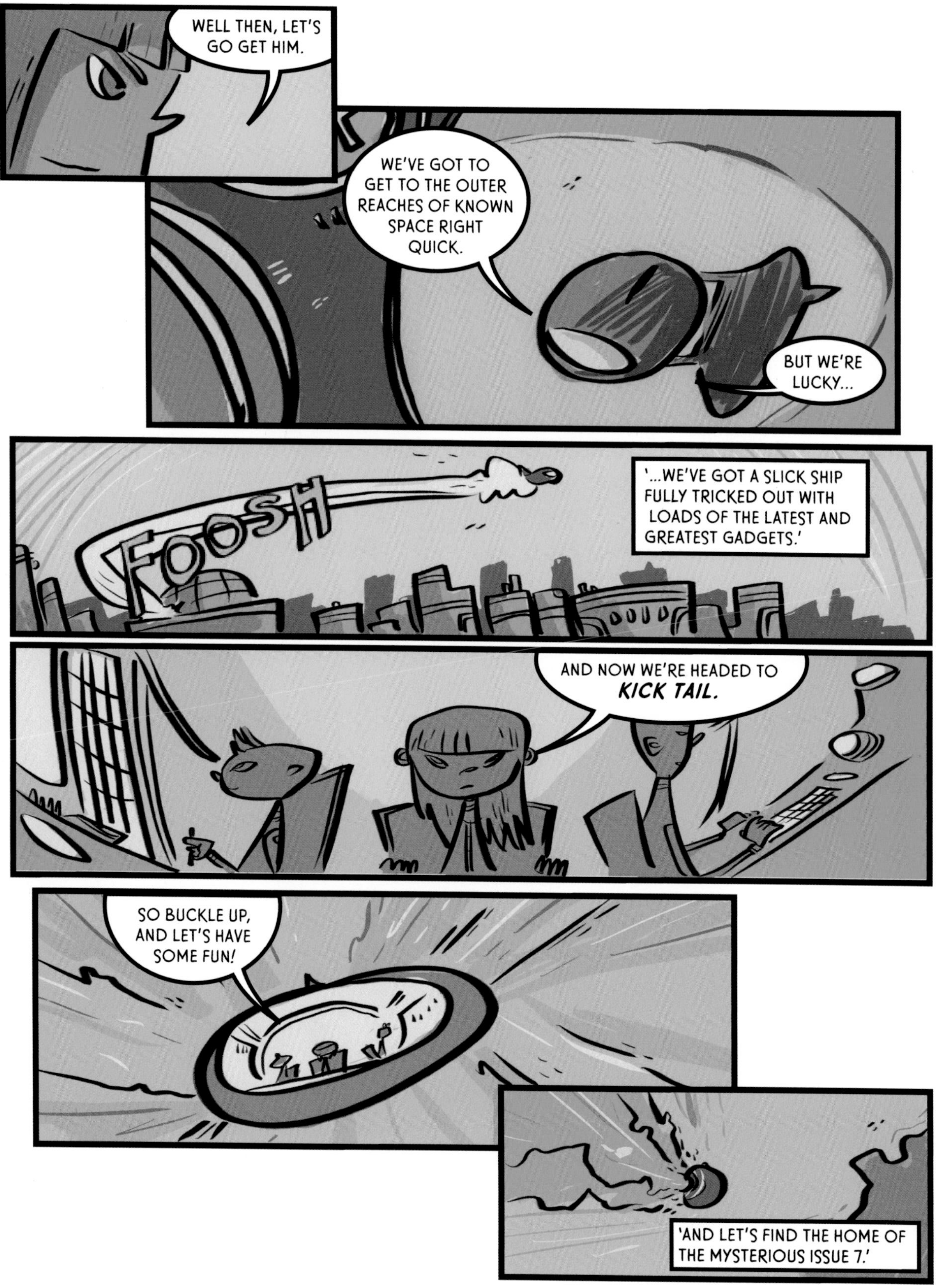
WELL THEN, LET'S GO GET HIM.
WE'VE GOT TO GET TO THE OUTER REACHES OF KNOWN SPACE RIGHT QUICK.
BUT WE'RE LUCKY...
FOOSH
'...WE'VE GOT A SLICK SHIP FULLY TRICKED OUT WITH LOADS OF THE LATEST AND GREATEST GADGETS.'
AND NOW WE'RE HEADED TO *KICK TAIL.*
SO BUCKLE UP, AND LET'S HAVE SOME FUN!
'AND LET'S FIND THE HOME OF THE MYSTERIOUS ISSUE 7.'

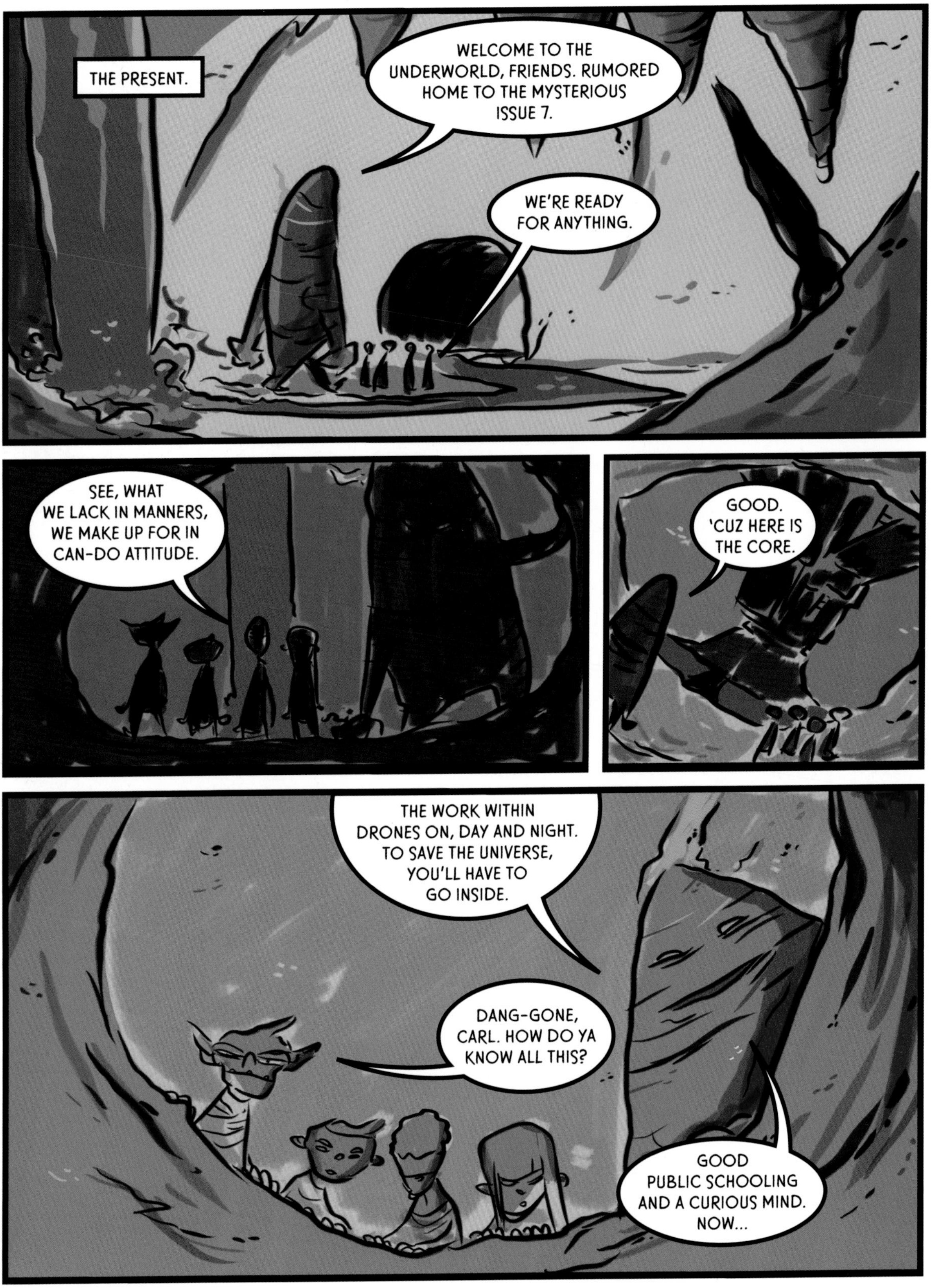
THE PRESENT.
WELCOME TO THE UNDERWORLD, FRIENDS. RUMORED HOME TO THE MYSTERIOUS ISSUE 7.
WE'RE READY FOR ANYTHING.
SEE, WHAT WE LACK IN MANNERS, WE MAKE UP FOR IN CAN-DO ATTITUDE.
GOOD. 'CUZ HERE IS THE CORE.
THE WORK WITHIN DRONES ON, DAY AND NIGHT. TO SAVE THE UNIVERSE, YOU'LL HAVE TO GO INSIDE.
DANG-GONE, CARL. HOW DO YA KNOW ALL THIS?
GOOD PUBLIC SCHOOLING AND A CURIOUS MIND. NOW...

YA BETTER GET INSIDE. THAT'S NOT A PROBLEM, IS IT?

OF COURSE NOT, CARL. WE LOVE A CHALLENGE. AND WE MEAN TO MAKE A BOLD ENTRANCE.

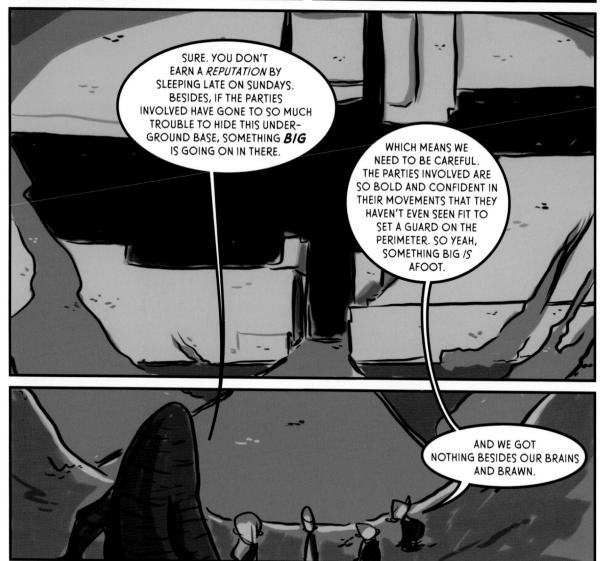

SURE. YOU DON'T EARN A *REPUTATION* BY SLEEPING LATE ON SUNDAYS. BESIDES, IF THE PARTIES INVOLVED HAVE GONE TO SO MUCH TROUBLE TO HIDE THIS UNDER-GROUND BASE, SOMETHING *BIG* IS GOING ON IN THERE.

WHICH MEANS WE NEED TO BE CAREFUL. THE PARTIES INVOLVED ARE SO BOLD AND CONFIDENT IN THEIR MOVEMENTS THAT THEY HAVEN'T EVEN SEEN FIT TO SET A GUARD ON THE PERIMETER. SO YEAH, SOMETHING BIG *IS* AFOOT.

AND WE GOT NOTHING BESIDES OUR BRAINS AND BRAWN.

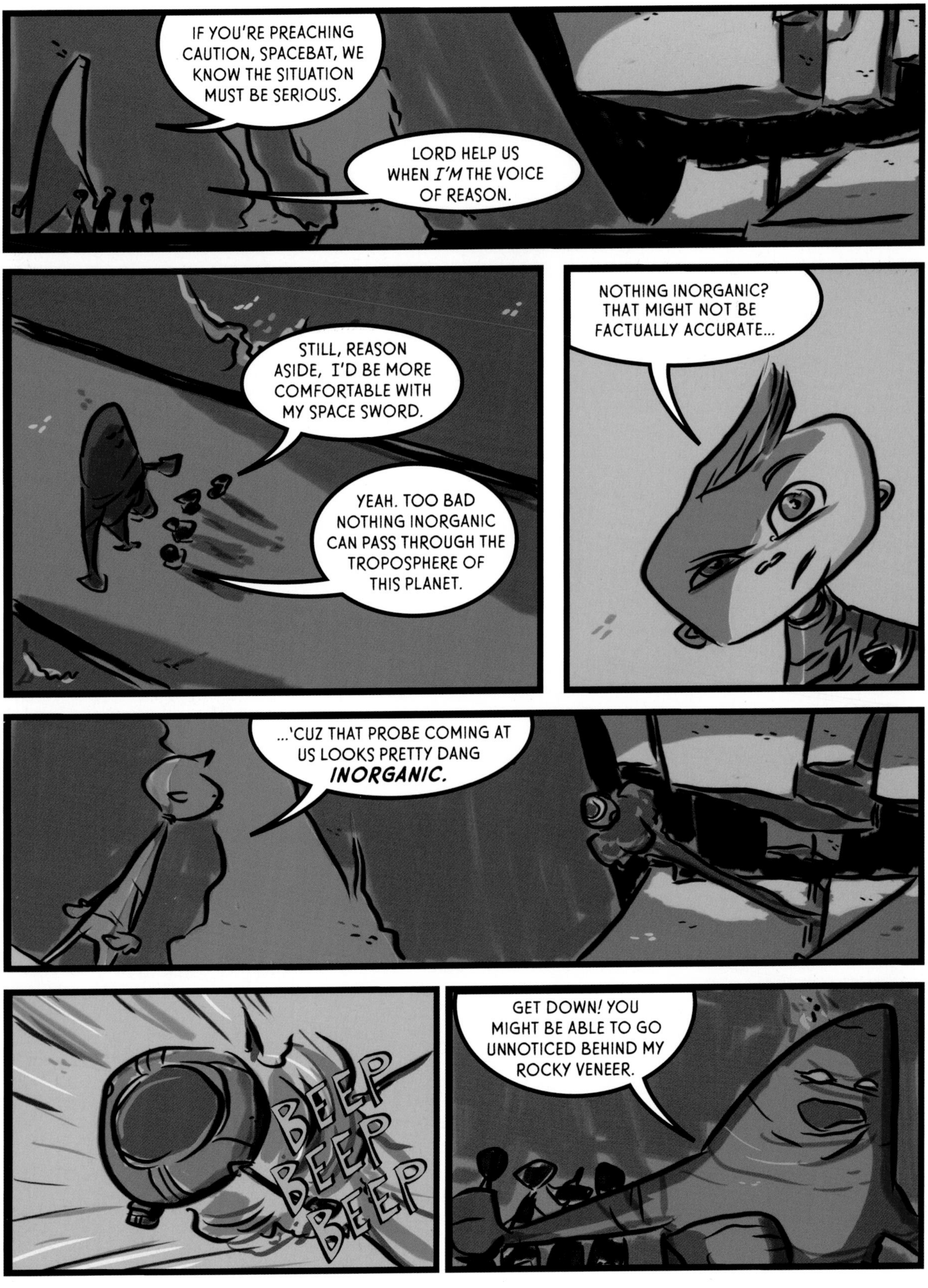
IF YOU'RE PREACHING CAUTION, SPACEBAT, WE KNOW THE SITUATION MUST BE SERIOUS.
LORD HELP US WHEN *I'M* THE VOICE OF REASON.
STILL, REASON ASIDE, I'D BE MORE COMFORTABLE WITH MY SPACE SWORD.
YEAH. TOO BAD NOTHING INORGANIC CAN PASS THROUGH THE TROPOSPHERE OF THIS PLANET.
NOTHING INORGANIC? THAT MIGHT NOT BE FACTUALLY ACCURATE...
...'CUZ THAT PROBE COMING AT US LOOKS PRETTY DANG ***INORGANIC.***
BEEP BEEP BEEP
GET DOWN! YOU MIGHT BE ABLE TO GO UNNOTICED BEHIND MY ROCKY VENEER.

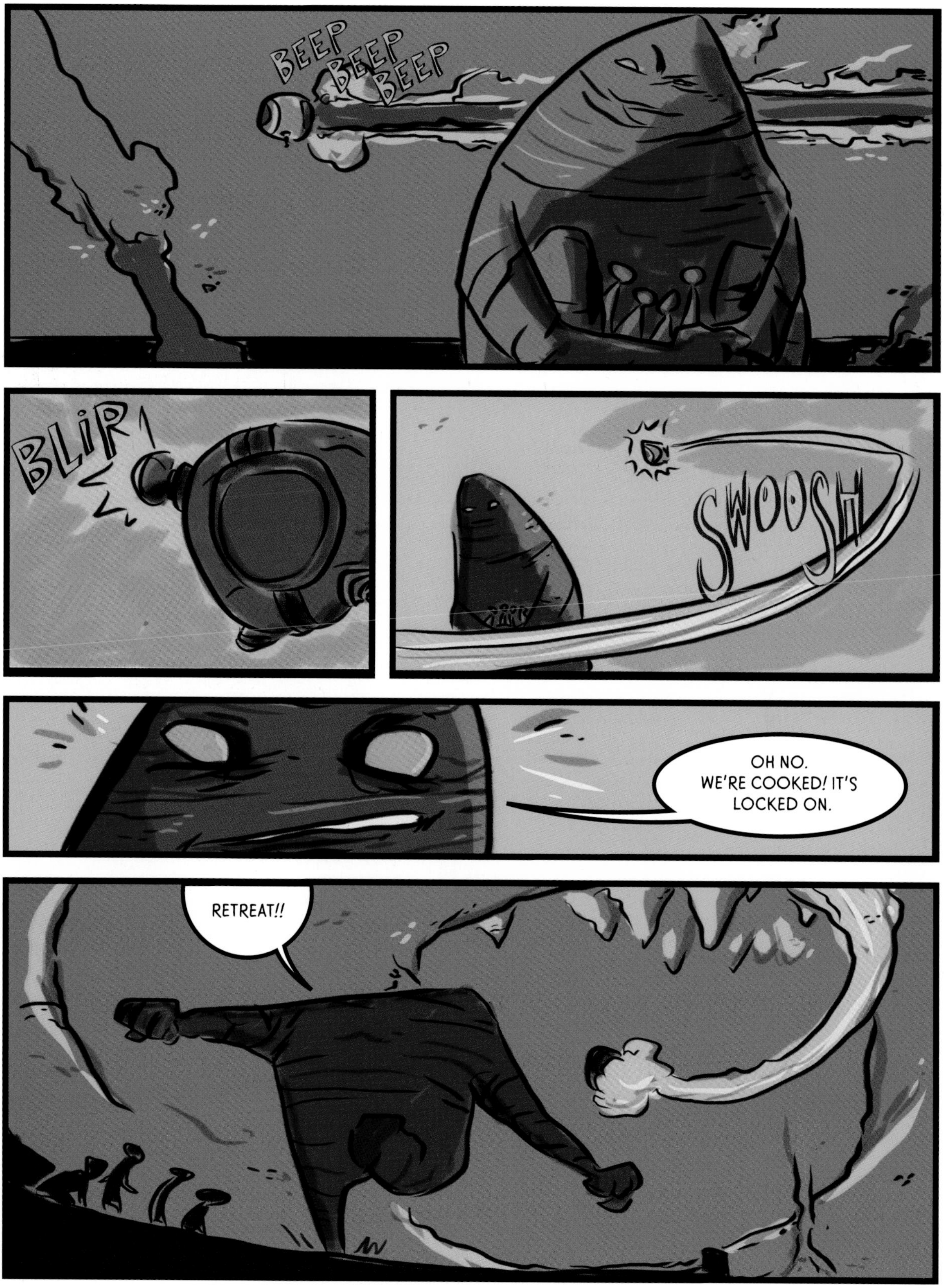
BEEP BEEP BEEP
BLIR
SWOOSH
OH NO.
WE'RE COOKED! IT'S
LOCKED ON.
RETREAT!!

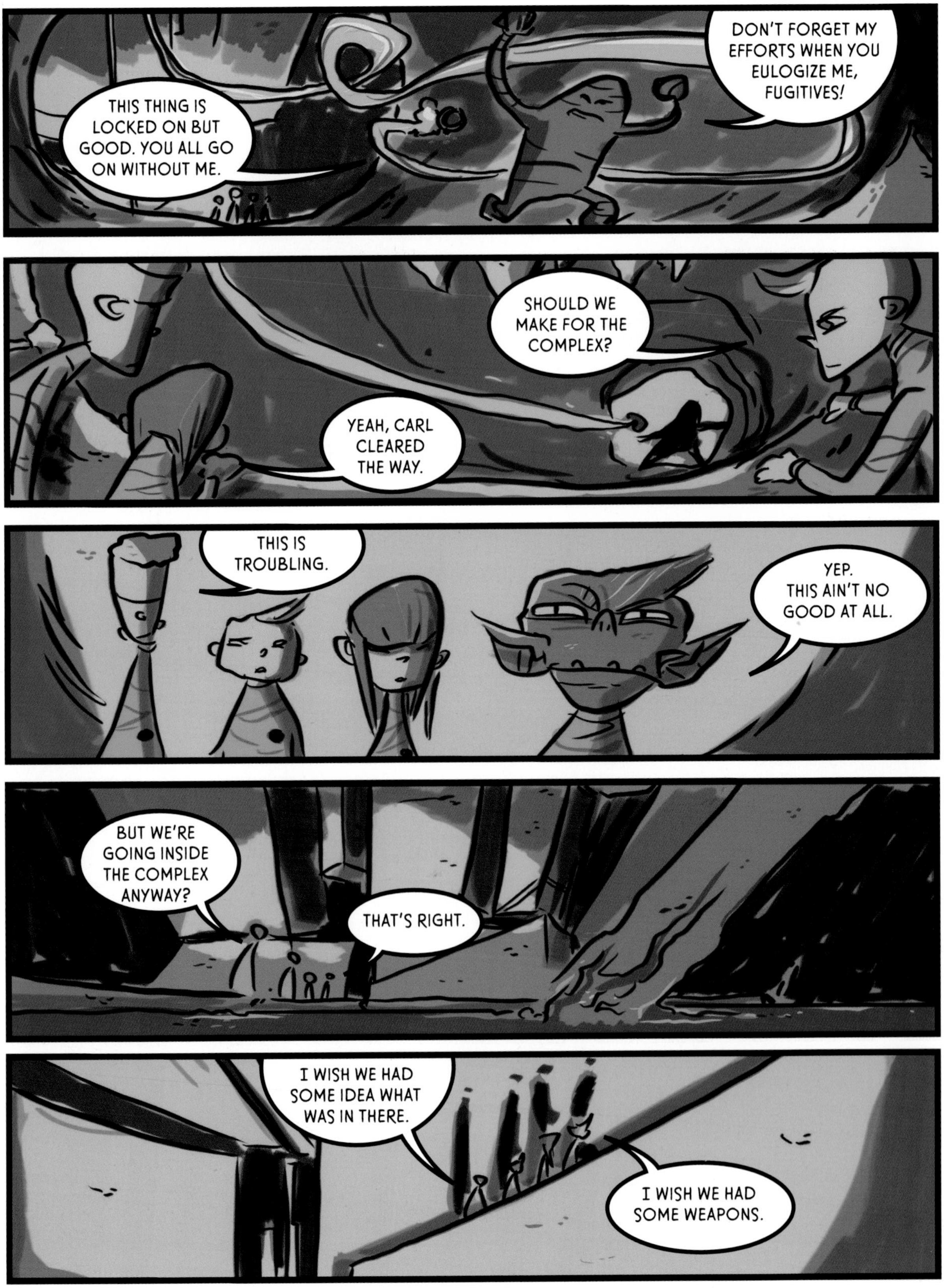
THIS THING IS LOCKED ON BUT GOOD. YOU ALL GO ON WITHOUT ME.
DON'T FORGET MY EFFORTS WHEN YOU EULOGIZE ME, FUGITIVES!
SHOULD WE MAKE FOR THE COMPLEX?
YEAH, CARL CLEARED THE WAY.
THIS IS TROUBLING.
YEP. THIS AIN'T NO GOOD AT ALL.
BUT WE'RE GOING INSIDE THE COMPLEX ANYWAY?
THAT'S RIGHT.
I WISH WE HAD SOME IDEA WHAT WAS IN THERE.
I WISH WE HAD SOME WEAPONS.

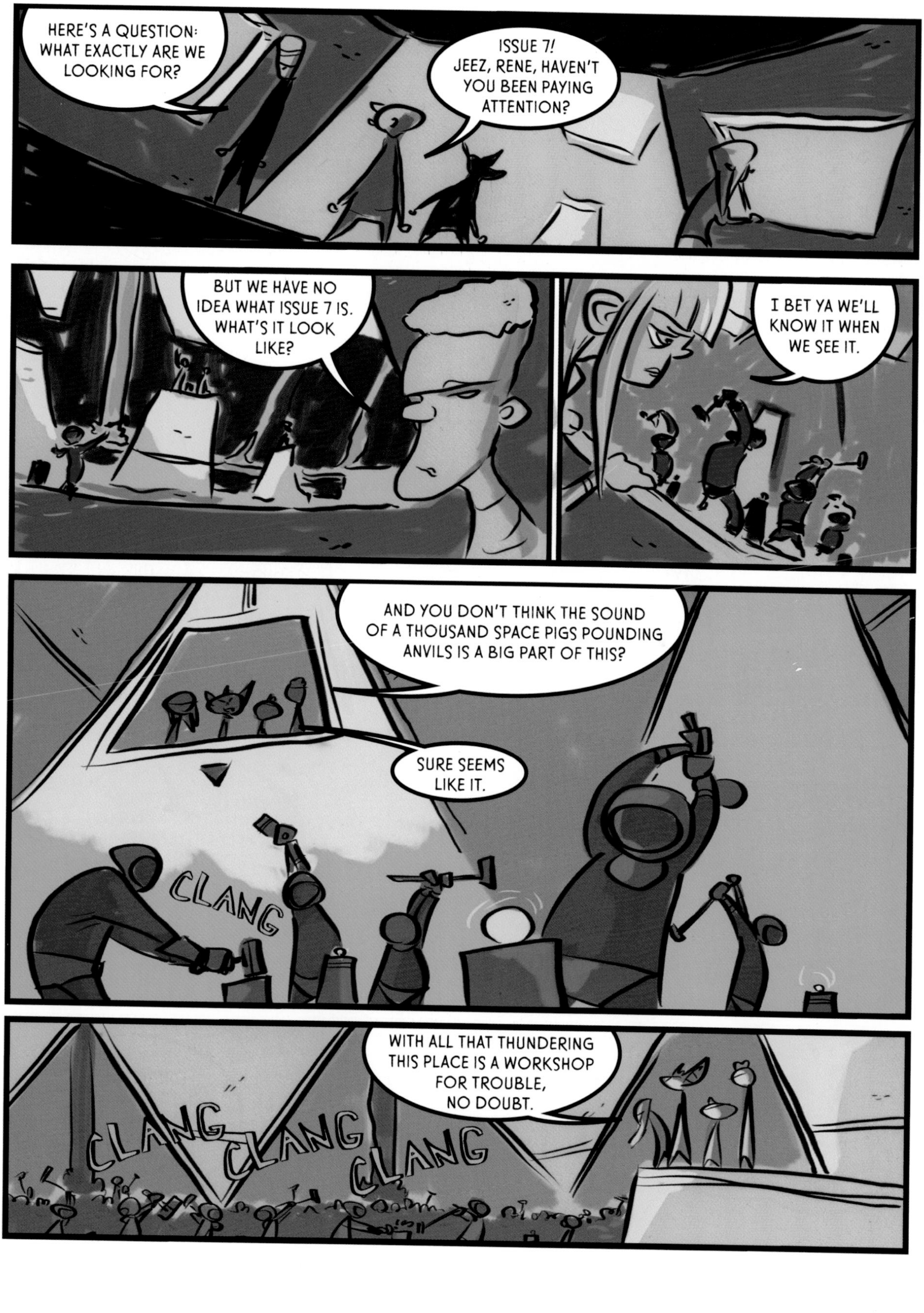
HERE'S A QUESTION: WHAT EXACTLY ARE WE LOOKING FOR?
ISSUE 7! JEEZ, RENE, HAVEN'T YOU BEEN PAYING ATTENTION?
BUT WE HAVE NO IDEA WHAT ISSUE 7 IS. WHAT'S IT LOOK LIKE?
I BET YA WE'LL KNOW IT WHEN WE SEE IT.
AND YOU DON'T THINK THE SOUND OF A THOUSAND SPACE PIGS POUNDING ANVILS IS A BIG PART OF THIS?
SURE SEEMS LIKE IT.
CLANG
WITH ALL THAT THUNDERING THIS PLACE IS A WORKSHOP FOR TROUBLE, NO DOUBT.
CLANG
CLANG
CLANG

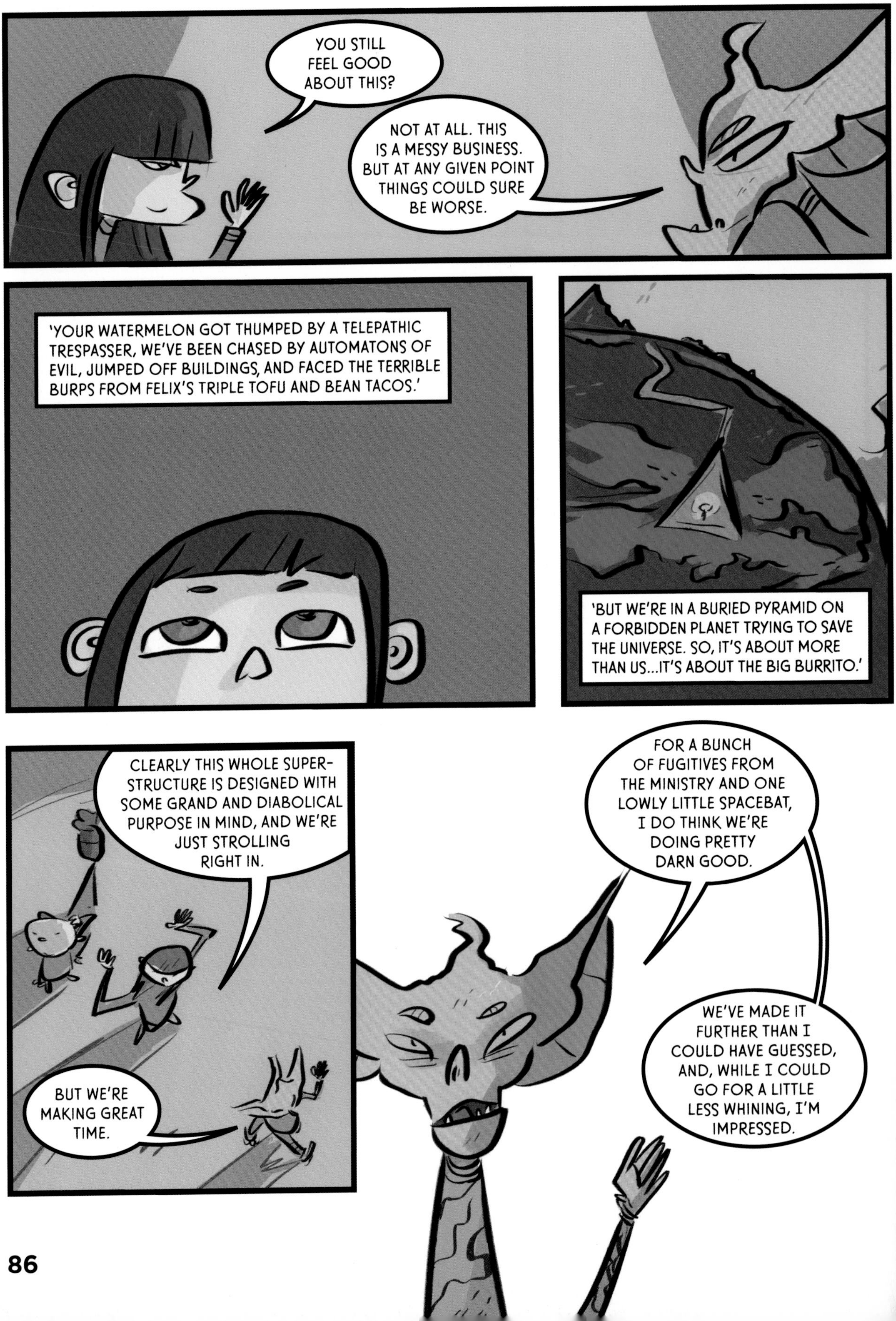
YOU STILL FEEL GOOD ABOUT THIS?
NOT AT ALL. THIS IS A MESSY BUSINESS. BUT AT ANY GIVEN POINT THINGS COULD SURE BE WORSE.
'YOUR WATERMELON GOT THUMPED BY A TELEPATHIC TRESPASSER, WE'VE BEEN CHASED BY AUTOMATONS OF EVIL, JUMPED OFF BUILDINGS, AND FACED THE TERRIBLE BURPS FROM FELIX'S TRIPLE TOFU AND BEAN TACOS.'
'BUT WE'RE IN A BURIED PYRAMID ON A FORBIDDEN PLANET TRYING TO SAVE THE UNIVERSE. SO, IT'S ABOUT MORE THAN US...IT'S ABOUT THE BIG BURRITO.'
CLEARLY THIS WHOLE SUPER-STRUCTURE IS DESIGNED WITH SOME GRAND AND DIABOLICAL PURPOSE IN MIND, AND WE'RE JUST STROLLING RIGHT IN.
BUT WE'RE MAKING GREAT TIME.
FOR A BUNCH OF FUGITIVES FROM THE MINISTRY AND ONE LOWLY LITTLE SPACEBAT, I DO THINK WE'RE DOING PRETTY DARN GOOD.
WE'VE MADE IT FURTHER THAN I COULD HAVE GUESSED, AND, WHILE I COULD GO FOR A LITTLE LESS WHINING, I'M IMPRESSED.

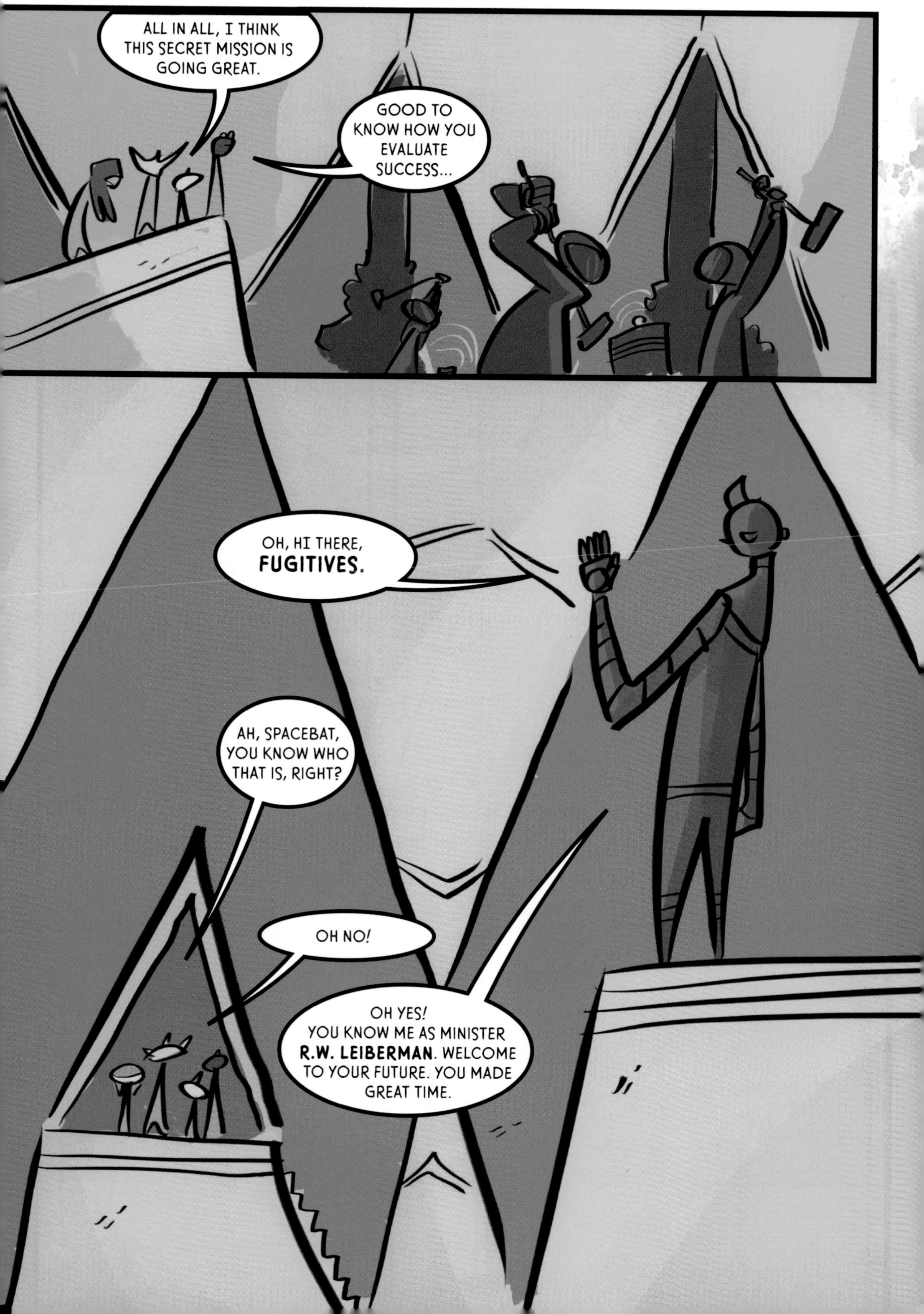
ALL IN ALL, I THINK THIS SECRET MISSION IS GOING GREAT.
GOOD TO KNOW HOW YOU EVALUATE SUCCESS...
OH, HI THERE, **FUGITIVES.**
AH, SPACEBAT, YOU KNOW WHO THAT IS, RIGHT?
OH NO!
OH YES! YOU KNOW ME AS MINISTER **R.W. LEIBERMAN**. WELCOME TO YOUR FUTURE. YOU MADE GREAT TIME.

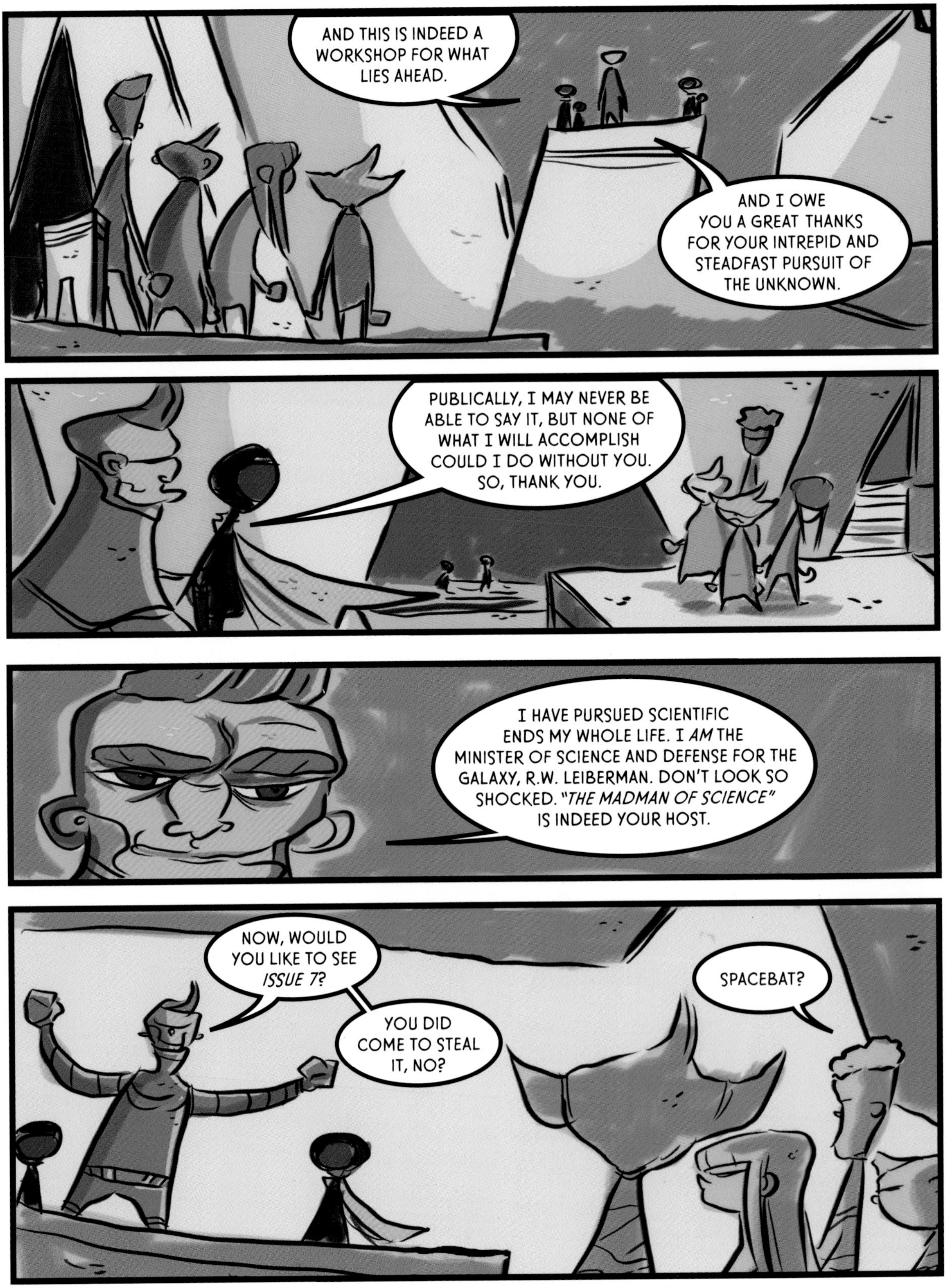
AND THIS IS INDEED A WORKSHOP FOR WHAT LIES AHEAD.
AND I OWE YOU A GREAT THANKS FOR YOUR INTREPID AND STEADFAST PURSUIT OF THE UNKNOWN.
PUBLICALLY, I MAY NEVER BE ABLE TO SAY IT, BUT NONE OF WHAT I WILL ACCOMPLISH COULD I DO WITHOUT YOU. SO, THANK YOU.
I HAVE PURSUED SCIENTIFIC ENDS MY WHOLE LIFE. I *AM* THE MINISTER OF SCIENCE AND DEFENSE FOR THE GALAXY, R.W. LEIBERMAN. DON'T LOOK SO SHOCKED. *"THE MADMAN OF SCIENCE"* IS INDEED YOUR HOST.
NOW, WOULD YOU LIKE TO SEE *ISSUE 7*?
YOU DID COME TO STEAL IT, NO?
SPACEBAT?

WE'VE HANDLED YOUR LITTLE MINIONS BEFORE, LEIBERMAN.

YEAH.

YES, LARRY HERE WOULD LIKE TO HAVE A WORD WITH YOU ABOUT THAT. SOMETHING TO DO WITH HIS BROTHER, MURRAY.

SPACEBAT.

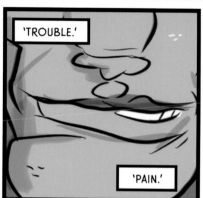

'TROUBLE.'

'PAIN.'

'AND A SETTLING OF SCORES...'

ALL THESE FISTICUFFS...FOR WHAT? TO REPEAT THE CYCLE OVER AND OVER? HOW PREDICTABLE. HOW BORING.

YOU GOT ANOTHER SUGGESTION FOR HOW THE WORLD SHOULD OPERATE, R.W.?

89

I HAVE *AN ANSWER*...BUT IT COMES AT A PRICE, SPACEBAT. AND IT INVOLVES YOU, THE FUGITIVES, HELPING ME CHANGE EVERYTHING.
I'M NOT ONE OF THE ***FUGITIVES***, THANKS.
OH, MY DEAR SPACEBAT, YOU ARE ALL FUGITIVES, AND ALL THE PERFECT CANDIDATES TO HELP. YOUNG. ENERGETIC. IDEALISTIC. ***NAÏVE.***
MAKING HEADLINES ACROSS THE UNIVERSE... BUSTING GOVERNMENT FORCES, TAKING OUT SECRET BASES, YOU HEARD ALL THE WHISPERS SPREAD, FOLLOWED THE BREAD CRUMBS, AND BUSTED IN HERE TO SAVE THE UNIVERSE. LIKE I SAID...
THE PERFECT PATSIES. HOW WOULD THE PUBLIC *NOT* LOVE THIS TALE?
...NAÏVE.
AND PERFECT IN YOUR CAPACITY TO BE BELIEVABLE.
'ALL THAT ENERGY TO FIND *WHAT*, YOU NEVER GUESSED AT *WHY*. NEVER REALIZED YOU WERE SETTING YOURSELVES UP TO HELP ME BY BECOMING THE PERFECT SUSPECTS TO STEAL THE ULTIMATE WEAPON...ISSUE 7. THE PUBLIC WILL LOVE THE TALE AND BELIEVE IT.'

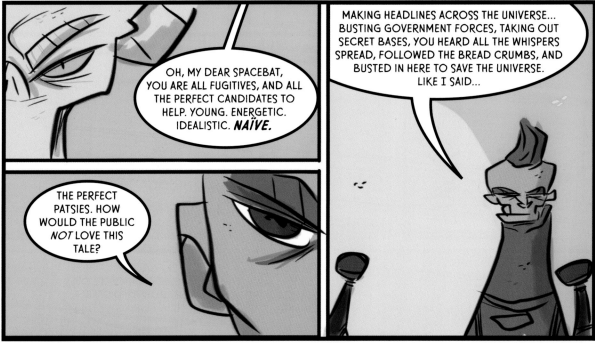

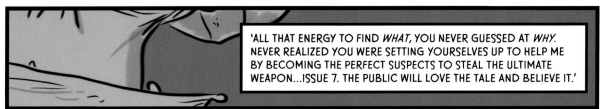

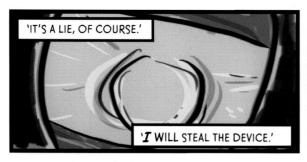

'IT'S A LIE, OF COURSE.'

'*I* WILL STEAL THE DEVICE.'

CLANG

SPACEBAT, THIS IS FROM THE VISION. YOU KNOW WHAT HAPPENS NEXT.

YEP...STAR-STUFF LEADS TO NOTHING GOOD.

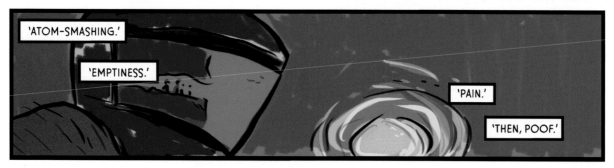

'ATOM-SMASHING.'

'EMPTINESS.'

'PAIN.'

'THEN, POOF.'

ISSUE 7 IS AN UNPARALLELED OPPORTUNITY TO CREATE SOMETHING NO ONE HAS EVER IMAGINED BEFORE, MUCH LESS SEEN. AND YOU ARE PART OF IT.

SO LOOK.

LOOK AND WONDER, MY DEARS. WITNESS THE FUTURE THAT IS UPON US! IT IS STRIKING, BOLD, TERRIBLE, AND RUNG IN BY THE SPACE PIG'S HAMMER.

CLANG

CLANG

CLANG

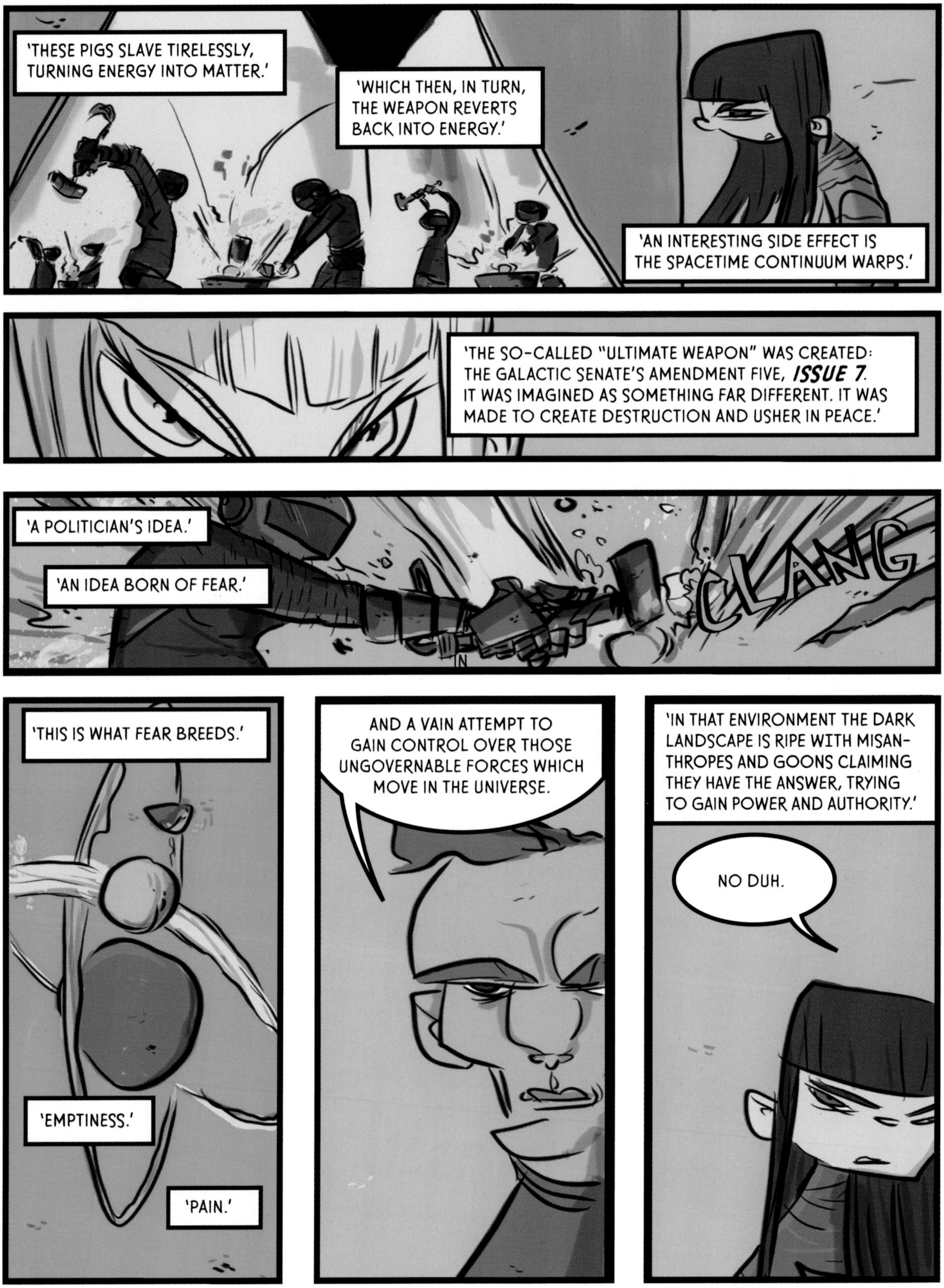
'THESE PIGS SLAVE TIRELESSLY, TURNING ENERGY INTO MATTER.'
'WHICH THEN, IN TURN, THE WEAPON REVERTS BACK INTO ENERGY.'
'AN INTERESTING SIDE EFFECT IS THE SPACETIME CONTINUUM WARPS.'
'THE SO-CALLED "ULTIMATE WEAPON" WAS CREATED: THE GALACTIC SENATE'S AMENDMENT FIVE, ISSUE 7. IT WAS IMAGINED AS SOMETHING FAR DIFFERENT. IT WAS MADE TO CREATE DESTRUCTION AND USHER IN PEACE.'
'A POLITICIAN'S IDEA.'
'AN IDEA BORN OF FEAR.'
CLANG
'THIS IS WHAT FEAR BREEDS.'
'EMPTINESS.'
'PAIN.'
AND A VAIN ATTEMPT TO GAIN CONTROL OVER THOSE UNGOVERNABLE FORCES WHICH MOVE IN THE UNIVERSE.
'IN THAT ENVIRONMENT THE DARK LANDSCAPE IS RIPE WITH MISAN-THROPES AND GOONS CLAIMING THEY HAVE THE ANSWER, TRYING TO GAIN POWER AND AUTHORITY.'
NO DUH.

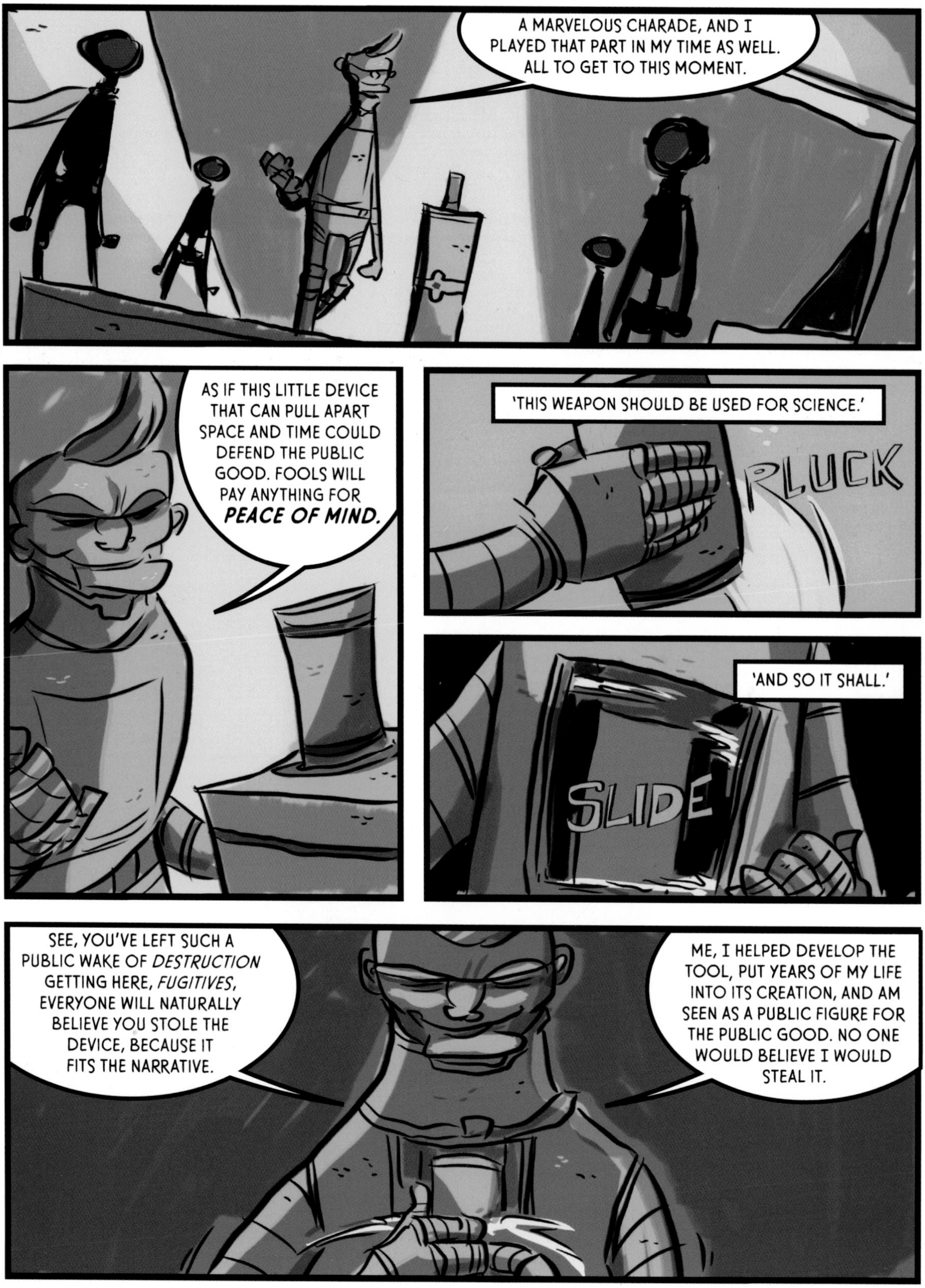
A MARVELOUS CHARADE, AND I PLAYED THAT PART IN MY TIME AS WELL. ALL TO GET TO THIS MOMENT.
AS IF THIS LITTLE DEVICE THAT CAN PULL APART SPACE AND TIME COULD DEFEND THE PUBLIC GOOD. FOOLS WILL PAY ANYTHING FOR *PEACE OF MIND.*
'THIS WEAPON SHOULD BE USED FOR SCIENCE.'
PLUCK
'AND SO IT SHALL.'
SLIDE
SEE, YOU'VE LEFT SUCH A PUBLIC WAKE OF *DESTRUCTION* GETTING HERE, *FUGITIVES*, EVERYONE WILL NATURALLY BELIEVE YOU STOLE THE DEVICE, BECAUSE IT FITS THE NARRATIVE.
ME, I HELPED DEVELOP THE TOOL, PUT YEARS OF MY LIFE INTO ITS CREATION, AND AM SEEN AS A PUBLIC FIGURE FOR THE PUBLIC GOOD. NO ONE WOULD BELIEVE I WOULD STEAL IT.

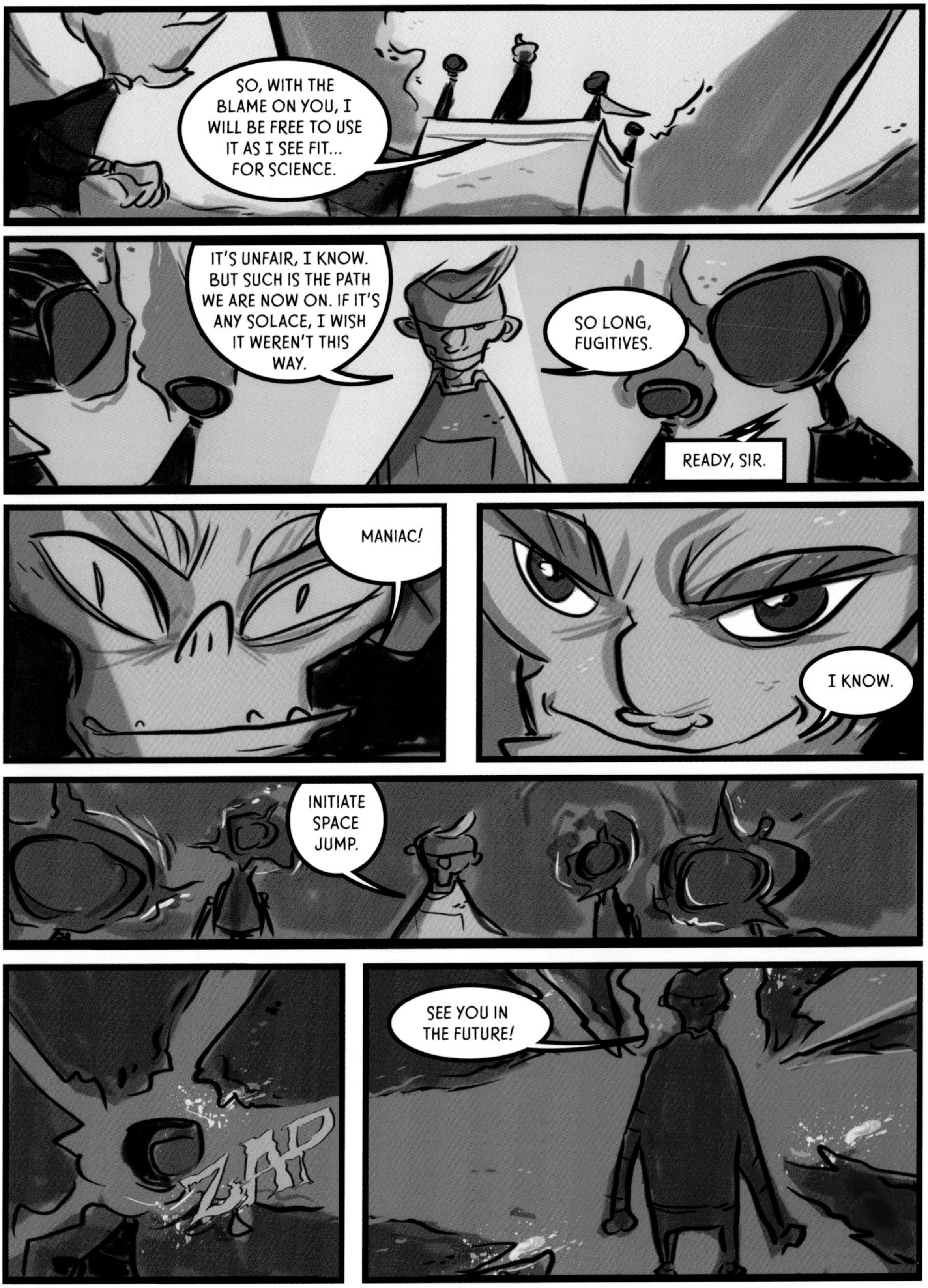
SO, WITH THE BLAME ON YOU, I WILL BE FREE TO USE IT AS I SEE FIT... FOR SCIENCE.
IT'S UNFAIR, I KNOW. BUT SUCH IS THE PATH WE ARE NOW ON. IF IT'S ANY SOLACE, I WISH IT WEREN'T THIS WAY.
SO LONG, FUGITIVES.
READY, SIR.
MANIAC!
I KNOW.
INITIATE SPACE JUMP.
ZAP
SEE YOU IN THE FUTURE!

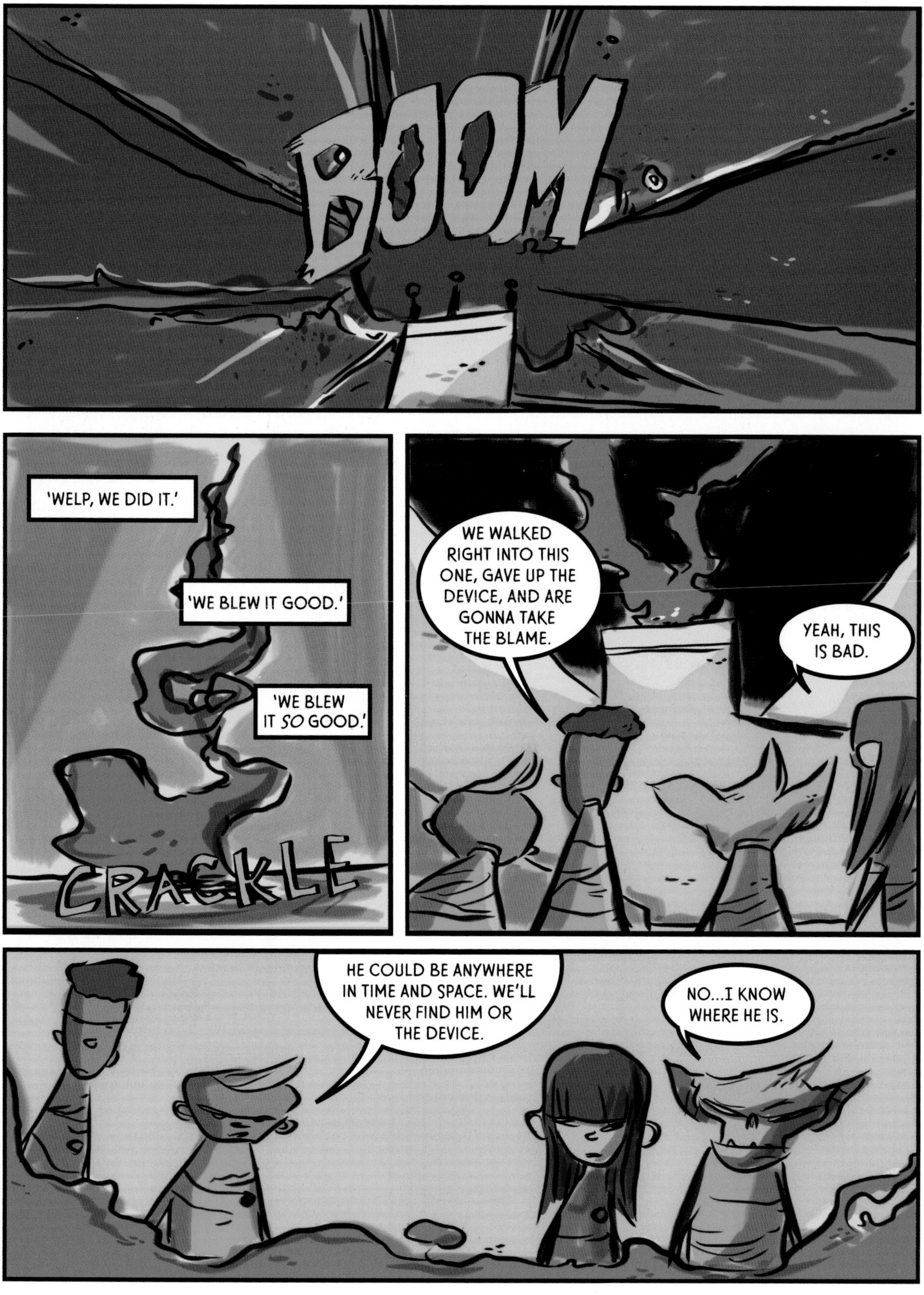
BOOM
'WELP, WE DID IT.'
'WE BLEW IT GOOD.'
'WE BLEW IT *SO* GOOD.'
CRACKLE
WE WALKED RIGHT INTO THIS ONE, GAVE UP THE DEVICE, AND ARE GONNA TAKE THE BLAME.
YEAH, THIS IS BAD.
HE COULD BE ANYWHERE IN TIME AND SPACE. WE'LL NEVER FIND HIM OR THE DEVICE.
NO...I KNOW WHERE HE IS.

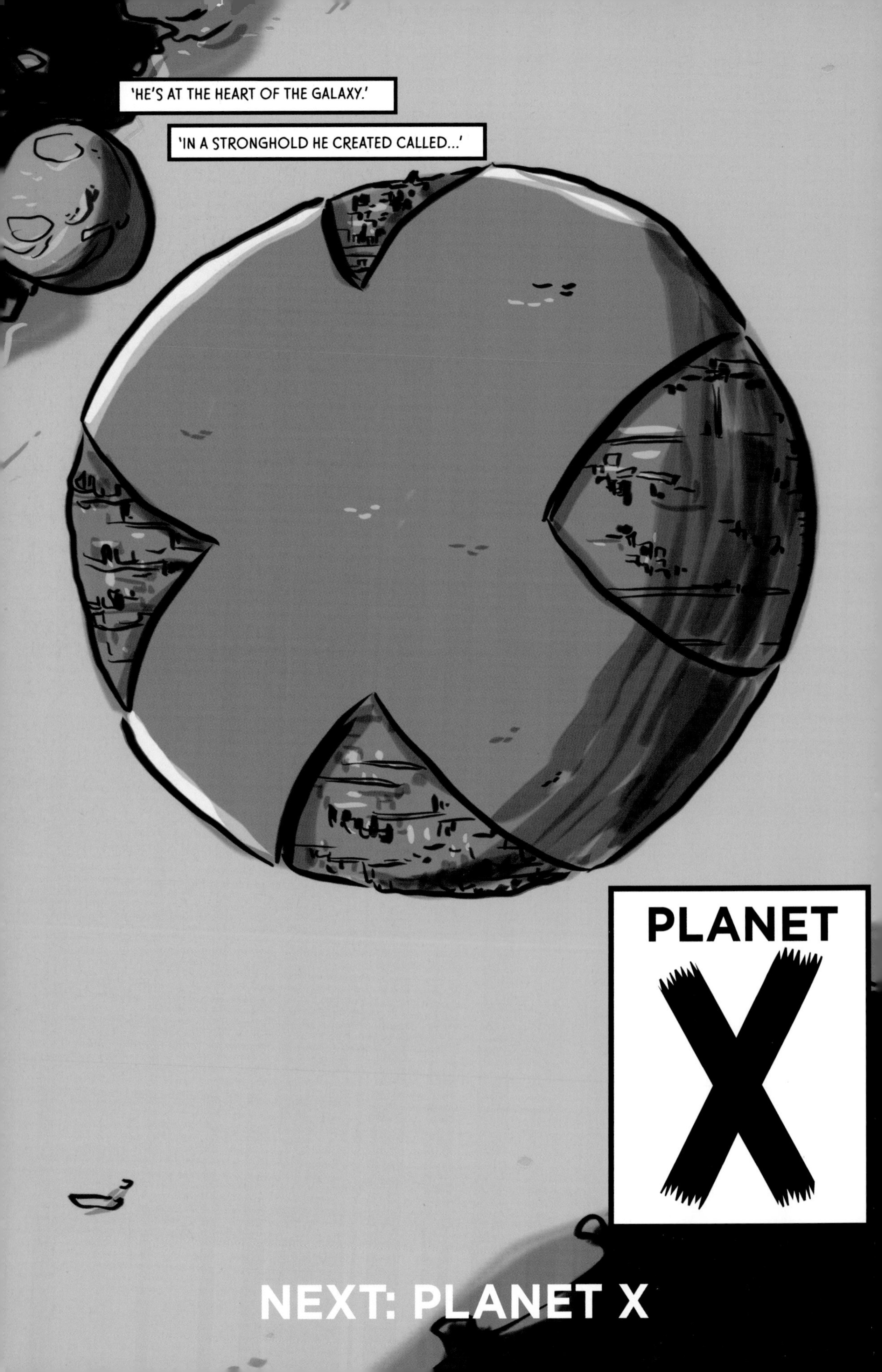
'HE'S AT THE HEART OF THE GALAXY.'
'IN A STRONGHOLD HE CREATED CALLED...'
PLANET X

NEXT: PLANET X

ISSUE FOUR:
PLANET X

BALL:
Take that ball outside to play!

-MOM

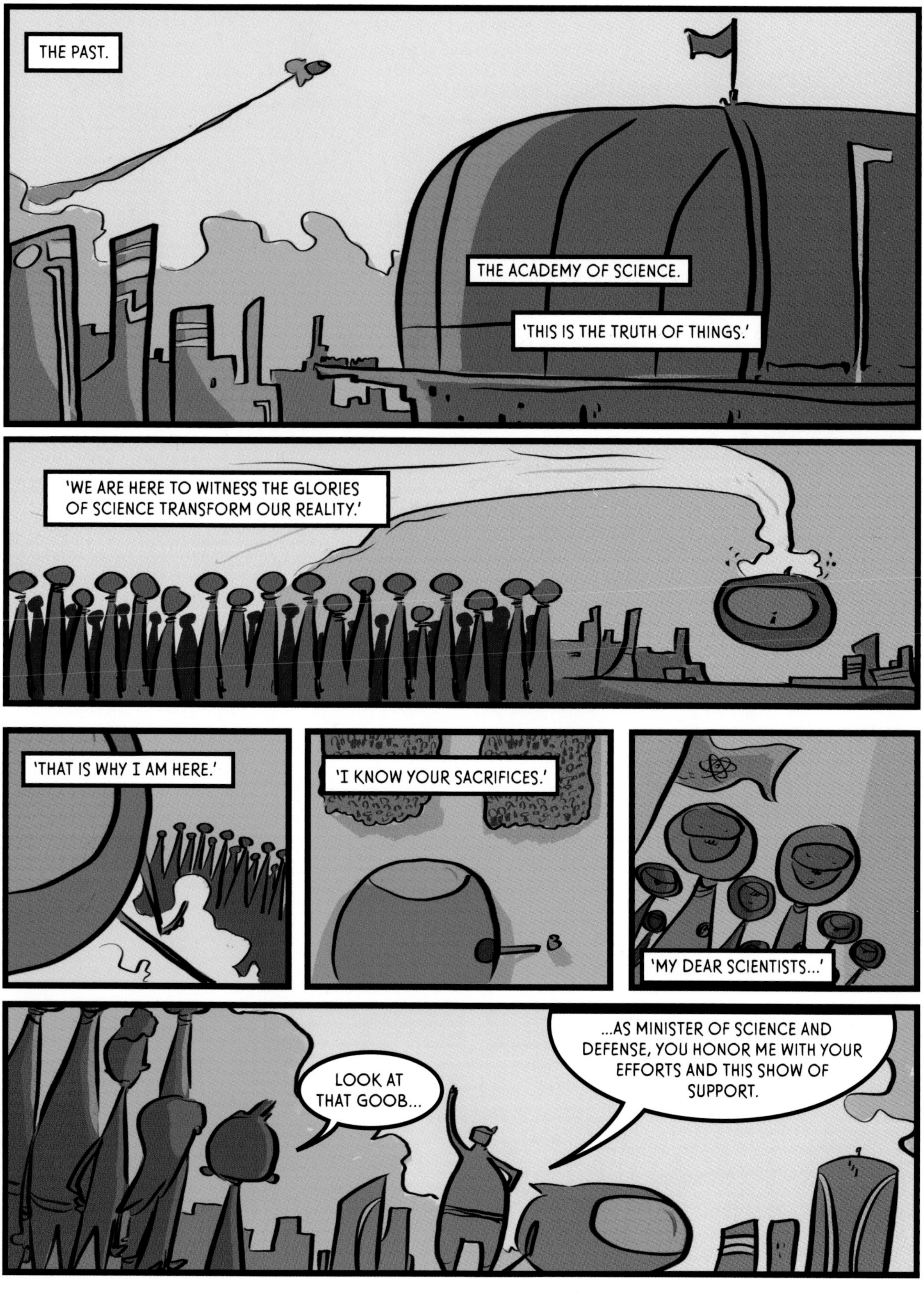
THE PAST.
THE ACADEMY OF SCIENCE.
'THIS IS THE TRUTH OF THINGS.'
'WE ARE HERE TO WITNESS THE GLORIES OF SCIENCE TRANSFORM OUR REALITY.'
'THAT IS WHY I AM HERE.'
'I KNOW YOUR SACRIFICES.'
'MY DEAR SCIENTISTS...'
LOOK AT THAT GOOB...
...AS MINISTER OF SCIENCE AND DEFENSE, YOU HONOR ME WITH YOUR EFFORTS AND THIS SHOW OF SUPPORT.

ONLY A FOOL WOULD DENY REALITY.
AND NONE AMONG US ARE FOOLS.
WE ARE HERE TO CREATE
SOMETHING NEW.

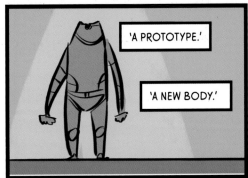

'A PROTOTYPE.'

'A NEW BODY.'

'A BODY THAT WILL NOT AGE.
IT WILL BE POWERED BY THE
GREATEST THING THERE IS...'

'STAR-STUFF.'

THIS WAY, MINISTER.
THE FACILITY IS
PREPARED.

VERY GOOD TO HEAR,
DOCTOR.

'MINISTER. I KNOW THE
TRUTH. IT'S UNDER YOUR
THOUGHTS, SO CLEAR.'

'YOU AREN'T FOOLING ME.'

'YOU'RE BROADCASTING
YOUR TRUE INTENTIONS.'

'NO DOUBT ALL YOUR ENERGY
AND AIMS ARE BENT ON IT.'

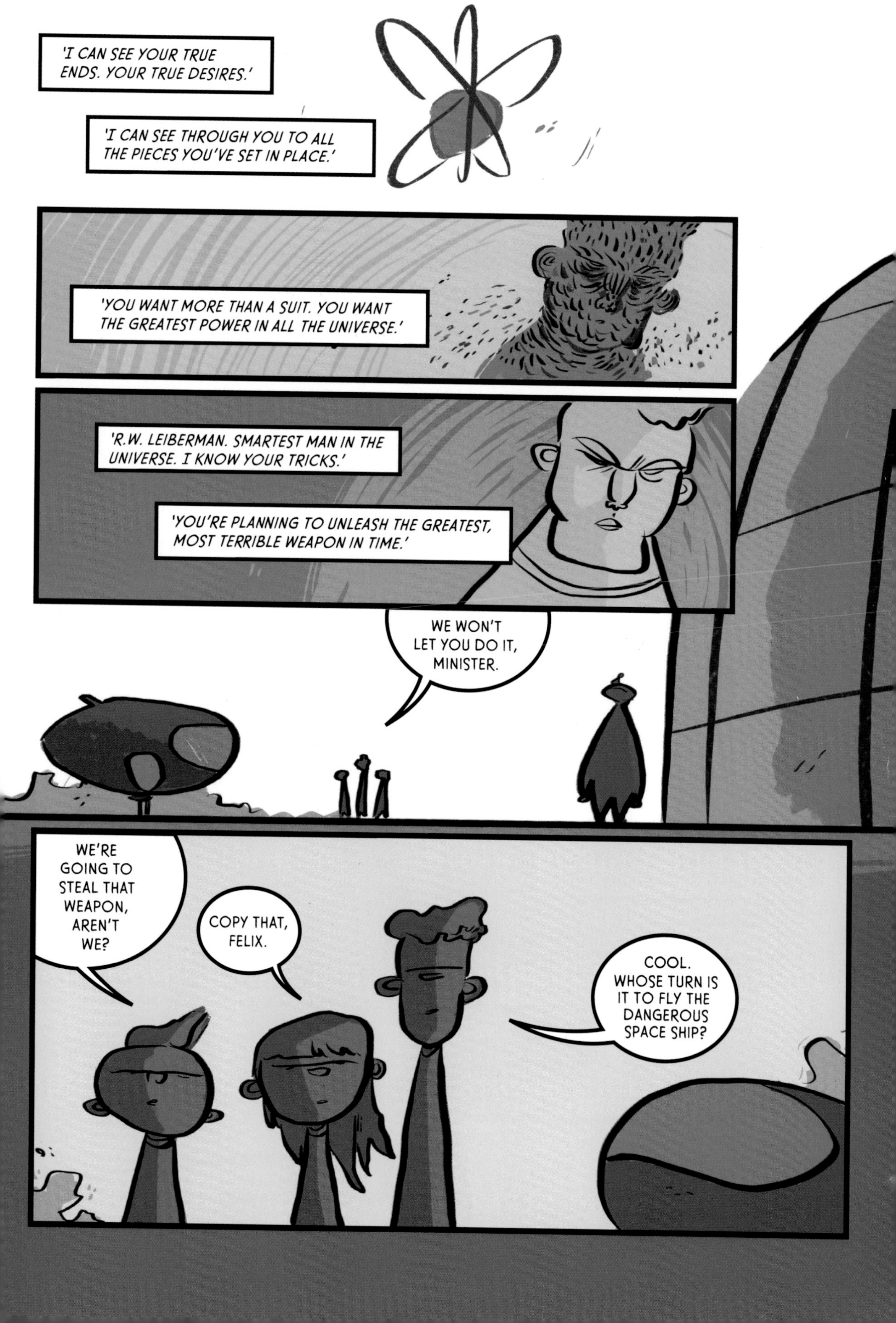
'I CAN SEE YOUR TRUE ENDS. YOUR TRUE DESIRES.'
'I CAN SEE THROUGH YOU TO ALL THE PIECES YOU'VE SET IN PLACE.'
'YOU WANT MORE THAN A SUIT. YOU WANT THE GREATEST POWER IN ALL THE UNIVERSE.'
'R.W. LEIBERMAN. SMARTEST MAN IN THE UNIVERSE. I KNOW YOUR TRICKS.'
'YOU'RE PLANNING TO UNLEASH THE GREATEST, MOST TERRIBLE WEAPON IN TIME.'
WE WON'T LET YOU DO IT, MINISTER.
WE'RE GOING TO STEAL THAT WEAPON, AREN'T WE?
COPY THAT, FELIX.
COOL. WHOSE TURN IS IT TO FLY THE DANGEROUS SPACE SHIP?

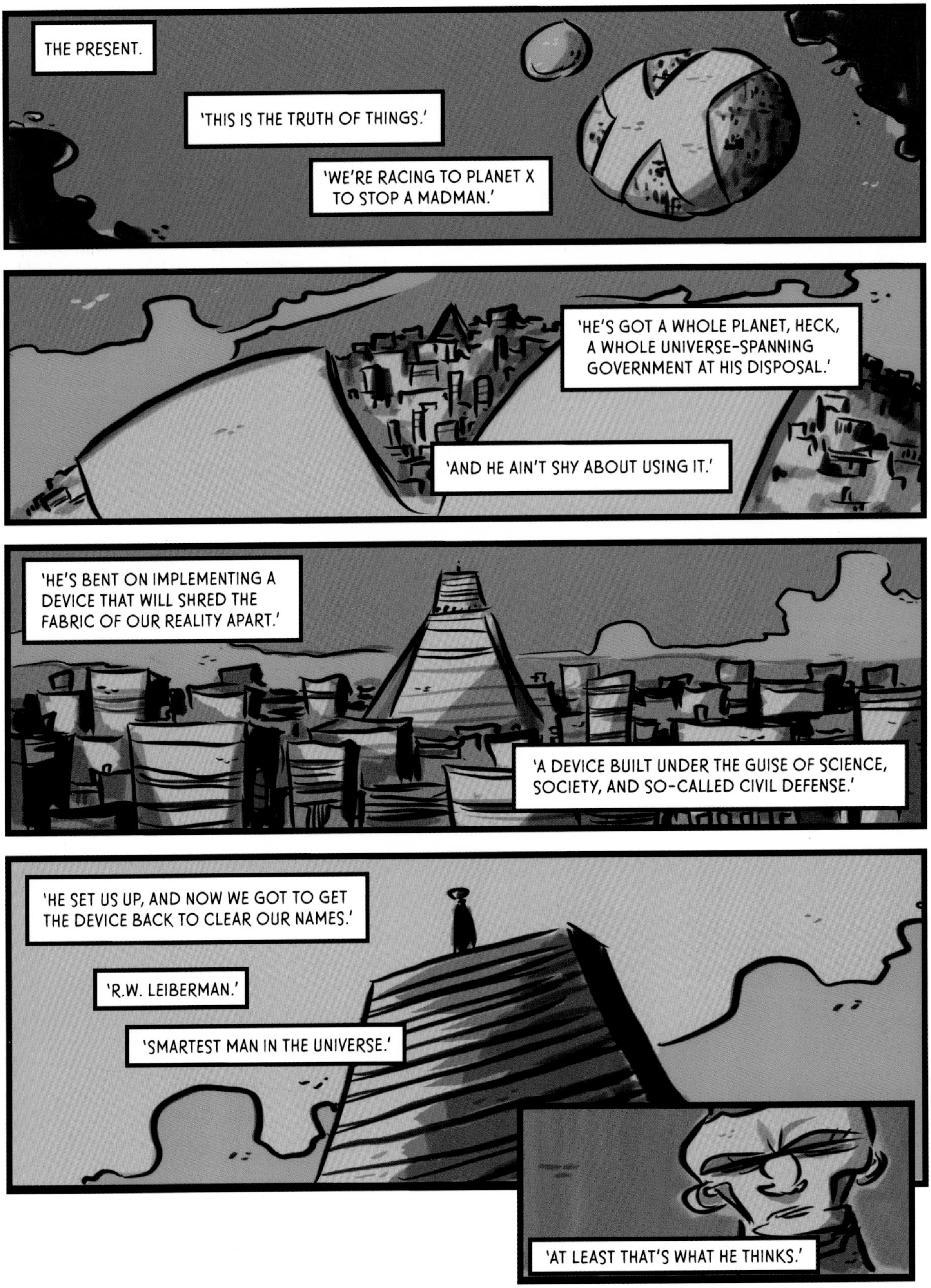
THE PRESENT.
'THIS IS THE TRUTH OF THINGS.'
'WE'RE RACING TO PLANET X TO STOP A MADMAN.'
'HE'S GOT A WHOLE PLANET, HECK, A WHOLE UNIVERSE-SPANNING GOVERNMENT AT HIS DISPOSAL.'
'AND HE AIN'T SHY ABOUT USING IT.'
'HE'S BENT ON IMPLEMENTING A DEVICE THAT WILL SHRED THE FABRIC OF OUR REALITY APART.'
'A DEVICE BUILT UNDER THE GUISE OF SCIENCE, SOCIETY, AND SO-CALLED CIVIL DEFENSE.'
'HE SET US UP, AND NOW WE GOT TO GET THE DEVICE BACK TO CLEAR OUR NAMES.'
'R.W. LEIBERMAN.'
'SMARTEST MAN IN THE UNIVERSE.'
'AT LEAST THAT'S WHAT HE THINKS.'

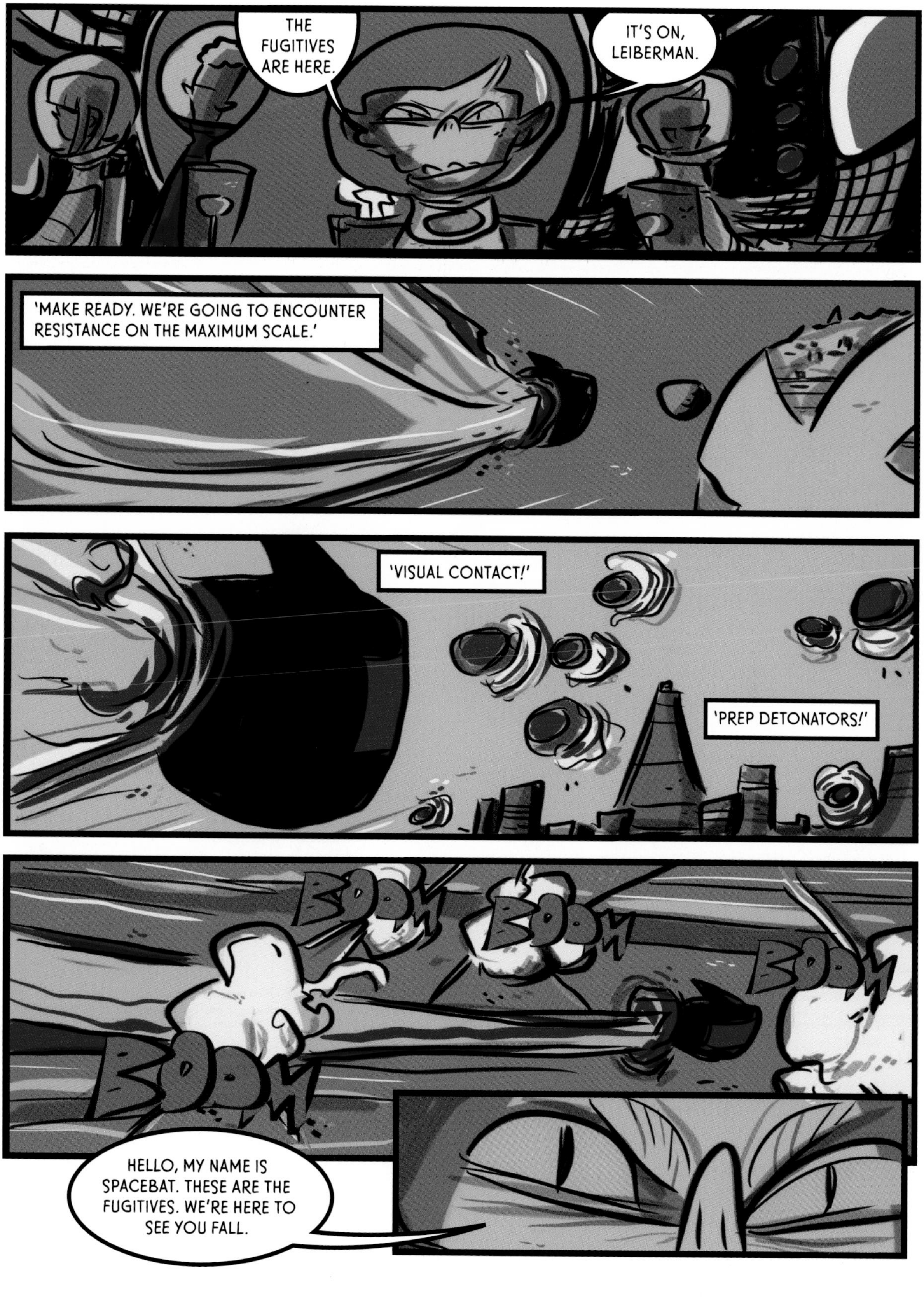
THE FUGITIVES ARE HERE.
IT'S ON, LEIBERMAN.
'MAKE READY. WE'RE GOING TO ENCOUNTER RESISTANCE ON THE MAXIMUM SCALE.'
'VISUAL CONTACT!'
'PREP DETONATORS!'
BOOM
BOOM
BOOM
BOOM
HELLO, MY NAME IS SPACEBAT. THESE ARE THE FUGITIVES. WE'RE HERE TO SEE YOU FALL.

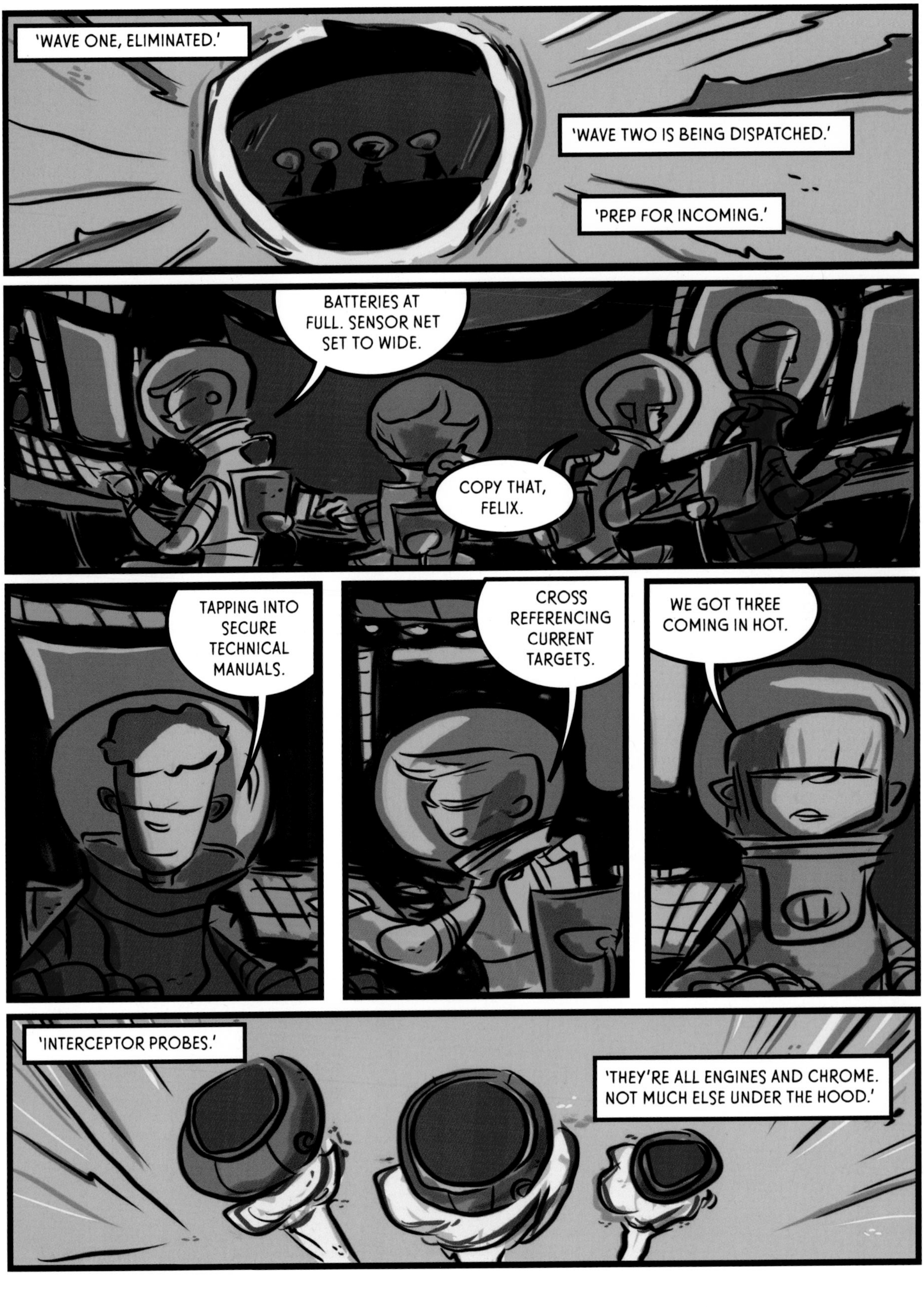
'WAVE ONE, ELIMINATED.'
'WAVE TWO IS BEING DISPATCHED.'
'PREP FOR INCOMING.'
BATTERIES AT FULL. SENSOR NET SET TO WIDE.
COPY THAT, FELIX.
TAPPING INTO SECURE TECHNICAL MANUALS.
CROSS REFERENCING CURRENT TARGETS.
WE GOT THREE COMING IN HOT.
'INTERCEPTOR PROBES.'
'THEY'RE ALL ENGINES AND CHROME.
NOT MUCH ELSE UNDER THE HOOD.'

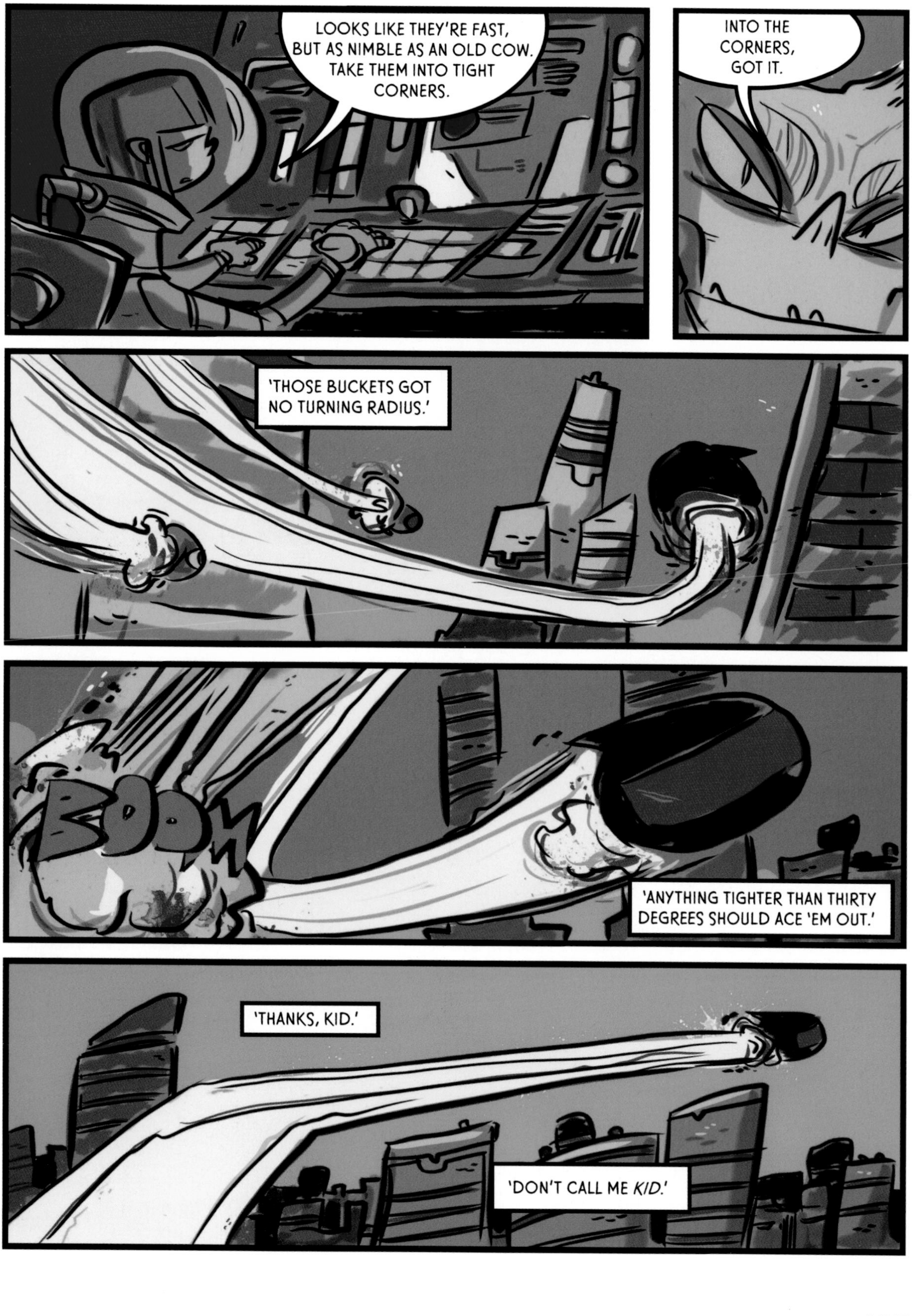
LOOKS LIKE THEY'RE FAST, BUT AS NIMBLE AS AN OLD COW. TAKE THEM INTO TIGHT CORNERS.
INTO THE CORNERS, GOT IT.
'THOSE BUCKETS GOT NO TURNING RADIUS.'
BOOM
'ANYTHING TIGHTER THAN THIRTY DEGREES SHOULD ACE 'EM OUT.'
'THANKS, KID.'
'DON'T CALL ME *KID*.'

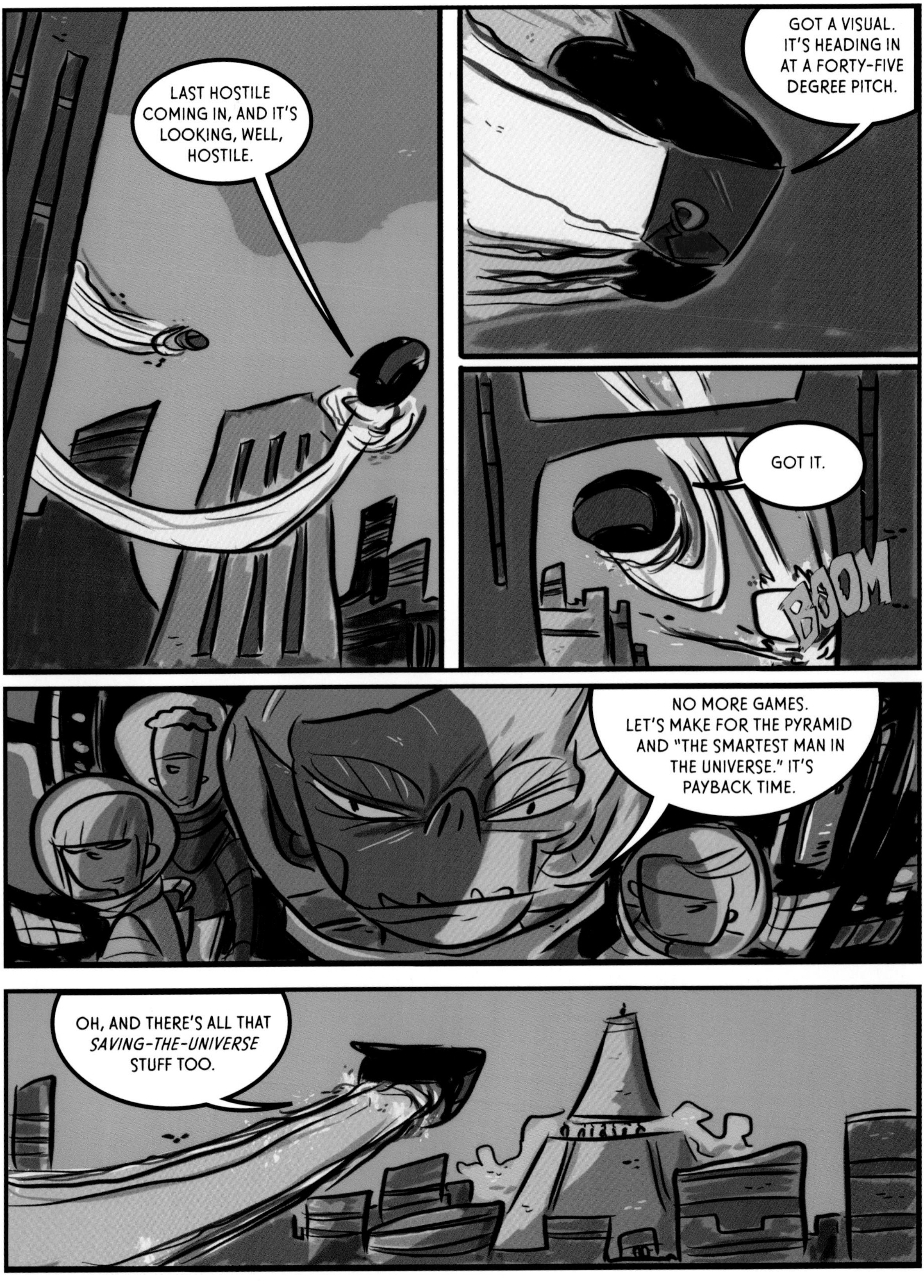
LAST HOSTILE COMING IN, AND IT'S LOOKING, WELL, HOSTILE.
GOT A VISUAL. IT'S HEADING IN AT A FORTY-FIVE DEGREE PITCH.
GOT IT.
BOOM
NO MORE GAMES. LET'S MAKE FOR THE PYRAMID AND "THE SMARTEST MAN IN THE UNIVERSE." IT'S PAYBACK TIME.
OH, AND THERE'S ALL THAT *SAVING-THE-UNIVERSE* STUFF TOO.

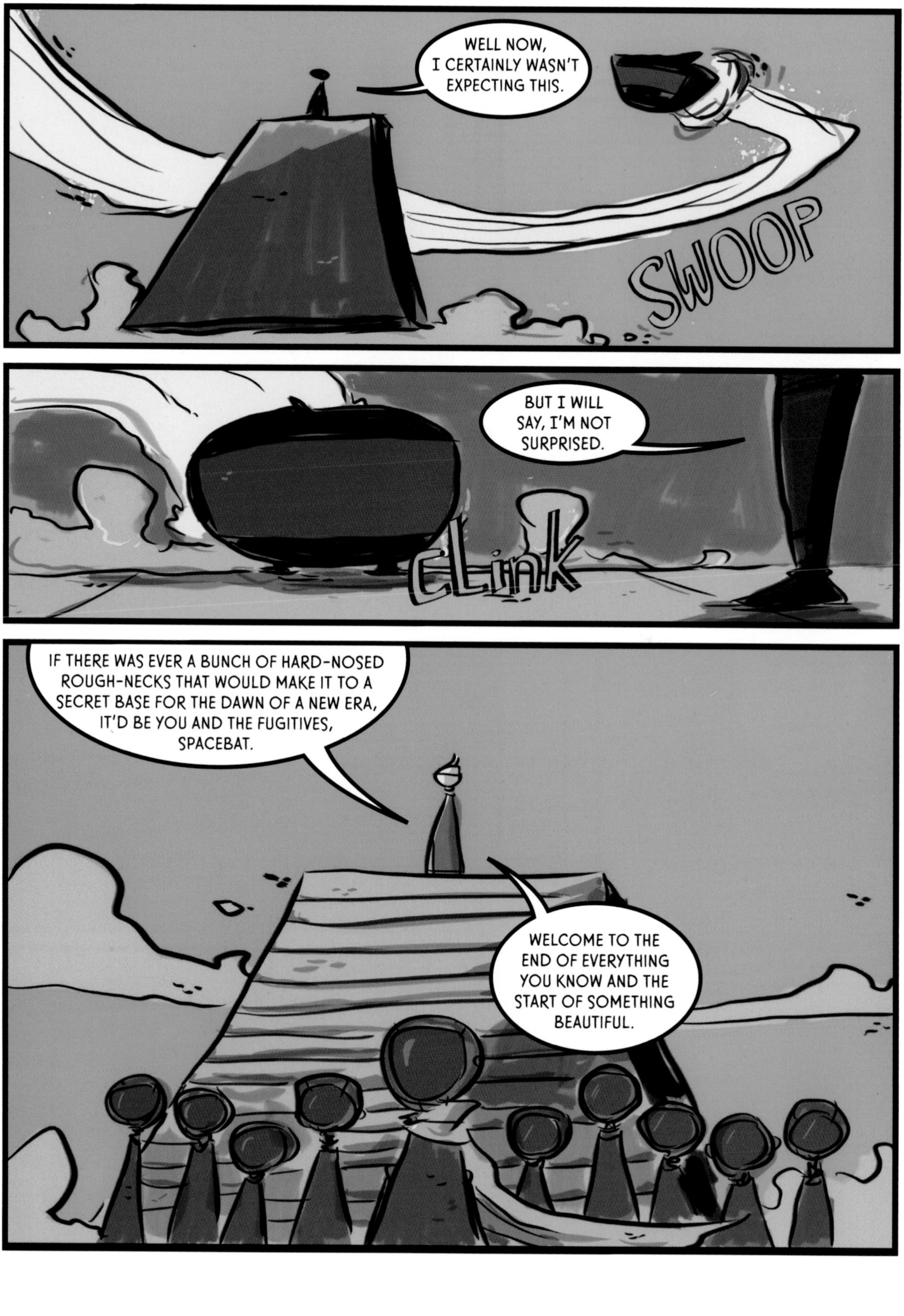
WELL NOW, I CERTAINLY WASN'T EXPECTING THIS.
SWOOP
BUT I WILL SAY, I'M NOT SURPRISED.
CLink
IF THERE WAS EVER A BUNCH OF HARD-NOSED ROUGH-NECKS THAT WOULD MAKE IT TO A SECRET BASE FOR THE DAWN OF A NEW ERA, IT'D BE YOU AND THE FUGITIVES, SPACEBAT.
WELCOME TO THE END OF EVERYTHING YOU KNOW AND THE START OF SOMETHING BEAUTIFUL.

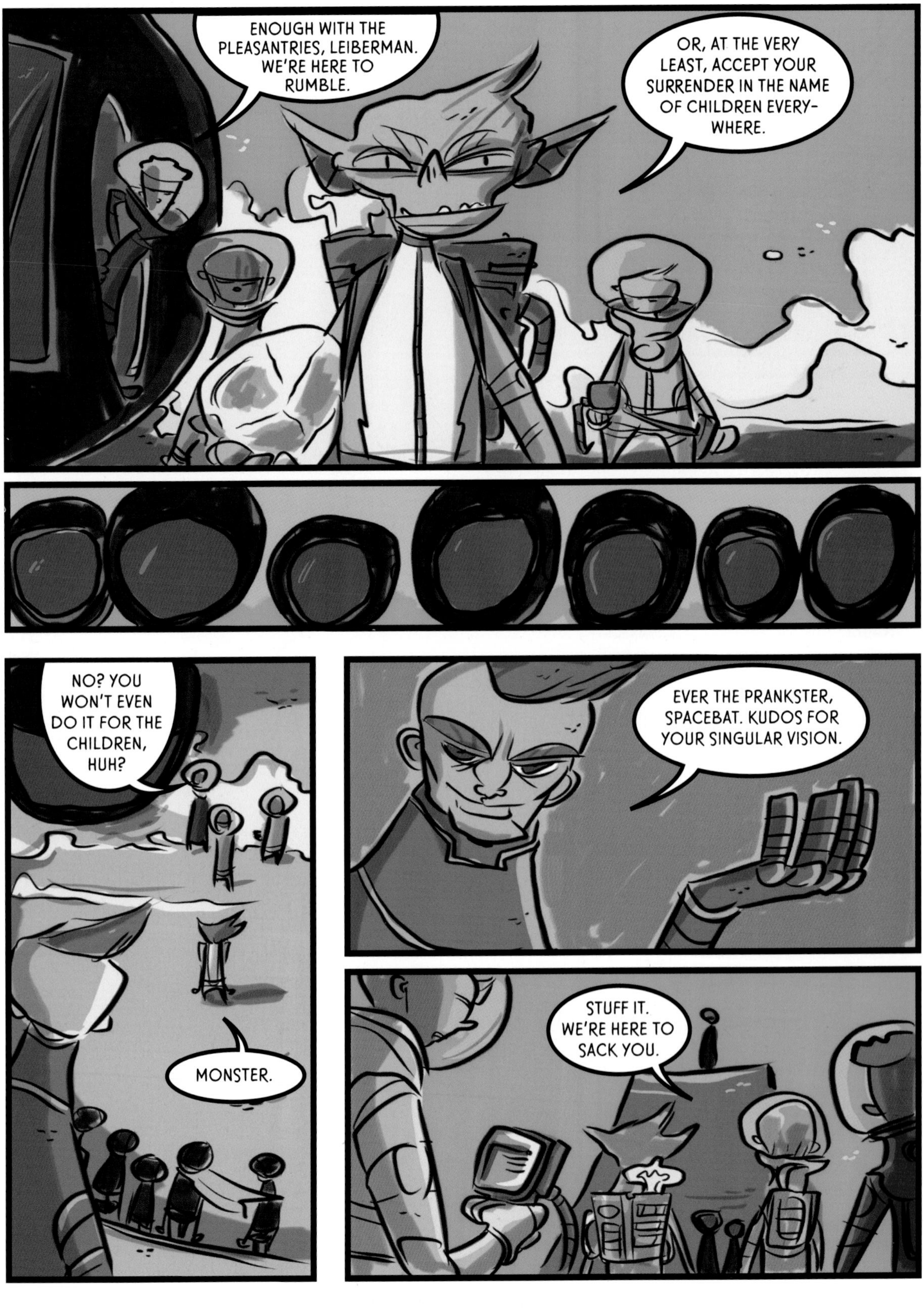
ENOUGH WITH THE PLEASANTRIES, LEIBERMAN. WE'RE HERE TO RUMBLE.
OR, AT THE VERY LEAST, ACCEPT YOUR SURRENDER IN THE NAME OF CHILDREN EVERY-WHERE.
NO? YOU WON'T EVEN DO IT FOR THE CHILDREN, HUH?
MONSTER.
EVER THE PRANKSTER, SPACEBAT. KUDOS FOR YOUR SINGULAR VISION.
STUFF IT. WE'RE HERE TO SACK YOU.

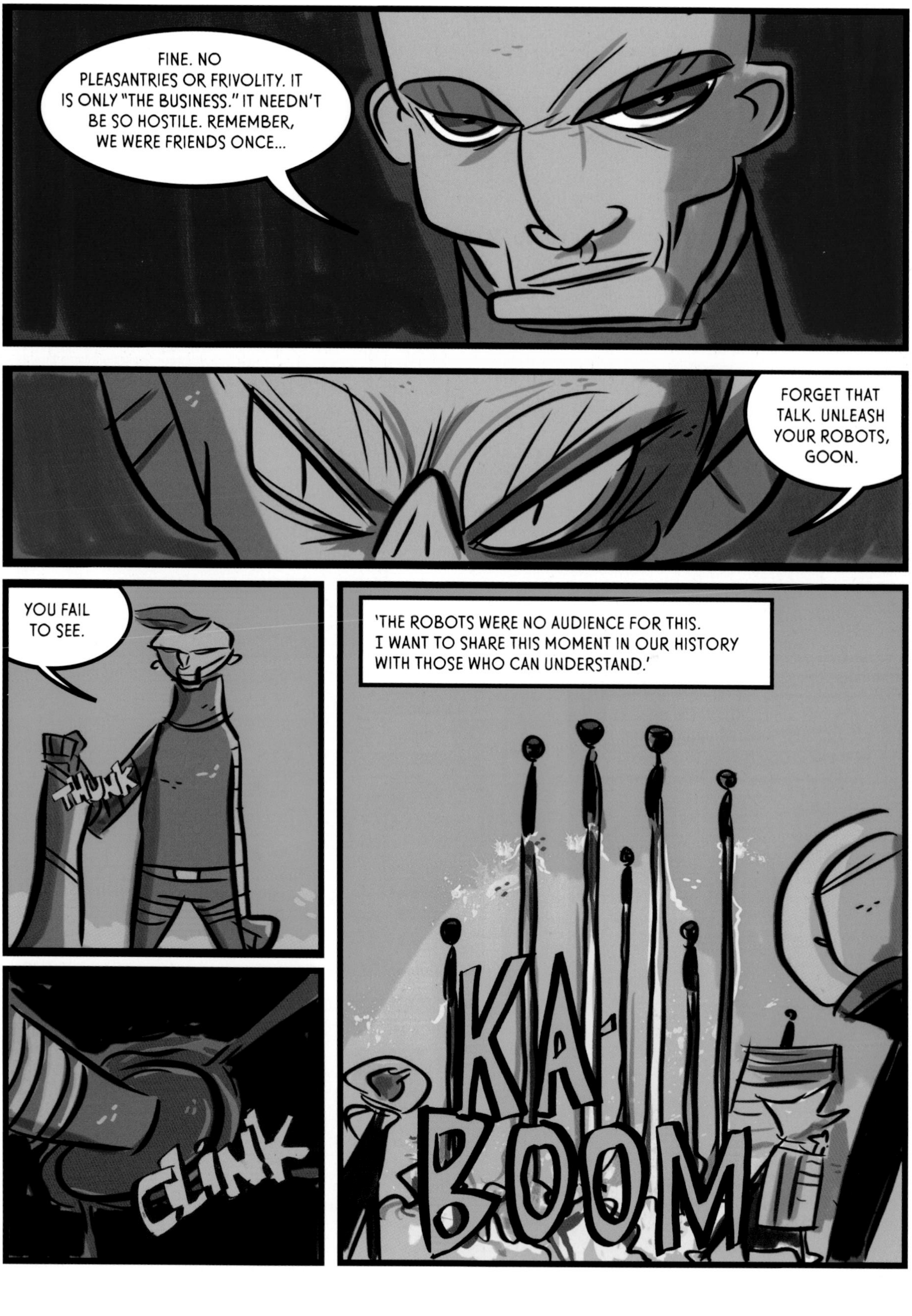

FINE. NO PLEASANTRIES OR FRIVOLITY. IT IS ONLY "THE BUSINESS." IT NEEDN'T BE SO HOSTILE. REMEMBER, WE WERE FRIENDS ONCE...
FORGET THAT TALK. UNLEASH YOUR ROBOTS, GOON.
YOU FAIL TO SEE.
THUNK
CLINK
'THE ROBOTS WERE NO AUDIENCE FOR THIS. I WANT TO SHARE THIS MOMENT IN OUR HISTORY WITH THOSE WHO CAN UNDERSTAND.'
KA-BOOM

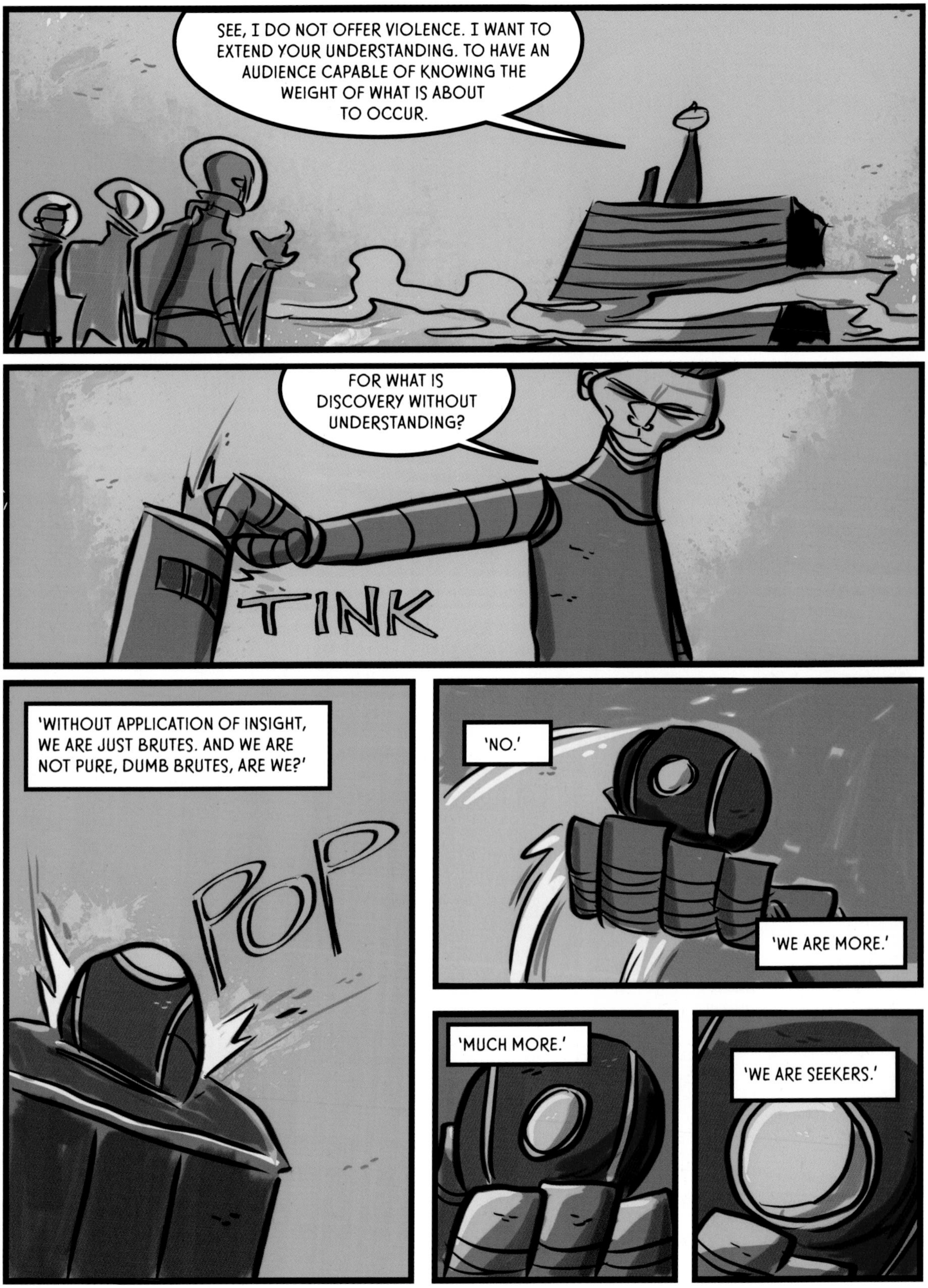
SEE, I DO NOT OFFER VIOLENCE. I WANT TO EXTEND YOUR UNDERSTANDING. TO HAVE AN AUDIENCE CAPABLE OF KNOWING THE WEIGHT OF WHAT IS ABOUT TO OCCUR.
FOR WHAT IS DISCOVERY WITHOUT UNDERSTANDING?
TINK
'WITHOUT APPLICATION OF INSIGHT, WE ARE JUST BRUTES. AND WE ARE NOT PURE, DUMB BRUTES, ARE WE?'
POP
'NO.'
'WE ARE MORE.'
'MUCH MORE.'
'WE ARE SEEKERS.'

WE DO NOT COWER AT THE HORIZON, WE RACE TO IT. AND WHAT I HOLD IS THE EDGE OF OUR KNOWLEDGE.

THE FUTURE? REALLY?

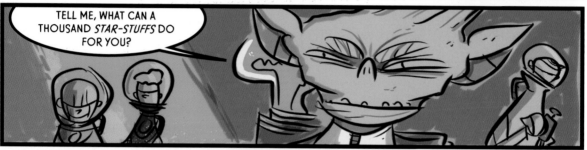

TELL ME, WHAT CAN A THOUSAND *STAR-STUFFS* DO FOR YOU?

'SPACEBAT, THINK OF THIS ENTIRE PLANET AS ONE *GIANT CIRCUIT*, AND WHERE WE STAND IS THE *DIAL* THAT RUNS THE MACHINE.'

'AND AS I AM A BIT OF A TRADITIONALIST, I WENT WITH AN ANCIENT SYMBOL...'

'A PYRAMID.'

'A PYRAMID IS OUR VEHICLE THROUGH TIME.'

'SO THOSE THOUSAND STAR CORES ARE AT THE CENTER OF THIS PLANET, CHURNING WITH RAW, UNBRIDLED ENERGY.'

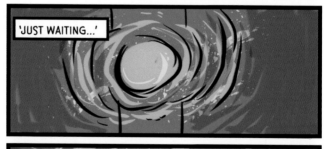

'JUST WAITING...'

'...TO BE UNLEASHED.'

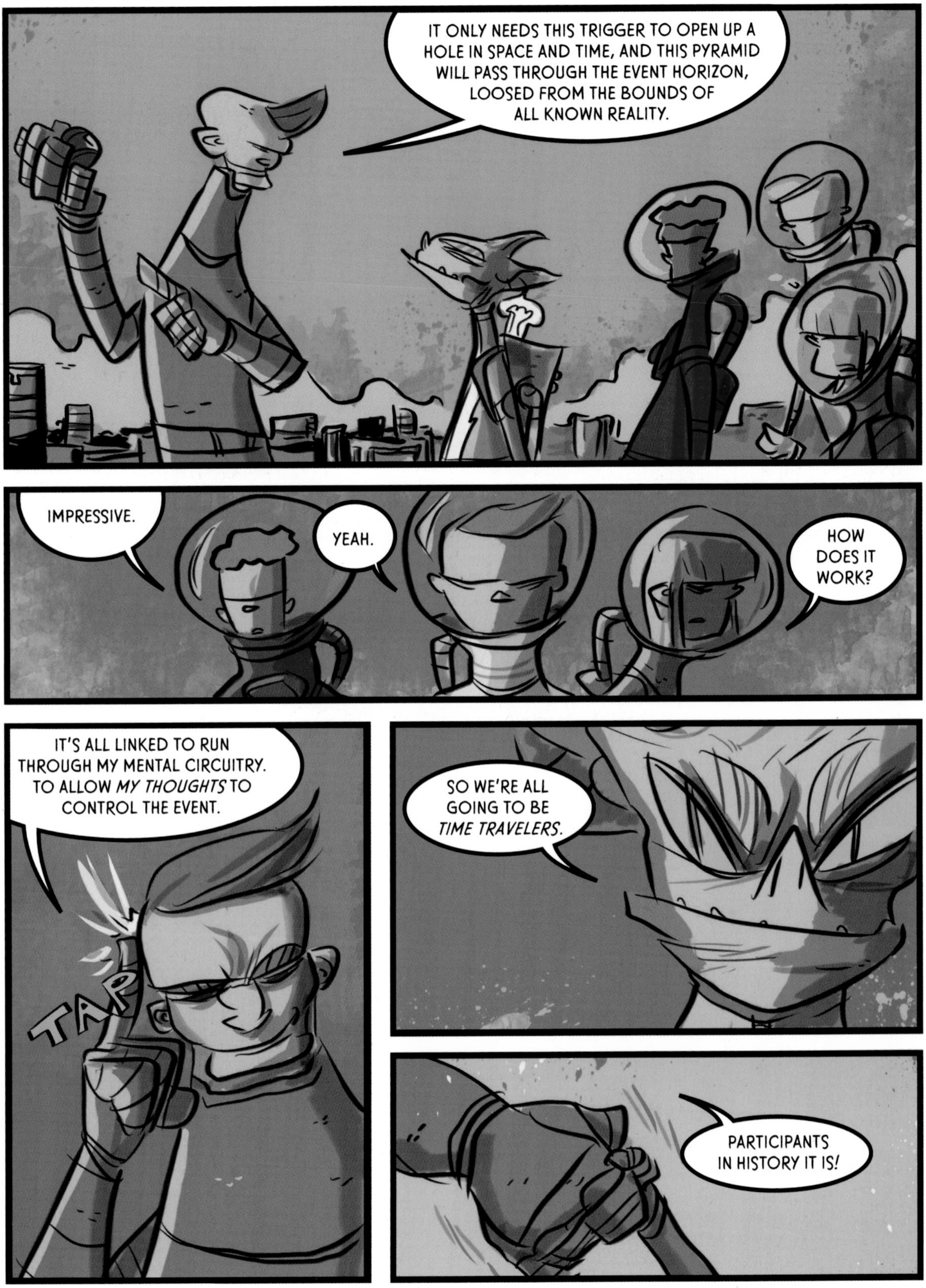
IT ONLY NEEDS THIS TRIGGER TO OPEN UP A HOLE IN SPACE AND TIME, AND THIS PYRAMID WILL PASS THROUGH THE EVENT HORIZON, LOOSED FROM THE BOUNDS OF ALL KNOWN REALITY.
IMPRESSIVE.
YEAH.
HOW DOES IT WORK?
IT'S ALL LINKED TO RUN THROUGH MY MENTAL CIRCUITRY. TO ALLOW *MY THOUGHTS* TO CONTROL THE EVENT.
TAP
SO WE'RE ALL GOING TO BE *TIME TRAVELERS*.
PARTICIPANTS IN HISTORY IT IS!

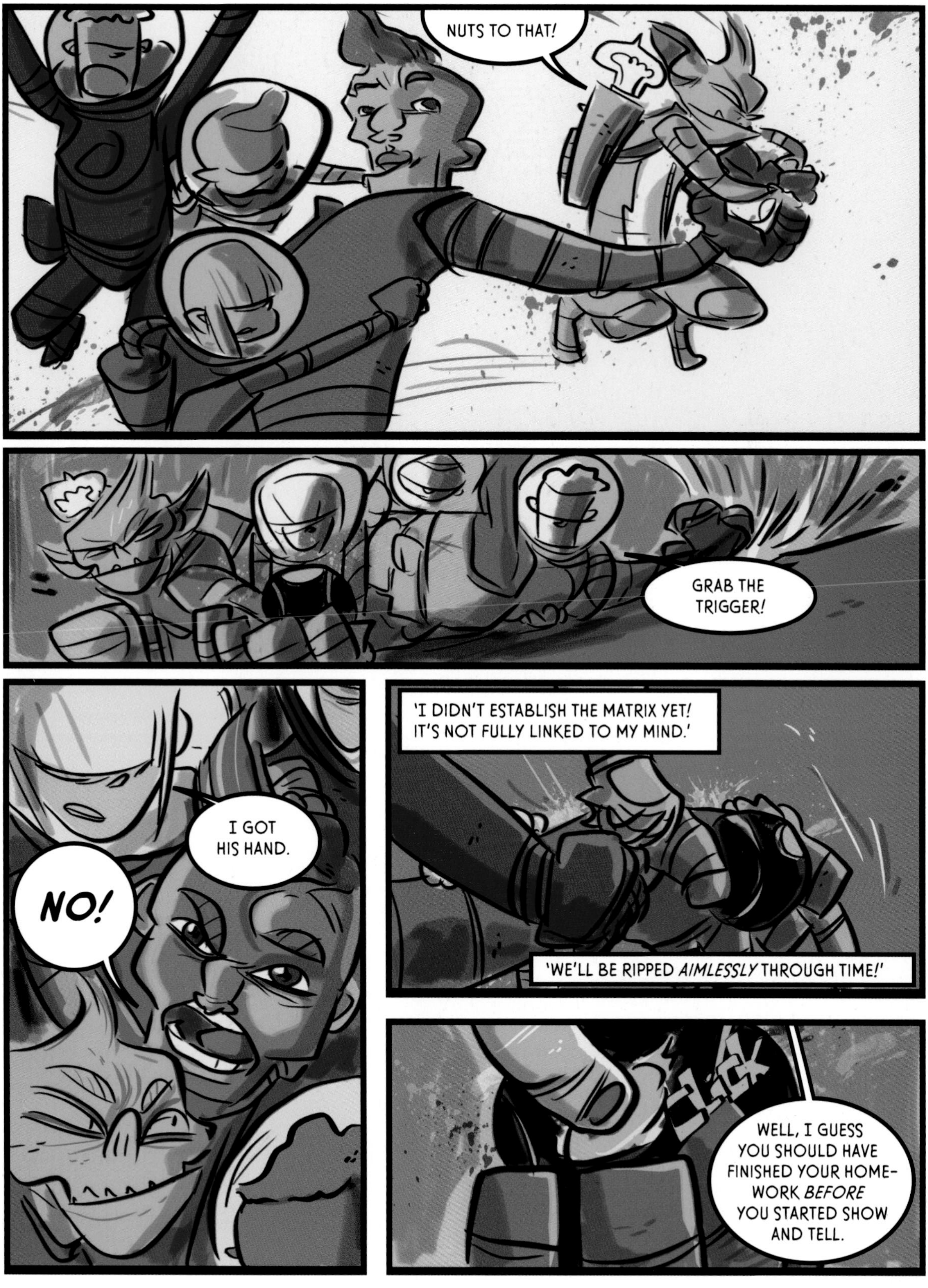
NUTS TO THAT!
GRAB THE TRIGGER!
I GOT HIS HAND.
NO!
'I DIDN'T ESTABLISH THE MATRIX YET! IT'S NOT FULLY LINKED TO MY MIND.'
'WE'LL BE RIPPED *AIMLESSLY* THROUGH TIME!'
WELL, I GUESS YOU SHOULD HAVE FINISHED YOUR HOME-WORK *BEFORE* YOU STARTED SHOW AND TELL.

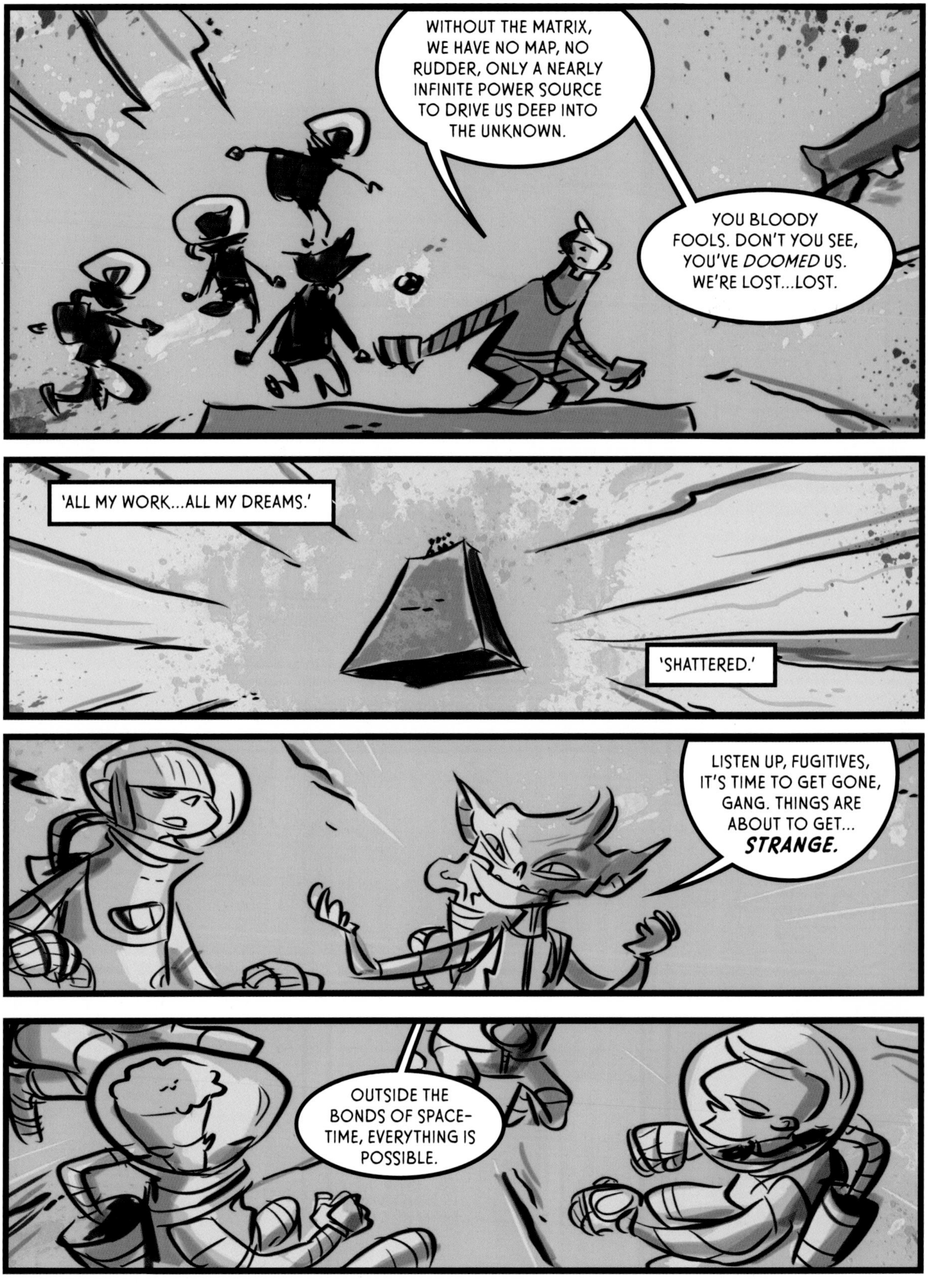
WITHOUT THE MATRIX, WE HAVE NO MAP, NO RUDDER, ONLY A NEARLY INFINITE POWER SOURCE TO DRIVE US DEEP INTO THE UNKNOWN.
YOU BLOODY FOOLS. DON'T YOU SEE, YOU'VE *DOOMED* US. WE'RE LOST...LOST.
'ALL MY WORK...ALL MY DREAMS.'
'SHATTERED.'
LISTEN UP, FUGITIVES, IT'S TIME TO GET GONE, GANG. THINGS ARE ABOUT TO GET... ***STRANGE.***
OUTSIDE THE BONDS OF SPACE-TIME, EVERYTHING IS POSSIBLE.

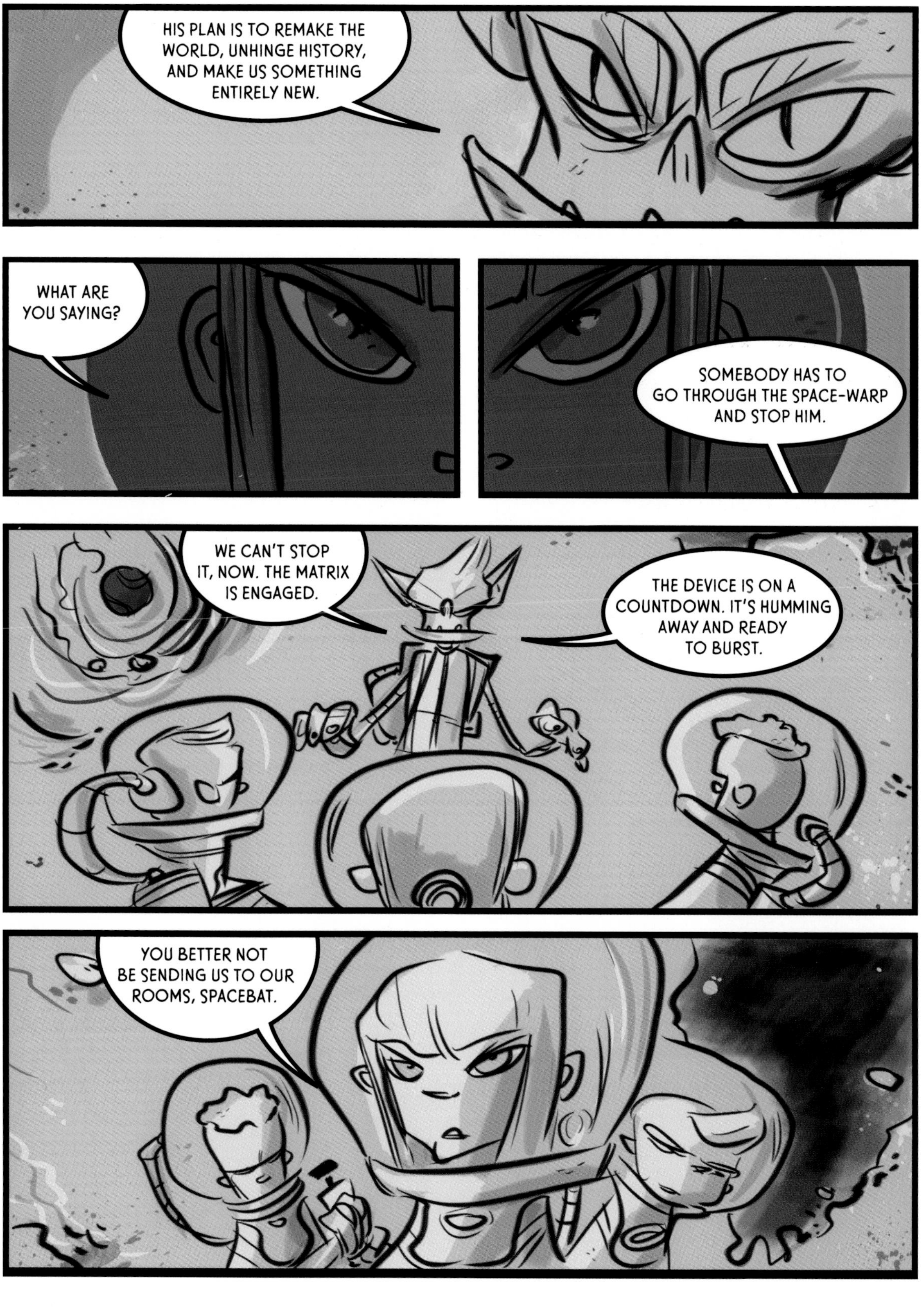
HIS PLAN IS TO REMAKE THE WORLD, UNHINGE HISTORY, AND MAKE US SOMETHING ENTIRELY NEW.
WHAT ARE YOU SAYING?
SOMEBODY HAS TO GO THROUGH THE SPACE-WARP AND STOP HIM.
WE CAN'T STOP IT, NOW. THE MATRIX IS ENGAGED.
THE DEVICE IS ON A COUNTDOWN. IT'S HUMMING AWAY AND READY TO BURST.
YOU BETTER NOT BE SENDING US TO OUR ROOMS, SPACEBAT.

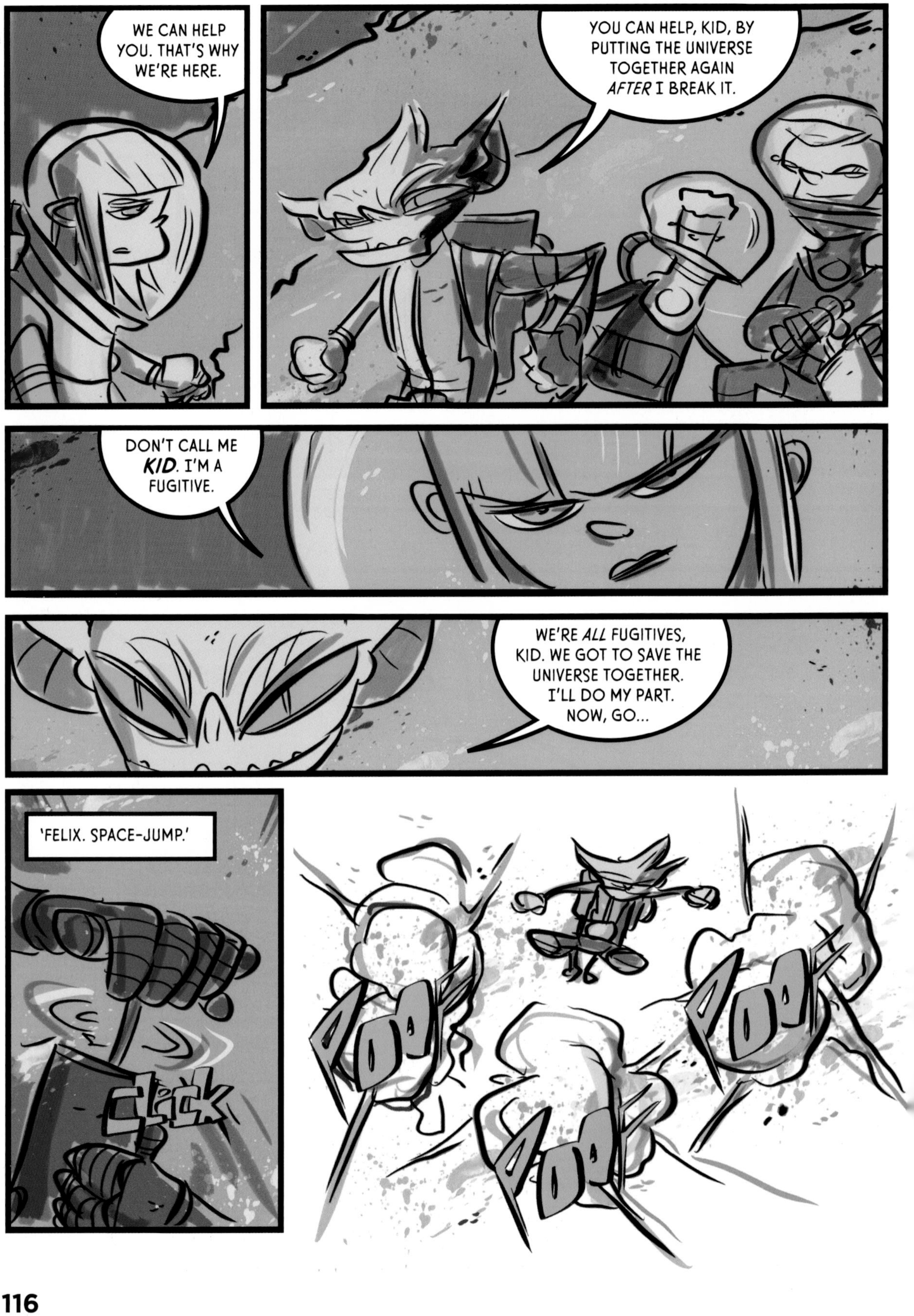

WE CAN HELP YOU. THAT'S WHY WE'RE HERE.
YOU CAN HELP, KID, BY PUTTING THE UNIVERSE TOGETHER AGAIN *AFTER* I BREAK IT.
DON'T CALL ME ***KID***. I'M A FUGITIVE.
WE'RE *ALL* FUGITIVES, KID. WE GOT TO SAVE THE UNIVERSE TOGETHER. I'LL DO MY PART. NOW, GO...
'FELIX. SPACE-JUMP.'
CLICK
POOF
POOF
POOF

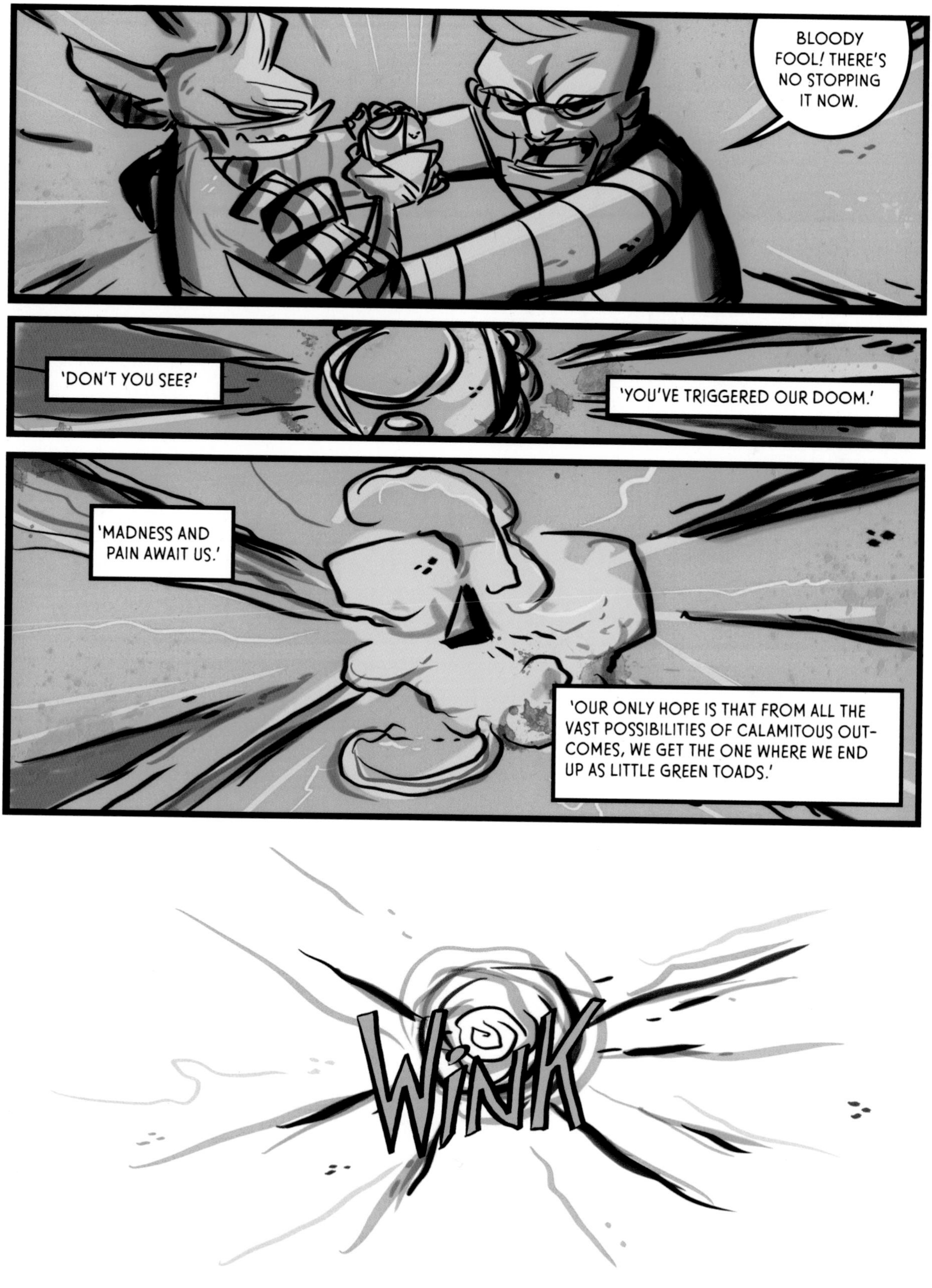
BLOODY FOOL! THERE'S NO STOPPING IT NOW.
'DON'T YOU SEE?'
'YOU'VE TRIGGERED OUR DOOM.'
'MADNESS AND PAIN AWAIT US.'
'OUR ONLY HOPE IS THAT FROM ALL THE VAST POSSIBILITIES OF CALAMITOUS OUT-COMES, WE GET THE ONE WHERE WE END UP AS LITTLE GREEN TOADS.'
WINK

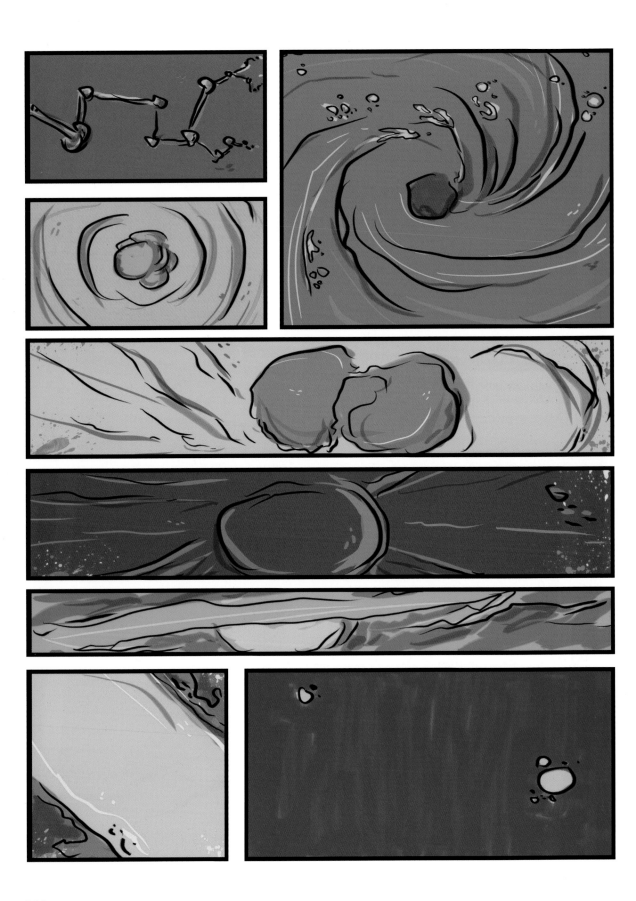

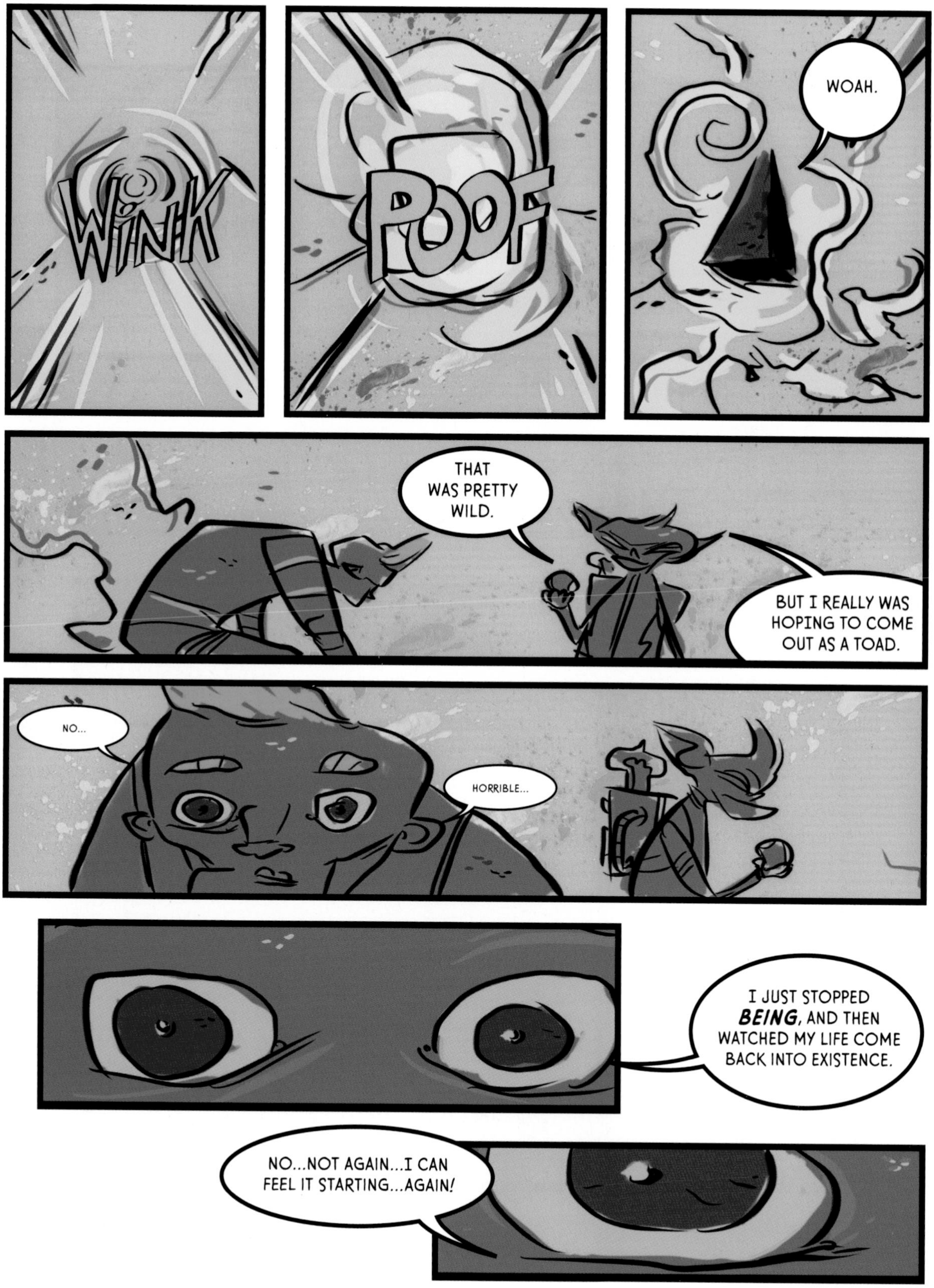
WINK
POOF
WOAH.
THAT WAS PRETTY WILD.
BUT I REALLY WAS HOPING TO COME OUT AS A TOAD.
NO...
HORRIBLE...
I JUST STOPPED ***BEING***, AND THEN WATCHED MY LIFE COME BACK INTO EXISTENCE.
NO...NOT AGAIN...I CAN FEEL IT STARTING...AGAIN!

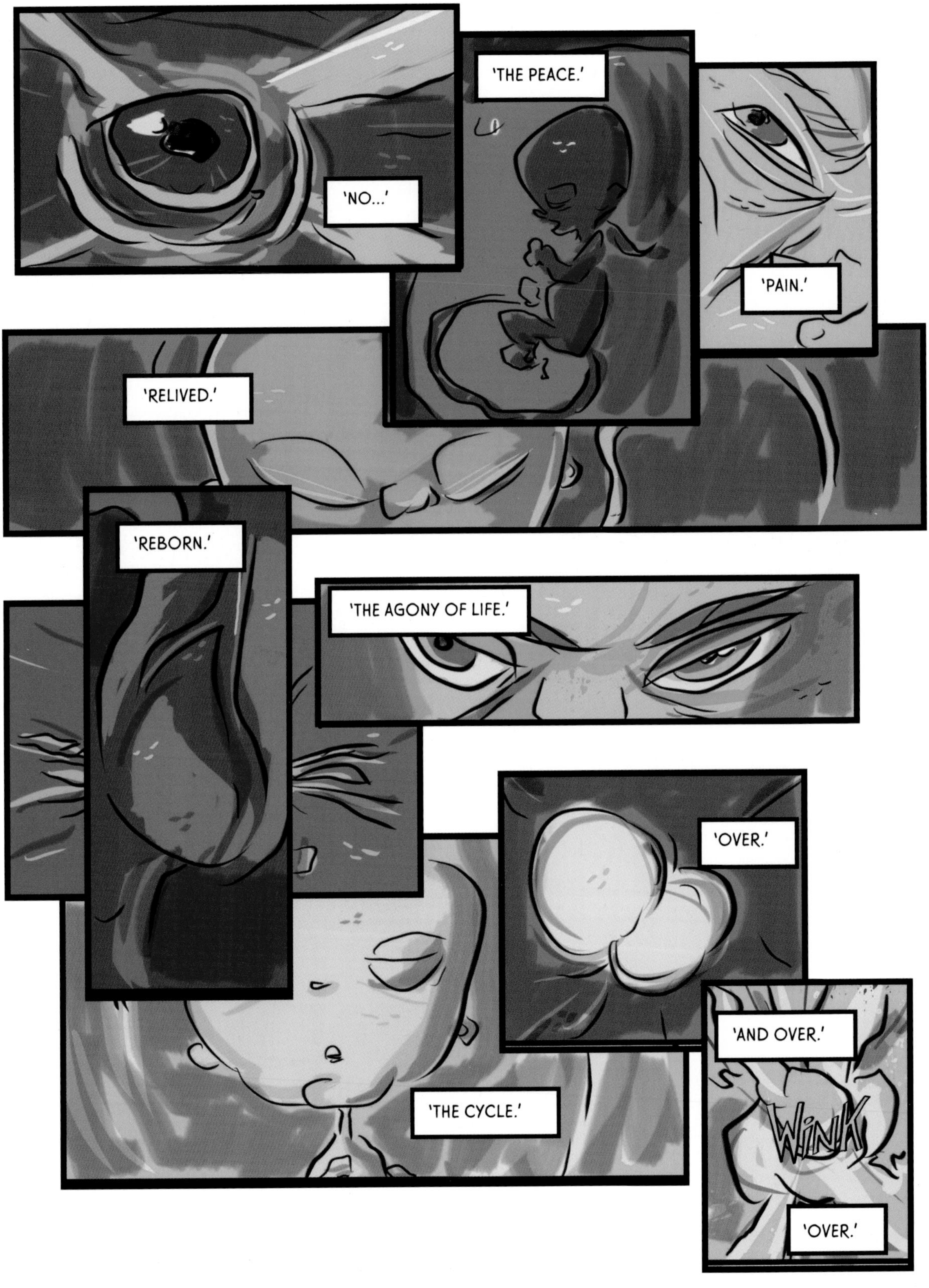
'NO...'
'THE PEACE.'
'PAIN.'
'RELIVED.'
'REBORN.'
'THE AGONY OF LIFE.'
'THE CYCLE.'
'OVER.'
'AND OVER.'
WINK
'OVER.'

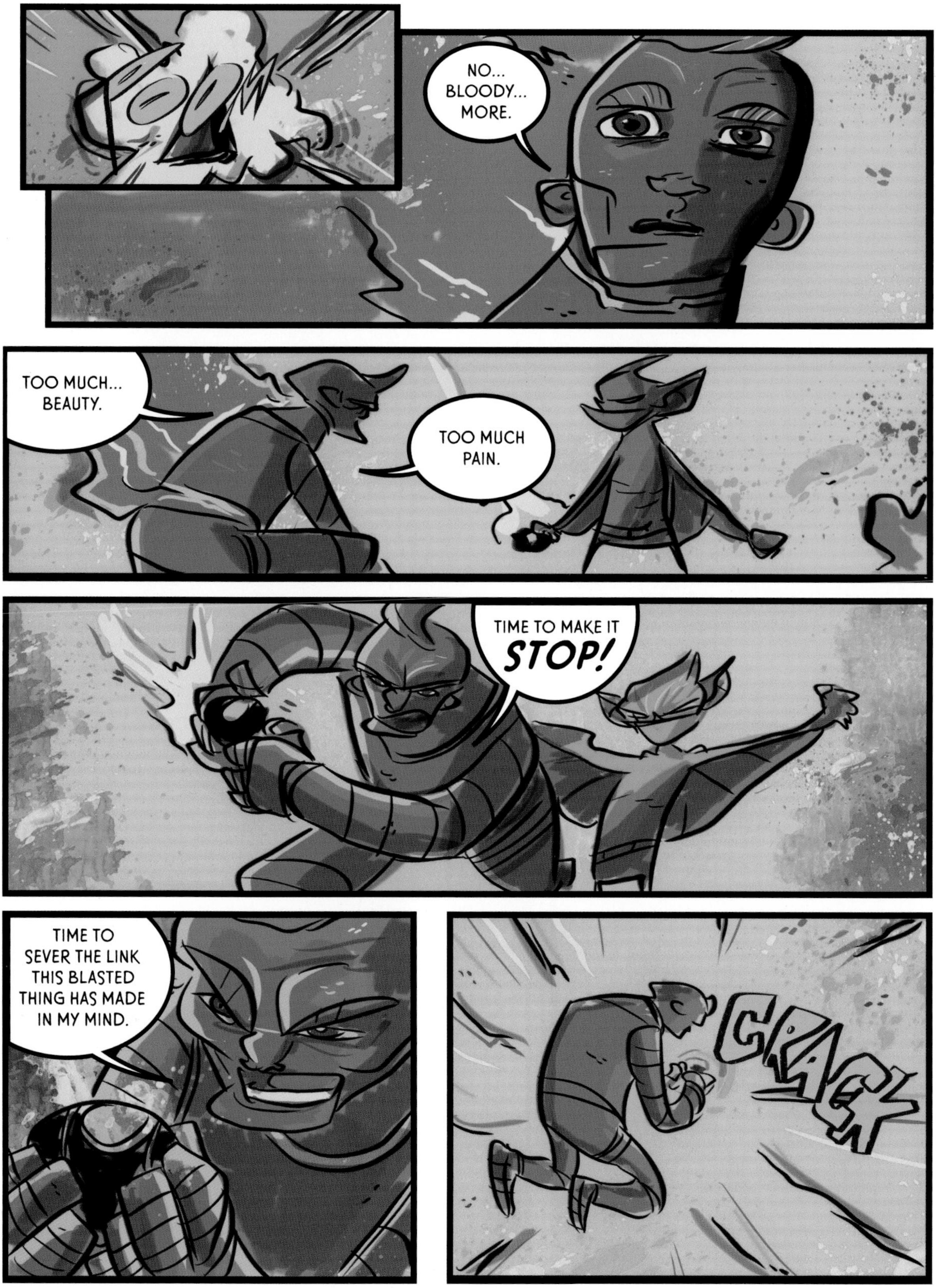

POOM
NO... BLOODY... MORE.
TOO MUCH... BEAUTY.
TOO MUCH PAIN.
TIME TO MAKE IT STOP!
TIME TO SEVER THE LINK THIS BLASTED THING HAS MADE IN MY MIND.
CRACK

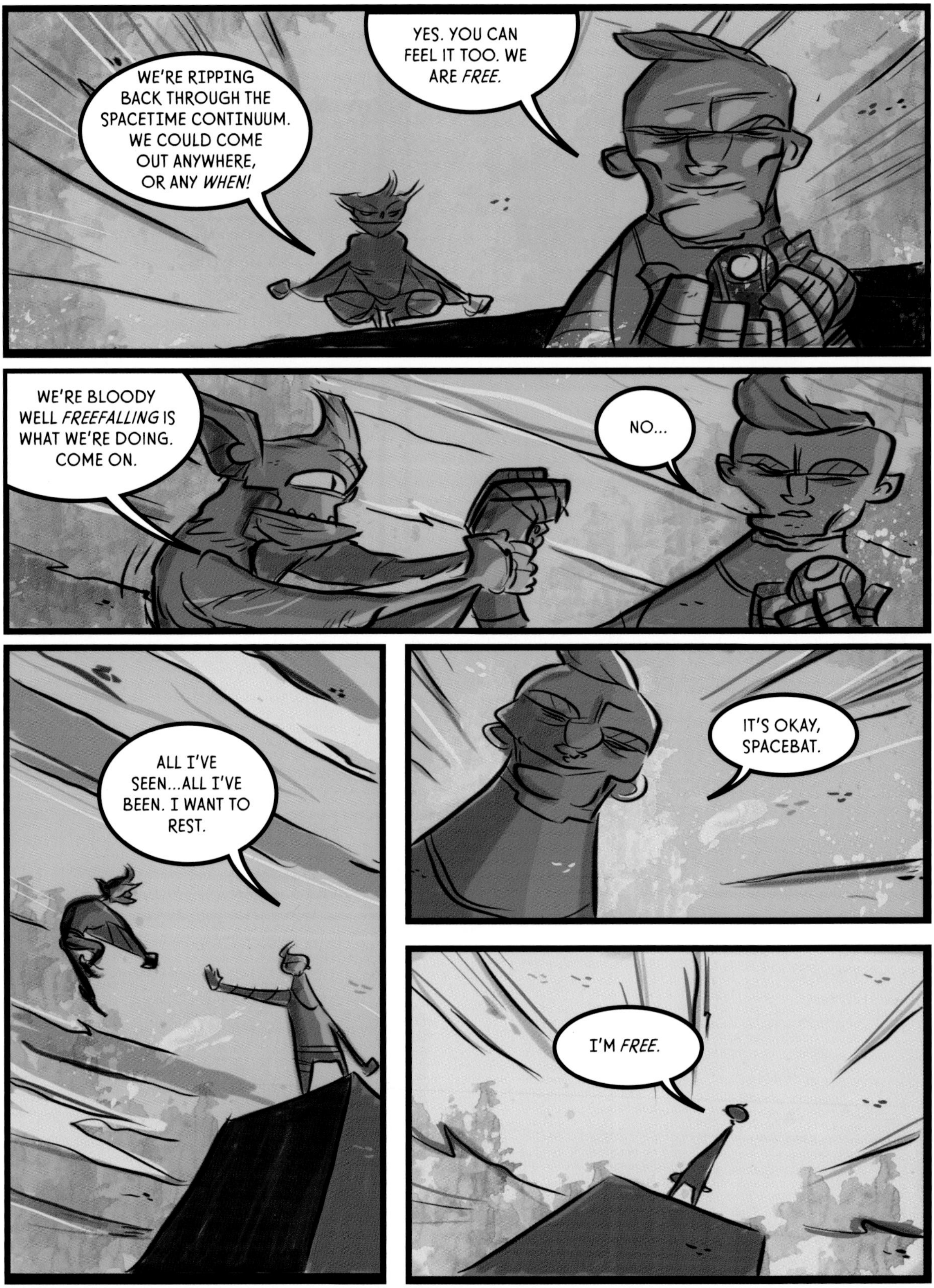
WE'RE RIPPING BACK THROUGH THE SPACETIME CONTINUUM. WE COULD COME OUT ANYWHERE, OR ANY *WHEN!*
YES. YOU CAN FEEL IT TOO. WE ARE *FREE.*
WE'RE BLOODY WELL *FREEFALLING* IS WHAT WE'RE DOING. COME ON.
NO...
ALL I'VE SEEN...ALL I'VE BEEN. I WANT TO REST.
IT'S OKAY, SPACEBAT.
I'M *FREE.*

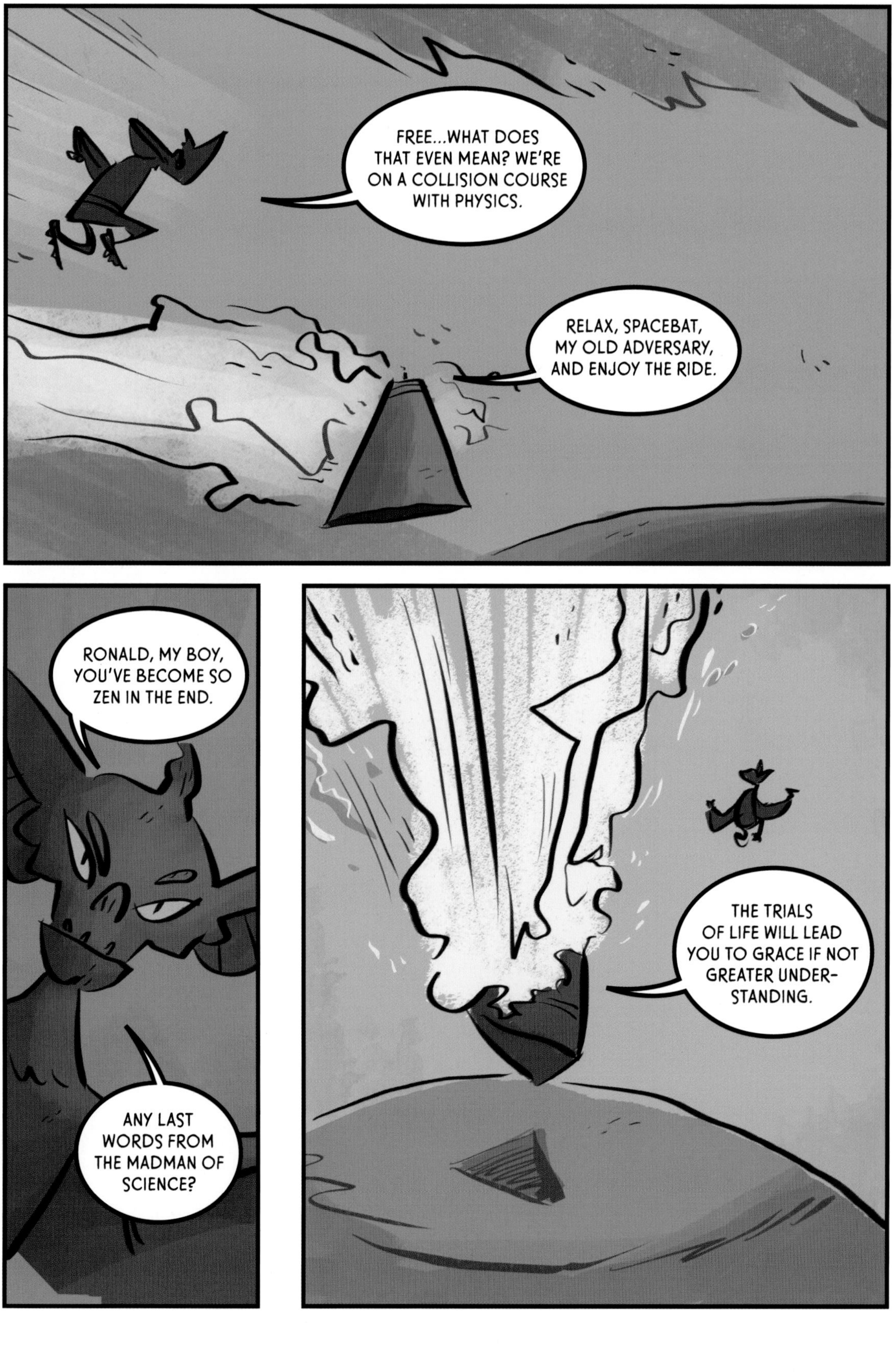
FREE...WHAT DOES THAT EVEN MEAN? WE'RE ON A COLLISION COURSE WITH PHYSICS.
RELAX, SPACEBAT, MY OLD ADVERSARY, AND ENJOY THE RIDE.
RONALD, MY BOY, YOU'VE BECOME SO ZEN IN THE END.
ANY LAST WORDS FROM THE MADMAN OF SCIENCE?
THE TRIALS OF LIFE WILL LEAD YOU TO GRACE IF NOT GREATER UNDER-STANDING.

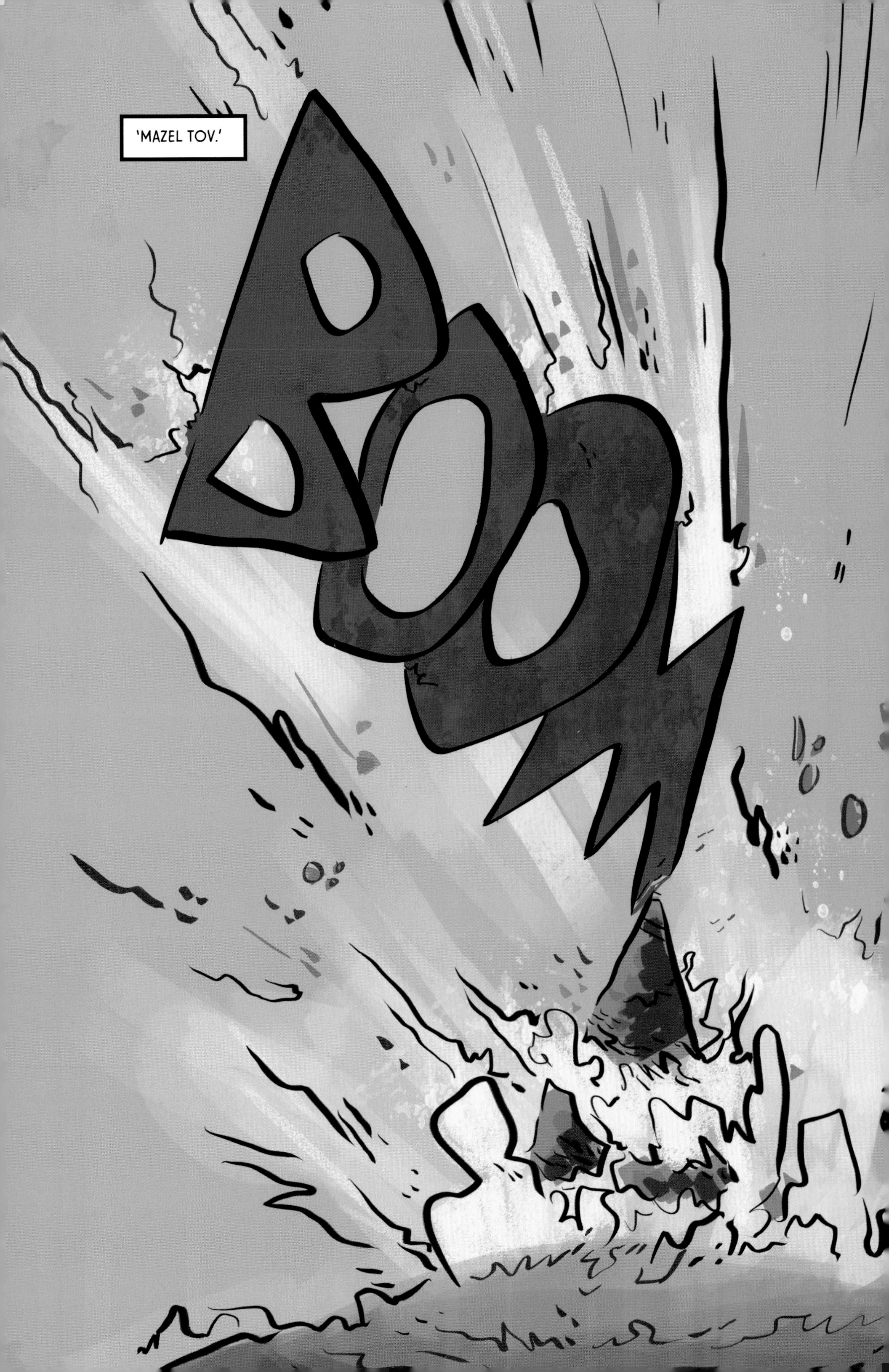
'MAZEL TOV.'
BOOM

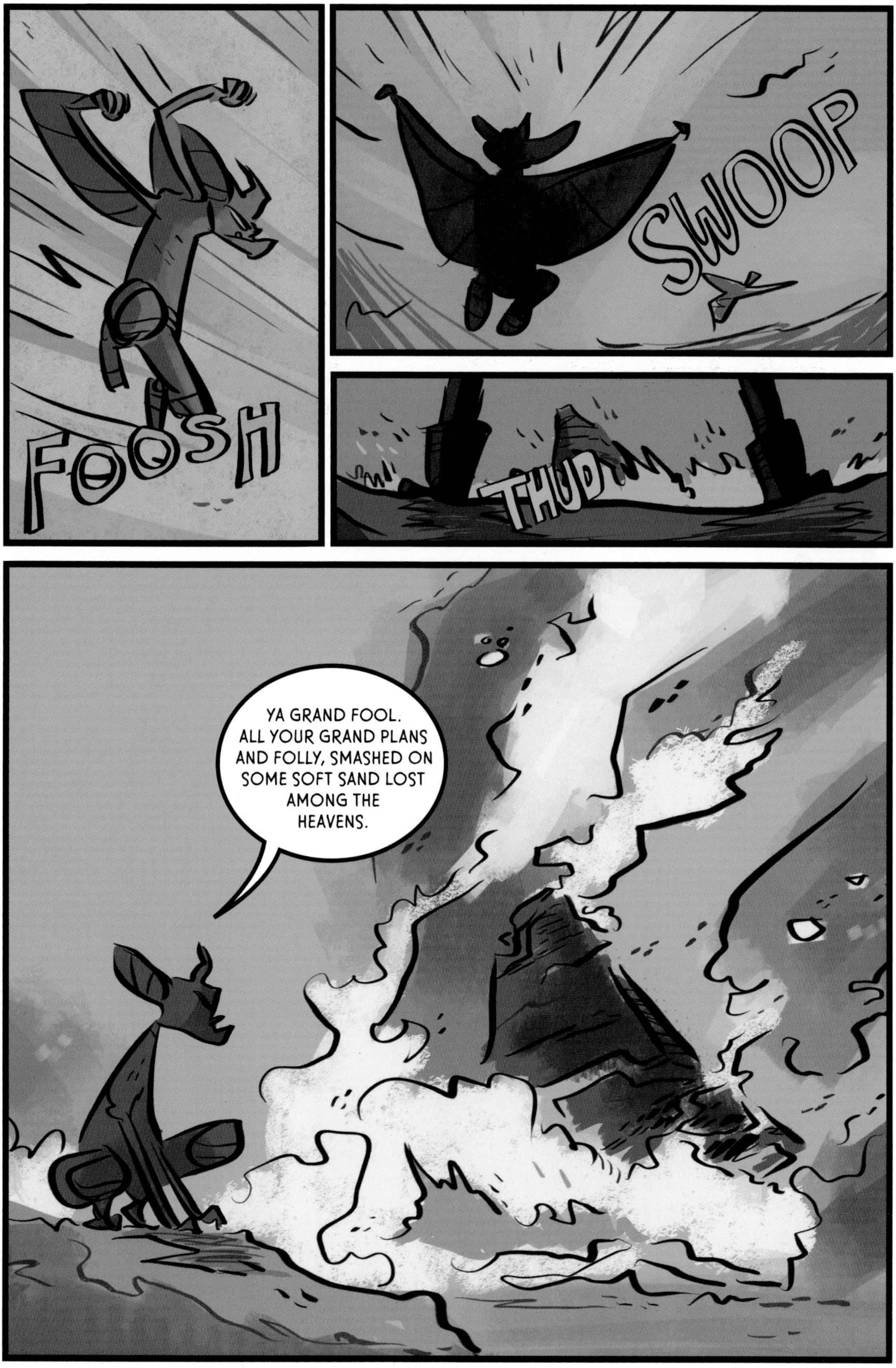
FOOSH
SWOOP
THUD
YA GRAND FOOL. ALL YOUR GRAND PLANS AND FOLLY, SMASHED ON SOME SOFT SAND LOST AMONG THE HEAVENS.

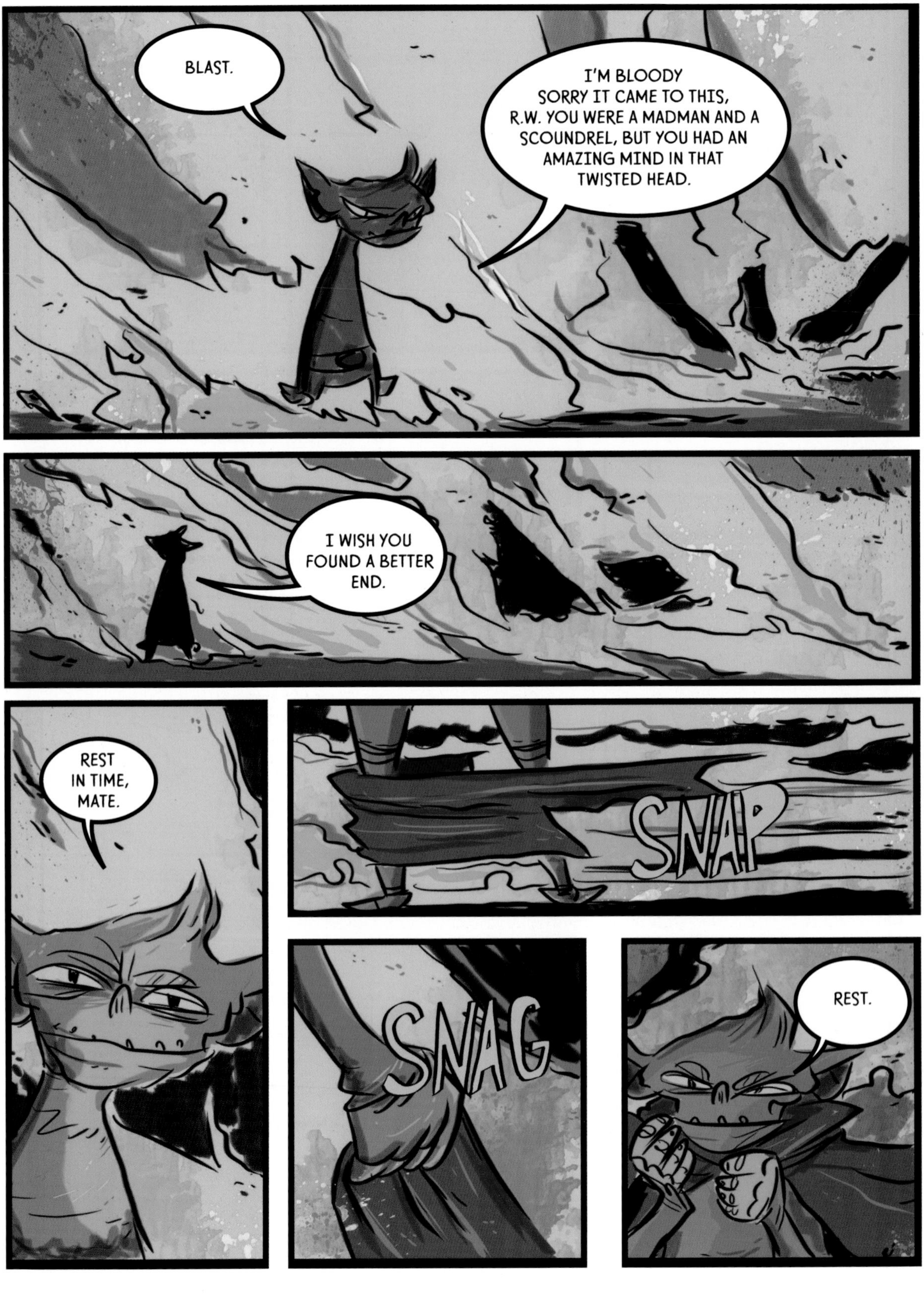
BLAST.
I'M BLOODY SORRY IT CAME TO THIS, R.W. YOU WERE A MADMAN AND A SCOUNDREL, BUT YOU HAD AN AMAZING MIND IN THAT TWISTED HEAD.
I WISH YOU FOUND A BETTER END.
REST IN TIME, MATE.
SNAP
SNAG
REST.

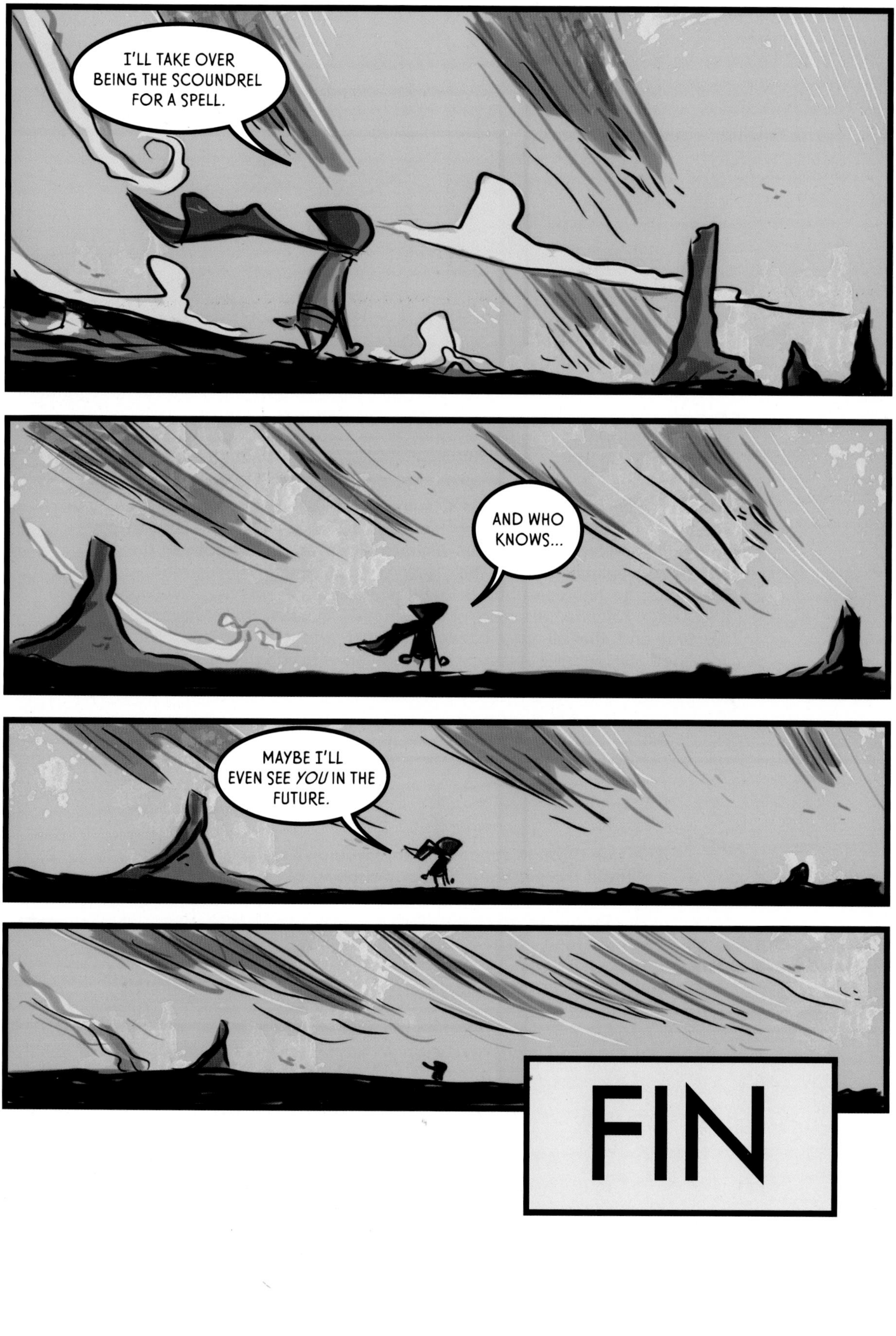
I'LL TAKE OVER BEING THE SCOUNDREL FOR A SPELL.
AND WHO KNOWS...
MAYBE I'LL EVEN SEE *YOU* IN THE FUTURE.
FIN

PHOTO BY KAREN OBRIST

CHRIS SHERIDAN is an illustrator, author, and designer calling the Great Northwest home. Born east of the Rockies, west of the island of Manhattan, Chris studied screenwriting, film, philosophy, and art in school and at university. He took a prize in a one-act play contest while living abroad in Dublin during his studies of theatre. After years traveling and trying his hand at various fields, he began studying graphic design. His distinct visual style combines the energy of animation with his love of rich, detailed illustrations. In comics, he has contributed to titles including *Plants vs. Zombies* and *Usagi Yojimbo*. His own graphic novels include *The Motorcycle Samurai* and the all-ages comic *Spacebat and the Fugitives* with Top Shelf. He currently lives in Seattle with his wife and their two bikes.

This ride through space and time wouldn't be possible
without the generous love and support of so many:

Thanks to Dad & Marion, Kate, Dave, Ollie, Omar, Michael, Margo, Henry, Willa,
and George & Frida. To Rich, Michelle, and Ellis & Dehlia. Elena, Adele, Remy, Kelly,
Dave, Emerson, Jess & Schoen, Lynds, Liz, Olive, Weez, Wild, Kyle, Joey, Jo, J.O.,
Meggs, Lola, and Garrett. Mom, Pop, & Ed C., Robert, Tricia, and Liz.

To Chris Staros for letting me play around again.
Zac B. for the effort & energy. Leigh W. for patience & persistence.
Chris R. for the pep talks and kicks in the can.

To Ted, Greg, Robbie, Laurie, Ryall, David, Sarah, Lorelei, Rebekah, Dirk,
and the rest of the family at the mothership.

To Mike A., Rich W., WJC, Fabian, Geof D., Jen V., Ibrahim, Tyler C., Matt K.,
Jeff L., Bill C., Brian H., Van, Churilla, Suriano, and Miles.
The gang at Arcane, the folks from Comic Dungeon, and Leo & Charles.